THE KABUL CONSCRIPT

M.E. Rostron

Michael E Rostron

Blaine, WA

Michael E Rostron
5545 Hillvue Rd.
Blaine, WA 98230
www.mikerostron.com

Publisher's Note: This is a work of fiction. Names, characters, places, and incidents are a product of the author's imagination. Locales and public names are sometimes used for atmospheric purposes. Any resemblance to actual people, living or dead, or to businesses, companies, events, institutions, or locales is completely coincidental.

Book Layout ©2017 BookDesignTemplates.com
Cover by Kenzie Mahoskey

Ordering Information: www.mikerostron.com

The Kabul Conscript/ M. E. Rostron. -- 1st ed.
ISBN 978-1-7335229-1-5

*To the people of Afghanistan, especially the women,
and their struggle against the forces of religious and
political oppression.*

The insolence of the Afghan is not the frustrated insolence of urbanized, dehumanized man in western society, but insolence without arrogance, the insolence of harsh freedoms set against a backdrop of rough mountains and deserts, the insolence of equality felt and practiced (with an occasional touch of superiority), the insolence of bravery past and bravery anticipated.

–Louis Dupree, "Afghanistan"

Kabul, 1973

Over three decades later David Stuckrath still retained a vivid memory of the tank lying on its side in the parched and littered channel of the Kabul River the day of the coup. The vintage World War II Russian machine had plunged over the steep bank into the dirty stream bed, killing one of its operators. Some said it was the only casualty that General Daoud's forces suffered in their well-planned and executed overnight takeover of the country. The old hand-me-down machine, looking vaguely insectile and strangely forlorn and helpless, would become for David a kind of metaphor for Afghanistan's misfortunes in the following decades.

Thirty-five years after the subsequent massacre of the ultimately unfortunate Daoud and most of his family, in an article buried on the inner pages of a newspaper, David would read that the remains of General Daoud and most of his entourage were finally discovered in a mass grave on the outskirts of Kabul. It would not surprise David that the secret of the leader and his family's burial place had remained unrevealed for so long, or that the new Afghan government then reinterred the previously discredited ruler with state honors. Such were the ironies of history, David would reflect—especially Afghan history.

As coup d'états go it was not a particularly notable one, but that upheaval would initiate a series of events which would eventually bring down the Soviet government and involve the United States in its longest war ever. There was some resistance from King Zahir Shah's personal guard that midsummer night of 1973. No exact figure was ever reported, but perhaps a few—probably less than a dozen—of the royal guard were killed or injured defending the conveniently absent king's palace.

The new ruler, Sardar Mohammed Daoud Khan, related by both blood and marriage to the king he deposed, and a previous prime minister under that same king, survived for barely five more years. Unlike the king he had ousted, Daoud did not have the foresight to leave the city before the next coup. He stubbornly held out a few hours until he and much of his family were exterminated by communist soldiers at the presidential residence during the so-called Saur Revolution of 1978.

The 1973 coup briefly interrupted international flights to Kabul, and caused only minor short term travel restrictions. Otherwise the nineteen sixties and early seventies were some of the best years for traveling in central Asia. But all too soon trekking on a small budget in the region would become a far more inconvenient and dangerous proposition.

For more than two decades following the end of the second world war the expansion of air travel, relatively cheap fuel, and peacetime prosperity had made it possible for nearly anyone with decent health, a desire for adventure, and a certain tolerance for the lack of modern comforts and conveniences to travel to areas once considered remote and obscure, or previously accessible only to the intrepid and generally well-financed explorer or expeditionary outfit.

The summer of 1973 was one of the last easy seasons for the network of backpackers and bohemian tourists on the routes that led from Istanbul all the way to Hong Kong, by way of Afghanistan and the Indian sub-continent. The young wanderers knew only that food, lodging, and drugs were cheap, the locals were mostly friendly and helpful, and all of the region seemed a vast playground where, with a modicum of discretion, they could indulge their youthful appetites with abandon. The ensuing years would bring terrorist attacks, hijackings, airport screening lines, fuel shortages, and a host of related inconveniences, but the young adventurers and expatriates could not imagine such a future that summer in Afghanistan.

CHAPTER 1

A Short Taxi Ride

On a day in July 1973 David Stuckrath stood next to a stalled taxi on a Kabul street under the intense midday sun. The driver of the dilapidated vehicle, in his eagerness to fleece the infidel, had run out of gas. It was always risky to take the cheapest cabs, and now his ride was blocking one of the busiest intersections in the city. A motley assortment of ruined Russian Volgas, sagging Chevys, dented Datsuns, listing lorries, and beat-up buses competed with pedestrians, bicycles, horse-drawn carts, and overladen donkeys. They came from the four cardinal directions, all struggling to get through the clogged intersection.

The frustrated commuters taunted and insulted his unfortunate driver in several languages as the man untied the frayed rope that secured the flapping trunk to retrieve the spare gas can, which proved—inevitably—to be empty. The smells, heat, and noise assaulted David's senses. Tempers flared. To David the scene began to feel uncomfortably similar to the mob mentality he had witnessed during the Viet Nam war protests back home. He imagined ants boiling out of a disturbed nest and swarming an unfortunate insect interloper.

Another taxi driver raised a fist at David's driver. David felt somehow responsible—western money and culture distorting yet another society. But of course David's civilization was only the latest of a series going back thousands of years the ancient city had seen. Through the veins of the taxi driver and his persecutors ran the blood of generations of the conquered and their conquerors—legions of hard men, going back to Alexander the Great and further—who had traversed scorched deserts and climbed the high mountain passes of the Hindu Kush to found new empires, only to be replaced in turn by other more powerful despots and their kingdoms. New religions, economic systems, and political ideas came and went over the centuries, but the people of the mountains, steppes, and deserts who made up the loose assortment of tribes known as Afghanistan endured, and enduring usually meant not being too particular about the source of your income.

Eventually the honking shouting horde began to find its way around the immobile taxi, as stampeding cattle divide around a downed comrade. David felt vulnerable, suspect, even more the foreigner. Even after more than a year in this city, and although he spoke Farsi, the primary trading language, and had a fair command of Pashtu, the language of the ruling tribes, there were always times like these—the sudden realization that you did not belong here, and there was no possible way of fully adapting or fitting in. Yet David was on his way to visit the one foreigner he knew in Kabul who seemingly had successfully integrated himself into the fabric of the city, though he, like David, was an American who hailed from the same Northwestern region of the country.

Feeling a twinge of guilt as he abandoned the hapless cab driver, David thought of Conrad Slocum as he slipped through the crowd, stepped over a reeking gutter, and turned down a quiet side street. He was close enough to walk anyway, he rationalized. He was at the edge of the part of Kabul called Shar-I-Nau, the 'New City,' where the more modern section gave way to the historic older neighborhoods. Here, painted concrete homes with electricity and running water neatly set along recently paved streets segued to mud-brick buildings and the narrow winding dirt alleys of the timeworn and organic polis.

The real heart of Kabul still beat here in the shops and old bazaars, where the world's currencies and products followed their mysterious paths of commerce, independent still of state controls. There were no multinational western style department stores here. No paper bags for your purchase. No cash register receipts. No stock reports. No shopping mall, for the great sprawling city itself was a huge living market, and almost any product you might desire could be found if only you knew where to look for it.

What David wanted this day were 'refreshments' for a party he was planning. David roomed with two other Peace Corps Volunteers, or 'PCVs,' as they called themselves, Dennis Butler and John Mesmer. Afghanistan was a difficult assignment for the young Americans, accustomed as they had been to the relative luxury and ease of their comparatively affluent backgrounds—at least compared to most Afghans. Not surprisingly Peace Corps Afghanistan had a high rate of attrition. David's group, only one year after arriving, was smaller now by more than half. Now Dennis too was leaving.

Dennis Butler, whose handsome dark brooding features and somewhat shy disposition so contrasted with David's ruddy complexion and exuberance. Dennis—tall, tanned, sharp featured, clean-shaven, and neat almost to obsession. David—bearded, with hair unruly and long (to the consternation of the Peace Corps brass), disheveled, and sometimes alarmingly informal. If opposites attract it was not surprising the two roommates, thrown together by their chance posting here in Kabul, had become good friends.

Dennis, unlike the more pragmatic David, was an idealist, and it was mainly for this reason that he was leaving Afghanistan, David understood. Idealists never lasted here. What looked good in planning almost never worked in practice in this country. Raised in a prosperous midwestern farming community with its neatly laid out streets, hardworking populace, and homogeneous society—as predictable and reliable as the Sunday sermon—Dennis had been frustrated from the very beginning of his posting with this archaic and Byzantine city.

He was going home after having served but half the normal two year Peace Corps term of duty.

David hoped to make this a very special bon voyage party, and Conrad was David's very special connection. It was true he could have bought opium from the same shopkeeper who sold hashish to the other Americans and Europeans in his neighborhood, but the truth was David was fascinated with Conrad, and went out of his way to find occasions to promote and cultivate their relationship. He made it his regular practice to buy in small quantities in order to come more often to Conrad's apartment. Pills of all kinds, legal or not, could be bought cheaply at the small drug stores, or in the bazaars. Hashish was more or less openly consumed and sold, and even easier to procure than decent wine or beer in this Islam city, but opium—David's drug of choice—he preferred to buy from a trusted fellow expat.

Conrad's apartment was located in a recently constructed concrete building situated at the border of the Old and New cities. It was a transitional location where a mixture of traditional walled compounds and modern multistoried concrete buildings awkwardly co-existed. It was appropriate that Conrad, a transitional specimen himself, lived there. He was the most 'Afghan' of any foreigner David knew. Like many of the Kabul natives he spoke both Farsi and Pashtu fluently. His dress was a mixture of modern western and traditional Afghan, which he varied according to his environment, much like the chameleons—those supremely adaptable creatures that were so ubiquitous in the city. Equally remarkable to the PCVs who knew him; Conrad appeared to eat the local foods and, so the gossip went, even drink the water without any obvious ill effects. Rumor was he did not even take the weekly anti-malarial tablets or the antibiotic doses the other westerners, and especially Americans, were so dependent on.

Conrad opened the door himself at David's knock. He was one of the few American expatriates David knew who did not have at least a part-time domestic or servant to cook his meals and perform the services of a butler and errand boy, though David was aware he did employ a woman to buy his groceries and do his laundry—the latter a task too demeaning for any man to be caught doing, even in relatively cosmopolitan Kabul. It was not due to lack of the money for household help. Stepping into Conrad's living room was like entering one of the rug bazaars. Like the traditional nomadic tribesmen, Conrad had come to regard the finely woven carpets as one of the few forms of reliable wealth in this country where the currency was subject to frequent unpredictable oscillations in value for inscrutable reasons. He had become an expert on the local and regional varieties of carpets, and supported himself partly through their export, though he had at least one source of income his Peace Corps friends knew nothing of.

One of Conrad's friends, the Italian artist Alighiero Boetti, owner of the notorious Number One Hotel above Kabul's one and only supermarket, had influenced Conrad's views on home furnishings. Boetti had observed that traditional Afghan homes were large-ly empty, with little furniture, and hence none of the objects normally associated with or placed on furniture in western homes. Conrad loved the simplicity of it. Like the traditional Pashtun tribesman, his apartment contained no sofa, chairs, or tables. However the flat's floors and walls were adorned with traditional carpets of all sizes, colors, and designs. Fortunately the lighting was diffuse, otherwise the effect would have been overwhelming. Sometimes, after several bowls of opi-um, David would contemplate the myriad patterns and geometric arrangements until their shapes and colors remained imprinted in his view long after he closed his eyes.

"You look like you could use a drink," Conrad said, ushering David into the strikingly decorated main room. He got two cans of Schlitz, the only American beer available locally, from the refrigerator, and handed one to David.

"Tashakor," David replied.

Some Farsi words were employed so often that David automatically used them, even with his English speaking friends and colleagues.

"My cab broke down, and I walked the last few blocks. I am a little dry."

"So what brings you out this way in the heat of the day? Is it business or pleasure?" Conrad asked after they had seated themselves Afghan style among the cushions on the floor, and opened their beers.

"Business serving pleasure." David answered. "I need some party favors."

"How much?" Conrad took a swig from his beer.

"An ounce should do it," David replied without hesitation.

"It must be quite a party—am I invited? Or are you developing a habit now, my friend? What will your teachers at the training center think of that, eh?"

David knew Conrad had no patience with most of the Afghan Peace Corps teachers, whom he considered to be prigs. It seemed to David that Conrad thought of the Peace Corps, and for that matter all the numerous foreign agencies in Afghanistan, as either inconsequential jokes, intelligence fronts, or both. David, who thought of himself as a member of Conrad's inner circle of friends, had no idea that much of Conrad's attitude was artifice. There were significant things about Conrad Slocum's life David did not know and would never learn, despite the fact that he considered him to be one of his closest confidants. Their relationship was not reciprocal, although Conrad for his part genuinely liked David and enjoyed his company.

Actually, David was in no danger of becoming an addict. In spite of his bohemian or hippie affectations, and his long hair and beard, he was more a dilettante in his drug use, and fairly conventional—a dabbler and occasional consumer of contraband, reliable at his Peace Corps position, and in essence not at all a political or social radical. David's experimentations with drugs and his sometimes nonconformist opinions were more in the way of what he himself would have characterized as the necessary profligacy of youth, not evidence of any serious commitment to a particular ideology or way of life. He considered it his intellectual and ethical duty to explore such controversial activities and ideas, as an essential aspect of completing his education. His was a romanticized view of life that owed more to immersion in the study of history and literature than to any current fashions or trends. Kabul, with its deep and convoluted past, its anachronistic present, and far enough removed from the familiar world of David's upbringing to appeal to his idealistic sensibilities, was in some ways an ideal setting for entertaining such notions in the early 1970s.

"I'm planning a party for Dennis next Friday. Of course you're invited—that's the other reason I came over."

He ignored Conrad's sarcasm. As Conrad and many of David's Kabul acquaintances knew, David was notorious for flaunting Peace Corps rules and formalities, but he had made himself valuable enough to the organization that he had so far avoided serious censure.

"Sounds like fun, and a lucky day too—that's Friday the thirteenth. In fact your timing today is fortunate as well. I just got some primo stuff in from Kandahar, but it will cost you a bit more."

Conrad left his guest briefly and returned with a wooden box elaborately inlaid with ivory and lapis lazuli, from which he extracted a plastic-swathed bundle. As the wrapping was removed the unmistakable aroma filled David's nostrils. He felt a shiver of anticipation. Conrad cut into the dark slab, revealing the lighter colored sticky interior. He offered a thin sliver to David. The pungent aftertaste was intense, and took a long time to fade away. It always reminded him of the time as a child his grandfather, a great practical joker, persuaded him to taste the juice of a certain 'milkweed' plant. Like biting into an aspirin, the bitter taste was never forgotten. Conrad began the smoking ritual, utilizing his prized museum quality gentlemen's smoking kit, crafted over a century earlier in Viet Nam—a serendipitous find from one of his early forays into a Kabul bazaar.

As they smoked, the intense dry heat of the summer afternoon gradually gave way to the cooling breezes of evening. Kabul, with an elevation nearly equal to that of Denver, and ringed with the even higher peaks of the Hindu Kush, often experienced sudden spectacular sunsets, one of which the two young men admired as its orange-red glow lit up the southwestern facing windows of the second floor apartment. They passed through the various stages of intoxication. After a time Conrad set aside the pipe. They had gone beyond words. Eyes closed, both drifted at the edge of sleep, each in his own private dream world.

David's reverie was of the lush green valley of his Northwestern birthplace. In his drowsy fantasy he rode in an open convertible through a countryside of vivid green hues. Stands of fruit and nut orchards alternating with straight-rowed plots of leafy green beans, fragrantly fecund mint, and waving dill from the rich farmlands of David's rural homeland were visible from the phantom automobile. He dreamt on, escaping for a short time, if only in his imagination, the muted browns and grays of this harsher land of stone and stubble.

Conrad too dozed in a blissful state of total relaxation that was not quite sleep. His straight dark hair and neatly clipped black beard framed a strong prominent nose, deep set eyes, and a small thin-lipped mouth. Though in his early twenties, he has passed for a decade and more older. His deeply tanned face has begun to take on the ageless look of the rural Pashtun tribesman.

In his own alkaloid phantasmagoria Conrad rides with the nomads, dreaming of a good steed and chill nights around the campfire—the stars preternaturally brilliant overhead—so many more visible through the thin clean air, with no artificial lighting to distract from an ageless scene of man, animal, mountain, and sky.

The visions brought on by the opium pipe are never identical. Sometimes Conrad, like David, experiences intense visions of his former life, only hours away by jet plane, yet for all that still centuries in the future as far as much of this land is concerned.

The foreigners who found themselves in this primeval province adapted to the unfamiliar culture in predictable ways. Most availed themselves of the sparse western subculture in the city, limited though it was. The few European or American style restaurants; the recently constructed Intercontinental Hotel; the USAID and USIS compounds, and other official agencies; and Kabul's one and only supermarket—all very recent additions to Afghanistan's most populous city. These were the places the western expatriates gathered to try and recreate feeble copies of their home societies.

But another choice, which some of the officials feared so much, was to 'go native.' The ancient city of Kabul was an amalgamation of disparate peoples and societies. Though primitive in many respects—no electricity in some neighborhoods, open sewage ditches—it was still a cosmopolitan city, complex and sophisticated in odd and unpredictable ways—multicultural and multiracial.

Conrad, mature and worldly beyond his years, has managed to adjust to and even thrive in this environment. He has begun to think almost as much in Pashtu or Farsi as in English. He regards both the Afghan and his native countryman's customs and habits as humorous, tragic, logical or irrational in turn, but ironically his feeling of alienation from any particular society makes it easier for him to make friends and establish social connections wherever he goes in the city. To him the Islam on his prayer mat, the Buddhist and his prayer wheel, the Hindu with his pantheon of gods and demigods, and the Christian in his pew all seem equally absurd. Likewise, the obsessions and subterfuges of the Soviet and Chinese communists and the western capitalists are but the latest chapter in the 'Great Game,' still being played out in Central Asia at

the expense of the mostly poverty-stricken and exploit-
ed or ignored inhabitants.

Conrad has shed much of the baggage of his heritage—a young man still in the process of assembling his
own unique ideology and credo from the many choices
available to him in this ancient city he has temporarily
adopted—a city still a crossroads and crucible of cultures, as it has been for more than two thousand years.

CHAPTER 2

July 4

July 4, the third day of Jumada al-awwal in the Islamic calendar, dawned torrid and still. The bazaar, although as usual open and active by five AM, seemed somewhat quieter, as if the storekeepers were conserving their energies for what promised to be a scorcher. This particular bazaar, located below David's apartment and comprising both sides of the street for two city blocks, was known to the foreigners as the 'toilet paper bazaar.'

Actually the shops sold an assortment of merchandise, including goods as diverse as juicy Jalalabad melons and the latest Japanese electronics; but the bazaar was especially known for its selection of a large variety, for Afghanistan, of paper products. In contrast to many shops in Kabul, one could choose from an amazing array of manufactured paper goods—toilet paper, paper towels, writing and typing paper, and even western brands of feminine hygiene products. Most of the toilet paper, David had observed, came from mainland China—a single ply, no frills unbleached variety bearing an uncomfortably close resemblance to newsprint in both appearance and texture.

The shops were mostly small, mere cubicles partitioned simply from the fronts of the buildings lining the street. Each store front had a cloth awning shading it from the morning or afternoon sun, depending on which side of the street it occupied. The upper story usually housed the shopkeeper and his (for all the store owners were male) family or close relatives.

At one end of the block a small drugstore sold a wide variety of western and eastern medicinal concoctions. Everything from Bayer Aspirin, and the other familiar brands of branded pills, to the more exotic Asian potions, such as ginseng extract and powdered Rhino horn. Even genuine Sandoz Laboratories LSD and Quaaludes were available—all of course without a prescription. Indeed, a prescription would have been exceptional, with about one licensed medical doctor for every one hundred thousand residents in Afghanistan.

The opposite end of the bazaar was anchored by the local bread bakery. Every neighborhood had one of these; a dome-shaped construction of mud-brick where the 'naan' or whole wheat sesame-seeded unleavened bread was baked fresh every morning and afternoon. The bread, roughly the shape and size of a snowshoe when purchased while fresh and warm, was remarkably tender and tasty, but had a shelf life of only a couple of hours. After that it began to harden, and by evening it would become brittle and virtually inedible—more suitable for use as a club or for swatting the ubiquitous flies that buzzed in jerky random flight around David's apartment above the bazaar.

It was the fresh savory version of naan that David Stuckrath and Dennis Butler greedily consumed that July 4 morning. As usual their domestic, Samot (whom they irreverently referred to among themselves as, 'Smut'), had prepared and served their breakfast; the fresh naan with imported peanut butter—a true luxury here—hot cereal, and the ever-present pots of green and black tea.

The kitchen noises had awakened David. Dennis Butler, an early riser by long habit, had already shaved and dressed even before Samot arrived. John Mesmer, their ailing third roommate, even when in good health often slept right through breakfast.

"Salaam alaikum."

"Wa alaikum salaam."

They exchanged traditional greetings every morning without fail in their cook's presence. Samot insisted the PCVs speak Farsi or Pashtu whenever possible, but the roommate's conversations normally relapsed into English as soon as he left the room. Though Samot had very low status as domestic help, in this way he maintained a kind of moral superiority over his employers. Even so, he genuinely felt he had an obligation to help his charges adapt to their foreign surroundings. He was a short, dark-complected man with the Mongolian features commonly found in the domestic class here. Although Moslem Afghanistan, unlike India, had no official caste system, the country had its own kind of not-so-subtle racial divisions and bigotry—a seemingly universal feature of the species Homo sapiens, David, the history graduate, had observed.

After some early misgivings the three have become fairly comfortable with the idea of having a servant, and of themselves as 'sahibs'—something which at first went against their working class egalitarian upbringing. Samot, having been weeded out years earlier as one of the reliable and relatively sanitary English speaking domestic workers suitable for hire by foreign residents in Kabul, made significantly better money working for foreigners than he would have earned in the same position for native Afghans. Samot played his role with expertise, and even entertained a certain amount of affection for the young infidels who paid so well.

For several months the roommates have been getting their hashish from the shopkeeper, Bagnur, directly below their flat. Bagnur was also the landlord and part owner of the apartment building. They had come to the conclusion that Samot was not to be trusted concerning such matters. This was mostly just doper's paranoia, though in fact Samot did not approve of hashish use. Samot did seem to spend a lot of time in conversation with Bagnur, and to the young westerners Samot appeared much too intelligent to be a mere cook and servant. Perhaps he was also reporting on their behavior. They suspect this, not really understanding the limitations of advancement available to a man like Samot in Afghanistan, regardless of intelligence and ability.

Yet their cook's culinary creations, even though necessarily somewhat repetitious due to their budget limitations, are tasty and attractively presented, and his movements in their small kitchen are practiced, efficient, even graceful. It was obvious even to his somewhat oblivious young employers that he took great pride in his work. Fatima, his wife, covered and mysterious under her 'chadaree' or 'burqa' would come today to gather the wash. This, in Afghanistan, was still woman's work, beneath the dignity of even the lowest of male domestics.

Dennis and David were nearly done with their breakfast by the time their roommate, John finally appeared.

"Fifth day in a row," he said matter-of-factly.

David noted that John looked even more gaunt than usual. At nearly six feet five inches and one hundred eighty pounds when he arrived in Afghanistan, he was lanky and angular even when in good health—all arms and legs with a huge bony head, scraggly beard, and thin balding hair that make him appear a decade or more older than his actual twenty-two years. Now, after nearly a week of dysentery, he is thinner yet, sallow and haggard looking.

"Did you get the stool sample in?" asked Dennis.

This was hardly genteel breakfast conversation, but certainly normal under the circumstances.

"I'm supposed to get results back tomorrow," John answered between mouthfuls of naan. "I sure as shit hope it's not amoebic dysentery—no irony intended."

John spoke with a pronounced Carolina drawl. Although he talked slowly, his movements were quick, precise, and agile. He was an accomplished artist and sculptor. He made two trips to the bathroom before the meal was over.

Throughout their breakfast Dennis was uncharacteristically quiet, and met any attempts at conversation with one or two word replies. The other two did not press him, knowing how torn he was about his recent decision to resign from Peace Corps and leave Afghanistan. The three of them had become close friends, having shared the same apartment for more than a year.

"Are you guys going to the party this afternoon?" David finally asked, referring to the Independence Day festivities to which all United States citizens and many local dignitaries had been invited. It was held every year on the grounds at the USAID compound.

"Sure, I wouldn't miss it," Dennis replied, between mouthfuls.

"I'll go if my guts let me," John answered hopefully.

"Well, I guess I'll see you there this afternoon, then. I'd better get going. I've got to pick up some books I reserved at USIS," David announced, unfolding from his cross-legged position.

There was no table in the main room of the apartment, which they used both for dining and as a general living space. They ate in traditional Afghan manner, seated on the floor around a cloth spread out at the beginning of each meal, and taken up at the end.

David was not going to pick up library books. He was off to see an Afghan friend, to make entertainment arrangements for Dennis' bon voyage party, which he and his roommates hoped to keep a surprise from Dennis—hence the subterfuge.

After a hot and dusty twenty minute walk he arrived at the Pashtoon Hotel tea room, which, because it catered to foreigners, featured a mismatched assortment of tables and chairs as well as the customary cushions and rugs on the floor. His Afghan friend, Shamsher, was already there and waiting at one of the tables. A samovar of tea, bowl of sugar, and several cups were laid out.

"Dennis is even moodier than usual these days. He definitely needs a good party to get his spirits up before he leaves," David said, after exchanging their habitual greetings in Pashtu and English, and pulling up a chair across the table from Shamsher.

"I would like to hire a traditional Afghan band—no sitars or Indian pop music, if possible."

Shamsher was a man of average height, very well built, with a prominent nose, swarthy complexion, and piercing gray-blue eyes. His face, at least from a distance, did not stand out in this city, but an astute observer might regard a more nuanced visage. The upper part of his face appeared stern, determined—even fierce—but his mouth was relaxed, reflecting his usual affable and agreeable temperament. The lines at the corners of his eyes suggested experience and hardship rather than age. In fact, he was just twenty-four. Shamsher had a pleasant speaking voice, with a lilting, musical quality. He spoke softly and deliberately. He had a fairly good, if not fluent command of English, which was in itself remarkable, and indicative of his determination and intelligence, for he was mostly self-taught, and came from an impoverished family.

In spite of the tremendous culture gap, Shamsher has become one of David's closest companions. They speak an odd patois of English and Pashtu. Shamsher always encourages David with his efforts at learning the difficult language, and in return David coaches Shamsher in the finer points of English grammar, pronunciation, and vocabulary.

"Yes, the music and movies of India are too much watched here," replied Shamsher in his soothing voice.

David relishes the thought of the search for the entertainment—today's adventure. Shamsher has already shown him much more of the authentic and historic old Kabul than he could ever have experienced without his local friend and guide. Shamsher is known to the small group of Afghan Peace Corps teachers, but they are somewhat wary of him. Shamsher in turn is secretly envious of their relatively secure and good paying positions, but having never attended even secondary school, let alone a university, he is not eligible for such employment.

In Kabul's complex and stratified society Shamsher's status is unique. He is a self-made man from a tough background, not a member of Kabul's young intelligentsia or literati, but descended from a one-time powerful and well-respected Pashtun family, impoverished now for several generations. Because of his heritage, intelligence, and sensitivity Shamsher has the rare ability to move between the more progressive and the traditionally minded factions of his generation in the city, but he is not fully a part of any social or political camp.

"We must have to go to the Old City. I know some very fine musicians there—in the true Pashtun tradition," Shamsher continued.

"That sounds like a great plan," David concurred.

They sat for a while longer and drank tea from the ancient and venerable samovar, its silvery skin now worn to a fine patina by the hands of generations of users. Though much dented and abused, and now in humble circumstances, if the old tea urn could have spoken it might have told tales of its opulent early years, when the nearly mythical English explorer William Moorcroft had been served fragrant brews by the servants of the great Dhost Mohammed himself, one hundred and fifty years earlier.

The floor of the Pashtoon Hotel had not seen a mopping recently, and the table cloth was spotted with dried grease and crumbs. The flies circled in holding patterns over their table. The latest hotel owner, like his recent predecessor, was not a stickler for cleanliness.

Several long-haired young Europeans sat on cushions nearby, passing a pungent pipe of hashish—no big deal in many Kabul establishments. A young Canadian couple with travel-weary faces and sunburned noses played backgammon two tables away. The hotel's owner and operator, Shamsher's uncle, Mahmud entered, stirred the charcoal under the samovar, and exchanged a few pleasantries with his nephew. He nodded deferentially to David, excused himself, and returned to the next room, which served as both his kitchen and office.

As Shamsher was refilling their tea cups, Conrad Slocum emerged from the hallway leading to the hotel rooms and courtyard, followed by a handsome but tastelessly dressed American man, and one of the prettiest girls David had ever seen—all the more attractive after more than a year in a country where the majority of women still revealed their faces only to their families and husbands, and walked about phantom-like in opaque tents, with only their shoes and hands exposed.

"Meet my new friends Karen and Brian. They are, for the time being anyway, staying right here in this fine establishment. They're new to Kabul, and I hope you will welcome them with your usual forthright generosity. They're looking to meet fellow Americans, so I took the liberty of inviting them to your going away party next week for Dennis. I hope I have not been too presumptuous," Conrad said, introducing the couple in a parody of urbane formality. He moved three more chairs over, and all five crowded around the small table.

David introduced himself and Shamsher. The American's handshake was strong and confident without being overbearing. David tried not to stare too intently at the striking girl.

"Of course it's okay! The more the merrier! The party is supposed to be a secret, but I imagine Dennis probably knows about it by now anyway."

David made a mental note to increase the number of expected visitors by two.

"How long are you staying in Kabul?" David asked.

"We don't know for sure—we'll just see how it feels. So far we like it here," Brian answered.

"We're thinking of renting an apartment or finding someone who needs a couple of roommates for a while," Karen suggested.

"I'll keep an eye out for you." David was thinking how nice it would be to play house with the girl. David had a habit—which often proved perspicacious—of judging people by his first impressions. He immediately liked the attractive couple.

"Have you heard about the Fourth of July party this afternoon? Any US citizen is welcome. Great food, volleyball, and free beer—American and cold!" David suggested.

Karen started to speak, but her boyfriend cut her off quickly.

"I've been a little sick the last couple of days—just the usual traveling bug—but my stomach is still acting up. I guess we'll just sit this one out, but we really would like to come to your party, if that's all right," Brian answered awkwardly.

Conrad did not comment, and appeared uneasy.

David was puzzled. Hadn't Conrad just said the couple wanted to meet some Americans? What better way than the annual Independence Day event? It was obvious to David there was more to it, but he decided it was not appropriate pry so soon after introductions. Perhaps Conrad would clue him in later.

"The ambassador won't be there this time. He's out of the country. I wonder which windbag will give the speech this year?" Conrad deflected the conversational focus felicitously, to Brian's relief.

"You also are going?" asked Shamsher.

"Of course. I'm a loyal American. I would not miss it for the world. Besides, it's our only chance to mingle socially with the royalty, other than the Christmas party."

David laughed at Conrad's sarcasm. The 'royalty' he referred to were the American and other foreign dignitaries, mostly from the embassies or other official government institutions that maintained a presence in Kabul. Many of these officials found some of the PCVs and the young tourists and trekkers (whom they referred derogatorily to as 'WTs'—short for 'World Travelers') to be too casual or disrespectful in their dress and comportment, and formal social encounters between the two groups could sometimes be uncomfortable.

"We had better get going. I want to finish our errand and get to the celebration before the booze is all gone," David said, after gulping the last of his tea. He and Shamsher both stood.

"We're off then. I'll see you at the party, Conrad. Great meeting you Karen, Brian—I hope to see you both again soon!" David said, really meaning it. He and Shamsher shook hands again with the young couple, leaving them in the competent care of their mutual friend, Conrad.

They hired a cab, which took them through the busy streets of Shar-i-Nau and some distance into the old quarter, but soon they were forced to leave the taxi, as the streets, laid out ages before the automobile, became too narrow for all but pedestrians and their beasts of burden. In this part of Old Kabul the denizens still dressed traditionally. They saw none attired as they were in modern western style clothing, but like many of the educated Afghans, Shamsher would not think of being seen with his fashionable Afghan or foreign friends dressed in traditional clothing. The men stared and gestured at them openly, while the women stayed hidden under their ghostly garb. The children in this quarter of the city, unlike in the more modern neighborhoods, seemed more restrained, and did not beg from the foreign 'potato heads.' David found it odd not to hear the constant call of "Hey, Meester Katchaloo!"—the one English phrase every child in Kabul seemed to know.

Lately he had taken to responding: "No—Meester Ree-jay!" Usually the children left him alone in astonishment after this riposte, doubly amazed that he could speak a few words of their language, and that the foreigner might actually eat rice as well as potatoes.

At last they arrived at their destination—a two floor brick and wood structure much like the others on the narrow lane. They knocked on the aged but stout wooden door, and were ushered in by a tall bearded man in traditional dress. On the top floor was a small gaudily carpeted room, illuminated by one dingy window and a smokey kerosene lamp. The room was dominated by a large samovar and an equally conspicuous hookah. The host offered both, but they accepted only tea. Shamsher was very critical of his countrymen's use of hashish and opium, as were many educated Afghans, so David rarely smoked in his presence.

"I no longer will smoke the hashish. Once, when I smoked too much, I got into a very bad trouble and must go to jail," Shamsher had told David on one occasion.

"What the hell did you do?"

"I got into a fight with someone and gave him a cut with my knife. His relatives had me put into the Tolkif jail."

This seemed so utterly out of character with what David knew of his Afghan friend, he had thought at first Shamsher was only trying to make excuses for not smoking, but upon subsequent questioning Shamsher explained how he had survived his jail term (a jail sentence in Kabul for a poor person could mean death, because of the primitive prison conditions) by having his mother and siblings bring food, and the bribes from his uncle which eventually got him released. David was finally persuaded to believe him, although he found it difficult to visualize Shamsher getting into any sort of situation he could not talk his way out of, stoned or not.

After serving the tea their host left the room.

"What happens now?" asked David.

"He has gone for the musicians," replied Shamsher.

"They will play for us. We will decide if they are acceptable. Only then will we discuss the cost. Also you must not accept their first price," he explained.

This was not unexpected. Every purchase in this city had to be haggled over, and this was doubly the case for foreigners.

Four men entered the room carrying their musical instruments. Their host began tuning a multi-stringed lute-like instrument called a 'rubab.' Another musician bowed a long-necked three stringed apparatus, known as the 'del rubab,' which was played upright like a cello. A third man warmed up on tablas. The fourth ran through a few rapid scales on the harmonium, a keyboard akin to the accordion, just becoming familiar to westerners because of the use of the instrument by the Hari Krishna sect and other performers from India. Although David had wanted a purely Afghan folk group for his event's entertainment, the fact was—in Kabul at least—local musicians had embraced the Indian tabla, as well as the harmonium—originally brought to India by French missionaries, as readily as blues and jazz performers had adopted the electric guitar in Europe and the Americas.

The music which followed was rapid and hypnotic. The rubab and harmonium played melody and counterpoint, while the del rubab supplied a constant drone, and the tabla player kept up a compelling rhythm. Frequently one of the musicians would break into a wailing vocal in either the Pashtun or Farsi language.

After the fascinating and enjoyable audition, there followed a contrastingly tiresome session of tea drinking and dickering over the cost of the ensemble's services. Finally they settled on a price of nine hundred afghanis—roughly fifteen American dollars—for six hours of entertainment starting at six and ending at midnight. The musicians bowed them out smiling broadly.

In the taxi after, Shamsher pointed out testily that they had paid four hundred afghanis too much.

"It's no big deal. I could not have stood another hour of haggling—my bladder is about to burst from all that tea. Anyway, I'm already running late for the July 4 party," David replied, glancing at his watch.

Shamsher shook his head in disgust at the extravagance. The overpayment would have bought food for his family for two weeks.

"Thanks for all your help, Shamsher," David continued. "I'm going straight over to the party, and I'll get the fare of course. The cabbie can drop you off wherever you want."

The weary Volga rattled on down the street. It was an uneventful trip, which, considering the state of repair of most of the taxis in Kabul, was something to be grateful for. They were soon in front of the metal gates of the USAID compound. David felt a little awkward not inviting Shamsher to the party, but he was not sure if he would be welcome at this patriotic event, especially since Shamsher had no official connection with Peace Corps or any other American government agency. David paid the driver, and the taxi pulled away, belching noxious gray smoke.

CHAPTER 3

Patriot Games

After a quick but careful scrutiny the Marine at the US-AID compound gate waved David in. The midday heat was oppressive, but cases of cold beer fueled the revelers for an energetic if amateurish game of volleyball—currently all the rage in Afghanistan. On one side of the net were a group of PCVs as well as a few younger American tourists who had gotten wind of the party. Like many, they were only there for the free beer and food. The combined hair and beard length of these players was easily over a dozen feet. On the other side of the net were some younger staff members, a couple of off duty embassy guards, and several young Afghan men of the ruling royal family, who had been invited to the celebration weeks earlier by the now absent ambassador.

As David was about to join the game, a man stepped up to the podium on the temporary plywood stage, which had been decorated with red, white, and blue bunting suitable to the occasion. The volleyball game stopped, but not without some rude and quite audible groans from a few of the players, especially from the hirsute side of the net.

The sound system squealed, and people began moving toward the stage—all except Dennis Butler, who remained where he stood with the volleyball in one hand and a beer—his sixth, in the other. He was shirtless, and his face was flushed and sweaty from the alcohol and his exertions in the hot sun.

"Who the hell wants to listen to this bullshit! I thought this was s'posed to be a party? I don't have to listen to that asshole!"

Dennis would have gone on, but David managed to get his attention with a punch to the shoulder and a whispered warning. A few heads turned their way, and an off-duty guard glowered at them.

The speaker began a tedious and lengthy introduction to an artless and meandering speech on the meaning of patriotism. Eventually he got around to the subject of president Nixon and the Watergate hearings, which were just then transpiring in Washington. The sun burned down on the fidgety audience. Flies landed on perspiring faces. Somewhere outside the high walls of the compound a stuck car horn wailed, grating on already frayed nerves. Dennis, along with several newly arrived Peace Corps Trainees and a few of the tourist guests, out of boredom and a sort of heat-intensified hostility, began lackadaisically to throw the volleyball around. Dennis ignored David's pleas to stop, and insisted in a raspy stage whisper that they should organize teams for another game.

"...and so, we must question the patriotism of any American who would doubt the word and judgement of our harried president. All Americans, especially those of us in foreign communities, should pull together as one for the common good in these troubled times, and support the administration until the ultimate discrediting of Nixon's detractors is accomplished. We should never forget..."

But at that point in his speech Dennis backed up to the chalked service line and let fly an impressive overhand serve. The ball sailed over the net and the heads of the impatient would-be players, bounced off the side of a PA speaker cabinet, and rolled to a stop on the stage. The orator paused in mid-sentence. Dennis, with an odd half-smile on his face, walked deliberately to the stage and picked up the ball. Except for the muted traffic noise from the other side of the thick concrete compound wall, there was total silence. He gazed up briefly at the perspiring rhetorician, uncomfortably overdressed for the day in his dark suit and tie. Abruptly Dennis turned to the gathering and spoke, not loudly but very distinctly, so that all could hear.

"Nixon's a lousy crook, and only an idiot or moron would defend that fuckin' bastard!"

That was as far as Dennis got before an off duty guard tackled him from behind and the brawl started. By the time David could get to him Dennis was on the ground, attempting to evade or block the punches of the Nixon sympathizers. Fortunately for his friend, with the aid of several of the volleyball players, David managed to drag his roommate out of the fray.

"Please—please! What kind of example are we setting here?" exclaimed the speaker, trying to recover control of the situation, but his efforts were in vain.

"Fuck you—and fuck Nixon!" a long-haired youth exclaimed, and let fly with a well ripened melon slice, hitting the speaker squarely in the face, and silencing him at last.

That action triggered an all out melee. The volleyball net came down, entangling several scrimmagers. The stage and those on it were pelted with the remains of the meal by a group of tipsy teenagers, who had been surreptitiously imbibing from the vodka-laced punch bowl. In the confusion, and not without a number of scuffles and detours, David and Dennis managed to make it to the front gate, only to find it closed and manned by the pair of husky and determined-looking guards, both armed with stout night sticks. Although they could not move from their assigned stations, the sentries were not about to let the two friends exit. Just then, David and Dennis saw a figure running rapidly toward them. It was Conrad Slocum.

"What kind of crazy shit is this? Follow me if you want to get out of here with your skins intact!"

He led them off in another direction to a grove of trees close beside the compound wall. It was an easy matter for the three fit and agile young men to climb up one of the trees and drop down to the other side of the barrier from an overhanging branch, making good their escape, and avoiding what was bound to be an uncomfortable situation once the tumult ended. They soon found a taxi cab, and were well away by the time the exhausted and overheated celebrants began to come to their senses.

Conrad looked at Dennis' face, already beginning to show the effects of the blows he had received at the hands of the angry Nixon apologists.

"You were damned lucky to get out of that with no broken bones. Those two Marines at the gate would have probably given you a lot worse than you did get, if I hadn't found you in time. They get real bored standing around all day long, with nothing to do but defend the compound from the occasional over-daring beggar. I imagine they were probably looking for a good excuse to practice their craft with those truncheons," he said, looking back at Dennis from his seat in the front of the taxi.

"Fuckin' pussies! If I could have taken 'em on one at a time instead of all at once, it would have been a different story!" Dennis replied, but his smile looked forced, and one eye was nearly swollen closed.

"Maybe so, but just in case someone decides to come looking for you, you had better hole up at my place for a couple of days anyway," suggested Conrad, and he gave the cab driver directions to his apartment.

<u>CHAPTER 4</u>

Brian And Karen

The evening of July 4 brought little relief from the day's heat. It was a cloudy, muggy night without the faintest stirrings of a breeze. The flies buzzed into her room through a gap in the rusted window screen, and occasionally a moth flittered in, battering itself senseless, or senselessly battering itself—she was not sure which was better—against the bare light bulb. Karen Truman was stretched out on the bed in cutoffs and a bra, where she alternated between writing in her diary and reading from "Been Down So Long It Looks Like Up To Me," a book Brian had recommended exuberantly. She had not made much progress in the novel, which so far had not piqued her interest, nor could she seem to finish a sentence in her erratically kept dairy. The flies and moths were distracting and the heat stifling, but more disturbing was her boyfriend's loud, incessant snoring.

Then, just when she had finally gotten somewhat accustomed to his noisy breathing, the snoring abruptly ended, and Brian began twisting and writhing on the bed, talking and moaning in his sleep.

He had drunk a fair amount of wine and smoked several bowls of strong Mazar 'i' Sharif hashish before falling into his troubled siesta. She wondered what kind of dream could possibly rouse him from his stupor.

Earlier that day they had argued over his refusal to go to the Independence Day celebration. It had ended with her in tears and Brian yelling: "Go by yourself if it means so fucking much to you!" They had made up afterward, but Karen still felt bad about the fight, and wondered now if it was the cause of his sudden change from noisy but contented slumber to this perspiring nightmare. She began to shake him gently.

The sun was burning down on him. No breeze brought relief from its merciless rays. He lay on the deck of an eighteenth century square-rigger. The sails above him were slack. The big man who stood over him, cat-o'-nine-tails in hand, looked familiar. He wore the uniform of a captain, but it was a modern uniform, not an eighteenth century one. What was he doing on this ship? The big man smiled, revealing tremendous fang-like canines. Brian tried to scream, but no sound would come from his throat. The sailboat vanished. He walked through a rice field, water up to his waist. He slipped and fell into quicksand. He opened his mouth to call out for help, and someone stuffed a filthy, stinking rag into it. The hut was small and dark. He came up to it slowly and cautiously. The enemy could be here. He heard noises from inside—muffled cries of pain and fright. Through the open doorway he saw a girl not yet fully ma-

ture, no more than eleven or twelve. The big man held her face down in the dirt with his right hand clamped around her thin neck, while his left hand bent her left arm cruelly behind her back. He was mounting her from behind, and through the window Brian could see the man was using her brutally, ramming into her in a frenzy of lust and anger. He shouted obscenities at the girl and beat her savagely as she struggled and cried out. Suddenly, there was movement behind Brian in the rice field. Somehow he knew it was the girl's parents returning. The man turned at the approaching sounds, and as he did so he caught sight of Brian's face in the window opening. The big man's mouth opened in a horrible leer, again exposing his preternatural canines. He let the girl go and stood up. He and his uniform were filthy with blood and grime. He took out his service pistol and shot the girl point blank in the temple. There was no sound, only the slow motion twitching of the girl and the slight jerk of the man's arm as the gun went off. The man stepped into the doorway of the hut holding his pants up with one hand and his pistol in the other. He shot both the parents. He turned once again to Brian. His teeth seemed to have grown even larger. The sun reflected off the gun barrel, blinding him. "All right?" the man said.

"Wake up Brian! It's all right! It's just a dream. Wake up —please!"

With Karen shaking him and the bare light bulb shining directly in his eyes, Brian Peccanter slowly emerged from his horrible nightmare. He sat up and rubbed his eyes.

"Christ, that was the worst one yet! God, is it hot in here! What time is it anyway?" He was still half-drunk and soaked with perspiration.

"Don't you think it's about time you told me something about these nightmares? You've been having them for weeks! It can't be healthy for a person to have as many bad dreams as you do. Why can't you just tell me what's really wrong?"

Karen had good reason for her worries, for this afternoon variant was only the latest incidence of Brian's all-too-frequent night terrors. Often during their travels he had awakened her, groaning, thrashing, and crying out in his sleep, and the frequency of his nightmares seemed to be increasing. At first she had been frightened, but as the dreams continued, along with Brian's stubborn refusal to tell her anything about them, her initial alarm changed to a more general concern for his mental state. She had even gone so far as to purchase a couple of popular psychology books at a used book store in Peshawar.

"Why don't you tell me about your dream? Perhaps all you need to do is talk about it. Maybe then they will go away," she offered, suggesting one of the techniques from her reading.

"These nightmares aren't going to go away anytime soon, because they're too close to reality. Maybe I should tell you, after all. God knows I've got to tell somebody sooner or later. If anything happens to me someone else must know, or he'll get away with it—the bastard!"

He didn't really want to tell her even now, but she was the only person he felt he could wholly trust, and the alcohol and hashish had eroded his inhibitions.

"Who, Brian? Who is going to get away with what?" Karen said, gently stroking his tattooed arm.

"That murdering bastard, Ramsy. This isn't a story for a young girl like you to hear, but who else can I tell? If I talk to the wrong person they'll have me arrested, and send me back for court martial. I'll never be able to bring charges against Ramsy because he has the whole thing rigged. He's got me set up for triple charges of treason, drug dealing, and desertion. I'm as good as dead if I go anywhere near an American embassy, or especially a military base or ship."

This all came as a shock to Karen, who had been under the impression Brian was just AWOL, which was bad enough. She had no idea of the punishment for desertion, but the punishment for treason was a different matter. No wonder he had balked at attending the Fourth of July celebrations, and no wonder he had refused to even consider turning himself in, when she had once suggested that he could not keep on the run forever.

"Don't you think this Ramsy guy, or whoever you think is after you, will already assume I know everything, since we have been together now for so long? So you might just as well explain what is going on.

Besides, it's not fair for you to keep something so serious from me," she pouted.

Karen looked as though she was on the verge of crying. Brian hated dealing with her tears, and that was the last straw. He decided then to tell her the whole thing. Sooner or later they would catch up to him, he reasoned, and he would rather she heard the truth from him than the lies others would tell her.

"All right then, I'll tell you, but it's not a very pretty story. It all started when we were on shore leave at Da Nang. Me and another guy happened to get hold of a jeep for the day. We decided to take a little ride out of that crowded city. We were headed south towards Hoi An, but took a wrong turn and ended up out in the countryside way off the main road. Hell, it was nice just to get away from that damned ship for a while. There wasn't much traffic, mostly bicycles and a few Vietnamese farmers with their kids and animals. It was a nice sunny day—not too hot at that hour of the morning, I remember. We had a bottle of scotch and some warm beer. We were technically AWOL, but we had made arrangements with the guards back at the ship to let us back in that night in exchange for some booze and smoke. Do we have any more of that wine?" he interrupted himself.

"There's a little left—here. Go on." Karen handed him the bottle. He took a swig.

"Yeah, it was a real fine day at first. We found a nice spot on the outskirts of a small village, and pulled out a blanket and some sandwiches we had bought along. We finished the beer and most of the whisky, and my friend—his name is Stan, fell asleep. I wasn't sleepy, but pretty drunk, so I decided I had better walk it off a little before getting back behind the wheel. Hell, I could have gone in any other direction and things would have been different. All this would never have happened—though of course I might never have met you."

He kissed Karen's neck in apology.

"I guess I walked couple of miles or so—over a little hill and down past a rice field. There was a sort of raised earth dike through the flooded fields I stuck to that so I wouldn't get my feet wet. I didn't worry about where I was 'cause this area was so close to Da Nang, and supposedly clear of gooks, and anyway—like I said before—I was definitely drunk. When I got to a certain point I noticed a little hut out by itself. It was no different from any of the others I had seen, except for the jeep in front of it. I was thirsty by now and getting a little tired of walking, so I decided to check the place out —maybe they might have something to drink. Also it seemed kind of funny that a military vehicle would be way out here, and it made me curious, but since I was technically AWOL, I was careful. As I got closer to the hut I heard noises. It sounded like muffled screaming, and being cautious, and by now a little spooked, I snuck up as quietly as I could. I don't know what I expected to see. I wasn't armed, or even in uniform, and I had a sick feeling in my guts. When I looked through the doorway I saw something I will never forget, and that's why I keep having these nightmares."

He took another shaky drink from the bottle.

Karen went pale. She felt suddenly naive and vulnerable—not at all the mature woman she had imagined herself only a few moments previously.

"Tell me what you saw," she insisted, in spite of her mounting dread.

"I saw a man raping a young Vietnamese girl. Even with his back turned he seemed familiar. I'll never forget that scene. It was too horrible for words! The man was finished with her before I could recover from shock. If I had walked up a few minutes later I would have witnessed an entirely different scene, and he probably could have convinced me that he had been attacked, or that they were enemy agents, or whatever—but as it was, I saw the captain of my ship—Captain Cecil Ramsy, brutalizing that poor girl."

Brian lifted the bottle to his lips once again, before continuing.

"As soon as he had finished—before I had time to react—he kicked her aside and pulled out his service pistol. I think I screamed just as he pulled the trigger and shot her point blank in the head. Then he pointed his gun at me. Smoke was still coming out of the barrel. He ordered me inside. I had no choice. There was some old rope inside, holding up a basket of food from a ceiling beam, so the rats wouldn't get it, I guess. He took the rope and tied my hands behind my back. I didn't even struggle—I was still in shock. What was the point anyway? He would have shot me just as he did the girl. When the girl's parents came in from the fields a little while later, he wrapped his shirt around the gun and shot them both too, without any warning or emotion. He killed them as casually as you might swat a fly or mosquito."

Brian stopped his monologue abruptly and stared blankly at the bed, avoiding eye contact with Karen. His hands folded and refolded a corner of the blanket.

"So this is what you have been dreaming about." She spoke as gently as she could, trying to hide her horror.

"The dreams are never exactly the same, but the parts where he shoots the girl and her parents are almost always just as it happened." Now that he had finally revealed his horrible secret to Karen, Brian felt numb. His voice was expressionless.

For a time neither of them spoke. Two moths bent on immolation flapped crazily around the light bulb. On the street outside their window a man could be heard cursing his stubborn and overburdened donkey.

"Tell me the rest." Karen finally insisted.

"Captain Ramsy took me back to Da Nang and had me locked in the brig. I was technically AWOL, and I had some pot in my pocket that he found when he was searching me. All the way into town he kept telling me I hadn't seen anything, and if I spoke I would never see the States again. I believed him then and I still do. A man like that wouldn't stop at anything. After a couple of miserable days in the brig he told me he had decided not to have me court-martialed because the ship was getting ready to leave, and he needed me in the radar room. I just assumed he wanted me where he could keep an eye on me. A couple of days later, before we left port, the MPs raided my room. They found photocopies of classified military codes and five thousand dollars under my mattress. They also found heroin in my closet. The stuff could have been planted easily while I was in the brig, or while I was on duty, but all the circumstantial evidence was against me, and in time of war—even if it's undeclared, a military man is guilty until proven innocent."

Brian paused, and took another drink.

"For some reason, Ramsy had changed his mind again about the court-martial. The prosecution, with Ramsy's help, was building a case that I was selling military secrets to the enemy to finance a drug habit. The fact that I did smoke dope didn't help things any. A few guys would have to testify they had seen me use drugs. They had no real evidence to convict me of selling codes, but the circumstantial evidence of the photocopies and money, along with my absence the day I was AWOL didn't help me any. Even my friend Stan would have to testify that when he woke from his nap that day I was gone, and he couldn't find me in spite of searching the rest of the afternoon. My lawyer advised me to confess, even though I kept on insisting I was framed. I couldn't give him any reason for the frame-up though. I knew no one would believe my story about Ramsy. A doper and suspected traitor's word against a respected career officer? I knew I didn't stand a chance, so when the opportunity came—while they were moving me across town—I managed to get away during a traffic jam. You know the rest. So here we are. What can I do but keep running?"

"We've got to find someone to help you! There must be someone who will listen to your story, and investigate it. There must be people back in that village who know something. That poor family! Maybe they have friends or relatives who saw something that day."

Karen held his hand tightly, as much to resist the feeling of hopeless dread she felt approaching, as to comfort her boyfriend.

"Yeah, but how can we do anything now? The Navy left Da Nang months ago—at least officially. We were working on clearing out of that place and turning assets over to the South Vietnamese while I was stationed there. It would be even harder to get in there now, and the VC guerrillas are everywhere. The locals are scared shitless of both the North and South Vietnamese military, and I doubt I would be allowed to wander around looking for evidence, even if I could somehow manage to go back there. No, the only solution I can see is to lose myself somewhere where I can't be found, or extradited even if I am. Maybe Ramsy will be content to just let me go if he thinks I'll keep my mouth shut. Still, I'd sure like to see that fucker behind bars, or better yet—in front of a firing squad—where he belongs."

"I think there is someone you should tell your story to right here in Kabul," Karen said, thoughtfully.

"Yeah—who?"

"You should tell Conrad. He seems to care about us. He's already helped us get settled in here—and I bet he has a lot of good contacts. Maybe he might know of someone who could help us. I think he likes us, and we can trust him."

"You mean he likes you!" Brian said, giving Karen a good-natured pinch. "He'd probably turn me in just to get a chance at your luscious little body," Brian teased, and they wrestled and tickled until they both collapsed laughing.

"Seriously Brian," Karen said, raising herself up on one elbow. She looked at him intently as he lounged next to her on the bed. "I do think he is someone we can trust."

"I think you're probably right, Karen. I get the same feeling about him. I doubt he can do anything to help me, but it would be good to talk to someone else about it, and besides—if anything happens to me I want someone competent around who knows what is going on, and can take care of things. This is not the best place for a girl out on her own."

"I'm not as helpless as you might think," she insisted. "What do you mean, if something should happen to you? You don't think that horrible captain knows that you are here, do you?"

"I'm sure the word is out all over this part of the world, but I don't know which is riskier—staying in one spot, or moving on. Every time we cross a new border, the more likely it becomes I will be found out—but the longer we stay in one place, the more people get to know us, and odds are sooner or later one of those people will be the wrong one. I don't know how efficient INTERPOL is. I agree with you that I can't spend the rest of my life running. Maybe Europe is our best bet; at least we won't stand out so much there," he said dejectedly.

"That sounds like a good idea to me. Anyway, I've never been to Europe, and I've always wanted to see Italy and Spain," she said with an artificial buoyancy they both knew was feigned.

Fortunately there was one sure way she did know of cheering Brian up. Smiling invitingly and reaching behind her back, she unfastened her bra, and let it fall.

CHAPTER 5

A Trip To Paghman

The following morning, July 5, David woke later than usual, sensing the sunlight entering the room at an unfamiliar angle. Then he remembered he was at Conrad Slocum's apartment, where he and Dennis had spent the night. After a breakfast of naan, melon, and tea, they set out for the Pashtoon Hotel to meet Shamsher for their planned outing to Paghman, a small town in the mountain range of the same name a few miles northwest of Kabul. Conrad had already left the flat, leaving a note telling them to make themselves at home, with no indication of where he had gone or when they would see him again.

Shamsher was at the hotel when David and Dennis arrived. After more tea, the three friends hailed a taxi. Paghman was not far from Kabul, but its elevation was even higher. The cleaner air and pleasant, slightly cooler climate, as well as the presence of a reservoir nearby, Lake Qargha, made it a popular day outing and picnic spot—and a welcome relief from Kabul's mid-summer heat, dust, and traffic.

Ignoring Shamsher's look of disapproval, Dennis lit up a hashish laced cigarette as the taxi headed out of the city. Unlike his more circumspect roommate, David, Dennis had no qualms about smoking in front of their Afghan friend.

"This must be one of the few places in the world where you can wipe your ass on toilet paper from Red China, and light up a joint with matches from Russia," he quipped, inhaling mightily.

The Russian match box cover showed a crude picture of a biplane, much like the ones that still, even in 1973, found service in the Afghan Air Force. The planes were actually quite useful in the rugged country—able to fly slowly into narrow mountain valleys where faster aircraft dared not venture.

Although Dennis' face was sore, bruised, and puffy from his scrap the previous day, he was in good spirits, and happy to be off on another adventure.

"There are few trees left in our country to make the paper from. Mainly they are in far away valleys, like Nuristan—very hard to get to," replied Shamsher, entirely missing the intended humor of Dennis' comment.

Soon their taxi slowed down and entered a narrow gravel road—really not much more than a wide path, and nearly covered over with arching tree branches. A previous king had erected a summer residence here years earlier, but the palace and adjoining grounds and gardens had since been turned into a park and opened to the public—supposedly as an indication of the generosity of the present king, Zahir Shah, but more likely because he preferred to spend much of his time in Italy, where he kept yachts and villas away from the worries of his troublesome nation. Although Afghanistan was one of the ten or so poorest nations on Earth, Zahir Shah's personal wealth was immense.

After a stroll and a mid-morning snack of fresh melon and grapes, bought from one of the local vendors in the park, the three decided to go to the neighboring reservoir for a swim. Afterwards they planned to take their lunch at a local 'chaikhanna' (tea house), that Shamsher insisted made the best beef kabob in all of Afghanistan.

The reservoir proved to be neither as cool nor as pleasant as the park, as its banks were pretty well denuded of trees, and exposed for the most part to the intense sunlight. Still, the heat made the water seem all the more inviting, and David was eager to swim in spite of the fact that Lake Qargha was known to be heavily polluted.

"That would be a pretty good swim to the other side," David observed.

"Yes, it is a good exercise—maybe two or three kilometers. We can change to our swimming clothes in those buildings," Shamsher replied, pointing to some incredibly dilapidated shacks close to the beach. They resembled nothing so much as decrepit outhouses.

"I'll just watch, if you don't mind. I'm not much of a swimmer—besides I'm blasted," Dennis said, spreading a blanket they had brought along on the hot sand.

David was at best a mediocre swimmer himself, but he occasionally swam in the pool at the USAID compound, and had become somewhat more confident, if not proficient. For a time he and Shamsher splashed about in the shallows, not doing any serious swimming, being careful to avoid the many broken bottles and other potential dangers of the lake bed, and diving from a group of rocks out where the bottom began to drop off.

"I will swim across the lake now," Shamsher said, finally.

He was graceful as a porpoise in the water, a model of power used efficiently. His neck, shoulders, and upper arms had the muscular but flexible look of an Olympic gymnast. Shamsher was all control and confidence, in direct contrast to David's ill-coordinated kicking and splashing.

"No way I can make it that far, but I'll swim part way with you," replied David. "I'll turn around when I've had enough."

They swam slowly toward the opposite shore, Shamsher adjusting his speed to David's erratic progress. After only ten minutes or so, David's breathing became short and ragged. Because of his general incompetence and inefficiency as a swimmer, the effects of the greater elevation, and his mild hangover from the previous day's partying, David had begun to tire unusually rapidly.

"I better turn around here," David sputtered. He panted and treaded water awkwardly.

About half way back, with the shore still many yards away, he knew he would never make it. As in a dream he could see Dennis on his blanket, dark glasses on, drinking wine from a bota bag and reading, oblivious to his friend's distress. A few Afghan men (Afghan women used another part of the segregated beach, and rarely swam.), mostly youths, lounged about on the beach some distance away from Dennis. There were no life guards.

David's lungs ached for air. He swallowed mouthfuls of water. His right leg was on the verge of cramping. His stomach knotted, and waves of nausea threatened his ability to stay afloat as he retched into the lake. Then, in an instant, it gripped him. A full-blown charley horse, incapacitating him with spasms of pain as the muscles in his right leg contracted and refused to unclench. He screamed and thrashed in the water.

Oh shit, what a stupid way to go—only a few yards away from shore in probably ten feet of water, he thought, as he felt himself sinking. But just as he was sure his lungs must burst, he felt a strong arm around his chest, and his head broke the surface. He sucked in a huge noisy breath of air. For once Shamsher was not smiling as he silently and efficiently supported David with one arm and pulled strongly toward the shore with the other. Once he was safely back on the beach, David explained what happened. By this time a small crowd had gathered around the three friends.

"...cramp in my leg," David gasped, collapsing next to Dennis on the blanket.

"I was stupid. I should never have tried that—forgot about the extra altitude. I thought I was a goner there for sure."

"Yeah, so did I," said Dennis. "No way could I have got to you in time, and I'm not much of a swimmer either. Lucky thing Shamsher was there."

"That's right—I was sinking like a stone. You saved my life, Shamsher," David said. His breathing slowed, and a wave of fatigue washed over him as the adrenaline dissipated.

"You would have made it by your own. It was not too far. I only helped just a little bit," Shamsher laughed, showing his fine white teeth. His normal relaxed and superficially light-hearted demeanor, like a mask, seemed to have slid back into place.

But for a brief moment David had caught a glimpse of the real person behind the disguise. Underneath the shallow exterior facade Shamsher habitually showed to the world was a power of will and the physical energy more than equal to the challenge of his environment. David felt a mixture of profound respect and awe for the man, along with the realization that he was only beginning to understand his Afghan friend.

"I think I will finish my swim now," Shamsher said. "I hope you will stay away from the water now," he smiled, wading back into the lake.

"You have nothing to worry about. I'm through with swimming—at least for today," David said as

Shamsher slipped into the water and began swimming rapidly and rhythmically toward the other shore.

"How do you feel now?" Dennis asked.

David settled back on the blanket and let the hot sun dry him. The small group of gawkers who had gathered nearby, seeing the drama had ended, lost interest and wandered away.

"I'm okay—the cramp is gone, but I really thought it was the end there for a minute."

"Did your life pass before your eyes, like they always say?" Dennis replied, teasingly.

"Shit no! I was too busy trying to keep my head above the water to think about my past sins," he answered. David was beginning to feel sleepy from the effort and the heat.

"You know, they say drowning is the best way to go," Dennis suggested. He shielded his eyes from the glare of the sun with his hand, and observed with admiration Shamsher's rapid progress across the lake.

"I've heard that too, but I'm still no authority on it, thankfully," David answered.

"Well, I know of one person who experienced it. I had a friend in high school who drowned when he was about sixteen. He was with a buddy in a boat, fishing. It was early spring and the water was real cold—the lake hadn't been ice-free very long. They were goofing around only a little way from shore when their boat capsized. They both went in. There were two fishermen on the shore who heard the commotion. They got to the one kid right away, but my friend had already gone under, and it took them a few minutes to find him. When they finally did, and got him to shore, his heart had stopped, and he wasn't breathing. His lungs were full of that freezing cold lake water. They squeezed the water out and gave him artificial respiration, but it still took a little while before he started breathing on his own. They figured he was out—really clinically dead for fifteen or twenty minutes. But he recovered completely, with no brain damage or any other problems as far as anyone could tell."

"So why does that make you think drowning is such a good way to go?"

"Because of what my friend told me he remembered of his experience just before he passed out. He told me he fought as long as he could, but he had on chest waders, and they had immediately filled with water and pulled him right under. He was only in a few feet of water, but he couldn't get those damn boots off. His lungs finally gave out, and he sucked in the ice cold water. He said at that point he suddenly experienced a flood of warmth all over, and along with it a sense of peace. He knew he was dying, but the panic vanished. He had a sensation of traveling down a tunnel—as though he was losing all peripheral vision. He could see nothing at the end of the tunnel except a bright point of light. He thought of his family and his girl friend, but they seemed unimportant and far away. Then things went black and he remembered nothing at all until he woke up later on the bank of the lake."

"Since then I have read that doctors can sometimes bring back a person who has drowned if they get to them soon enough. The body has some sort of protective ability—almost like hibernation. It seems the younger you are and the colder the water the better your chances are, even if you have been out a long time. Like I said, the water was really, really cold—just above freezing—and my friend was just a teenager at the time. I've heard of other similar cases too."

"So his life didn't pass before his eyes either," David said, shivering a little as he thought of his panic just minutes earlier. He gazed across the reservoir and saw the disturbance in the water that was Shamsher, still swimming steadily, and nearly to the far shore.

"Did he seem at all changed by the experience afterward?" David was intrigued.

"Yeah it definitely affected him—and the funny thing is, the experience turned him into an atheist almost on the spot," Dennis continued.

"When he got older he liked to refer to it as his 'negative conversion.' He used to regularly piss off the religious people at school by calling himself a 'born-again atheist.' He spoke of his drowning as a 'baptism into materialism.' When his minister heard about my friend's experience, he wanted to talk to him. I guess he thought he could get him to give one of those heart-warming testimonials to the congregation. You know—really tear 'em up with visions of Christ and the angels, and a bright light, and all that stuff—the kind of stories they like to print in Guidepost or Reader's Digest. The minister was pretty upset when my friend told him how it really was. He was even more upset when my friend said he had become an atheist. Those religious types really thrive on sudden conversion stories, and I guess the minister just hadn't thought it could happen in reverse. After that the pastor wouldn't speak to my friend, even though the rest of his family still went to the same church."

"I still don't understand why the near-death experience affected him that way," David said, perplexed.

"Well, the way he explained it to me—it wasn't what happened, so much as what did not happen. You see, he and some other kids at school were heavily into ESP, telekinesis, precognition, and that sort of thing, at the time."

"Yeah, I remember reading Rhine—the guy from Duke University who was doing all these experiments with specially designed card decks. Apparently some government intelligence idiots were afraid the Russians were way ahead of us with some sort of secret program to invade our minds. It embarrasses me to admit it now, but I even sent away for some of the cards and wrote a paper on ESP for an English class. I thought I could prove the existence of a non-physical world as something separate from the physical world by showing that ESP didn't obey the natural laws of physics. My logic and metaphysics were pretty screwed up at the time. I feel sorry now for the poor teacher who had to read that awful thing!" David laughed.

He felt his drowsiness finally dissipating. In the distance they saw Shamsher, standing on the opposite shore, stretch briefly before diving back into the water for the return trip.

"You know what I'm talking about then," Dennis went on.

"After that my friend began to read those stories by people who die in hospitals and see angels, their ancestors, God, or Christ, and then are brought back to life by the doctors, and are compelled from then on to tell everyone about it. He really did a serious amount of research on the subject, collecting those stories until he had hundreds of them by the time he graduated from high school."

"I get it now—so when your friend drowned and didn't see God or a choir of angels with harps, he figured it was all bunk," David said.

"Yeah, that's only part of it though. He also told me the whole thing was accompanied by a very strong and positive feeling that God—at least in the normal religious sense, did not exist; that Christianity was a big lie, and that he should live for the moment—not for some sort of pie-in-the-sky afterlife. That's why he always referred to it as his 'born-again-atheist-vision.'"

Dennis paused in his monologue and took a long swig of wine from the bota bag.

"The whole thing was emotionally charged for him. He really upset his family and some of his friends for a while. I mean the guy was like some sort of old testament prophet, only in reverse. He went around telling everyone at school he had died and seen what was on the other side and it was nothing, so they better start thinking about the here-and-now and forget about heaven or hell. He really irritated some people. You gotta understand this guy was real popular—class president, high honor roll, a letterman in track and football. Nobody had the guts to fight him, but he lost a lot of friends, and somehow never got a couple of scholarships that had been promised to him. After he got out of high school he mellowed out, though. I guess he figured out people would rather hang on to their comfortable illusions, and there was no point in upsetting them."

Dennis dug one foot lazily in the warm sand, enjoying the feel of it on his bare toes.

"I saw him again spring break my senior year in college, just before I graduated and went into Peace Corps," he went on, after a moment.

"He was in the process of collecting more near-death stories for a paper he was writing for a psychology class. This time he had collected stories from around the world—not just in America, as he had in high school. There were quite a few from America and Europe where people did have Christian-type visions, although there was a fair amount of variability even in those stories. Predictably enough the stories he collected from Hindus or Buddhists often featured their own mythological figures. But to him the most interesting stories came from the so-called 'primitive cultures,' mostly African, Australian, and New Guinean He thought he was beginning to find some sort of pattern. I can't remember just how he put it—something about imprinting in childhood that establishes what a person near death will visualize as his brain goes into oxygen starvation or sudden shock, if I am remembering it right."

"So what do you think?" David asked.

"Well, you already know I'm agnostic, and I've had too much psychology to doubt that these experiences are anything more than just another example of the sort of tricks our brains are capable of. Anyway, the incredible variety of experiences he had collected were enough to convince me, or any halfway intelligent person, that those experiences depended mostly on the culture the person had grown up in. There was no single vision of reality at death, just as in life."

"That seems like a reasonable conclusion," David replied.

"Shit, my favorite story was one he collected from an Australian Aborigine. It seems this tribesman nearly died of appendicitis, but they got him to some miserable little outpost clinic just in time, and the doctor managed to bring him back from the edge. After he regained consciousness he started raving about a giant penis he said inhabited the spirit world in the afterlife, or dreamtime. What was even funnier was that it was not even a human penis, but a kangaroo dick of incredible proportions—unattached and fully erect! Apparently this Aborigine started a minor religious movement in the area—a sort of Kangaroo Penis Cult. For a time you could see the tribesmen busily carving away, making hundreds of kangaroo pricks. I guess they were real hits with the tourists and art collectors."

Dennis chuckled, recalling his friend's story. He felt a sudden twinge of acute homesickness, and remembered he had only a few more days before he would be on his way back stateside again.

"I didn't see a giant cock or a choir of angels, but I guess I didn't get close enough to really drowning," David said. "And even if it is a pleasant way to go, I would just as soon stay around for a while longer. The only thing I felt out there was panic, and a sense of my own stupidity and vulnerability."

Just then Shamsher emerged from the water, smiling and dripping. David could only marvel at his strength and endurance. He had rescued a drowning swimmer, then immediately swam the breadth of the lake and back at a good pace. He was only mildly winded.

"Is anyone hungry?" Shamsher asked, toweling himself off, as though nothing at all out of the ordinary had occurred.

"Damned right!" answered David. "Let's check out that chaikhanna you were telling us about earlier. I'm more than ready to try that legendary kabob now. Drowning sure works up an appetite!"

CHAPTER 6

David Stuckrath

"Men do not know how real love should be. Nothing they have can ever satisfy them. They're always dreaming dreams, building up new duties, going to new countries and new homes. Women are different. They know that life is short and one must make haste to love, to share the same bed, embrace the man one loves, and dread every separation. When one loves one has no time for dreams."—Camus, The Misunderstanding

David Stuckrath awakened, as he did all too often, from some murky erotic dream featuring Clio, or a woman very much like her. He lingered in bed and thought back to the confusion and emotional turbulence of those last weeks at college. What he had not appreciated in his grand plans for a future without Clio was the sheer physical ache of life without her. If he had been able to really envision the loss of their casual day to day skin to skin contact, the lazy Sunday morning sessions in bed, or the occasional quick assignations between classes, when their different schedules might allow, perhaps he might never have left her. He had not foreseen just how difficult daily life would be without her—the sound of her voice, the easy intimacy, and the daily routine as it had been his last two undergraduate years at the university.

He had to be honest with himself about this. He had chosen, brutally and finally, to leave her. In the end there could be no real justification for his actions in the rigorous reptilian logic of the emotions—his or hers. In the deep recesses of his limbic brain where only the strict dichotomies of pleasure and pain, desire and fear, comfort or stress held sway, an insistent voice accused and would not be stilled. And ultimately—many months later, and so far from home—he was not sure that the more primitive part of his mind was not wiser than the fully conscious part which had made the decision to break up their relationship. For his decision to join Peace Corps, as much as he might rationalize it as a wish to travel and learn more about the world, or as the presumption that he was too young and immature to let this love affair run its natural course, was really a decision not to commit to their relationship at all—or at least to ensure that what they had could not evolve into anything more permanent.

David had not believed at the time that it was possible to experience authentic love, let alone to commit to marriage and all that implied at such a young age, or that his feelings were more than a youthful infatuation, and he had been willing to sacrifice his happiness as well as Clio's for those conceits.

David's first two years at the university were unremarkable. The routine of weekday classes, punctuated in the normal undergraduate fashion with weekend and holiday gatherings of fellow classmates for the usual binges—a perfectly typical undergraduate lifestyle. There were the occasional one night stands and a couple of girls who held his interest for several weeks, but until he met Clio nothing very memorable or satisfying.

Clio was the first bright glimmer in that otherwise bleak and lonely summer—a summer hot and languid as any other in the agricultural heartland of that west coast state. The fields of hay and grain surrounding his tiny rented house were tall and golden in the early evening of his walk, and though the sun's intensity had eased somewhat, the air temperature still hovered in the low eighties. She was walking down the country road near his house, soaking wet from a dip in a local irrigation canal. Her dripping shirt and cut off shorts clung to her, and she wrung the water from her hair, flaxen as the fecund fields, as she walked. For David it was lust at first sight. She had a sun-freckled face and an awkward gait that reminded him of a colt at play. She seemed to have not quite adapted as yet to her new woman's body.

He had pursued and ultimately won her with a mental and physical intensity that he had not known himself capable of until then. He had run the gauntlet of the friend and family gatherings, impatiently waiting for his moment as she played him off against several other suitors. He had endured long evenings of polite conversation while he longed only to lay his naked body next to hers. He had known instinctively that although she was obviously attracted to him too, she would not decide in his favor unless her family and friends approved of the match. And suddenly, unaccountably one evening, she was his. A quiet dinner at his place, a bottle of wine, the couch, and then her suggestion—not his!— that the bed might be more comfortable.

It did not take long for them to agree that sharing accommodations would not only be more convenient and fun, but would also save them money. But from the day they had moved in together it had seemed to him the relationship had gathered an independent momentum over which David had no influence or control. Their families and friends assumed it was only a matter of time before they would announce a marriage date. Perhaps after college graduation, several of Clio's friends speculated.

The series of events which led to his current status as a Peace Corps Volunteer in Afghanistan had started with a seemingly insignificant decision to eat at a certain restaurant. That decision came in turn from David's exasperation with the constant grinding poverty that had attended all the years of his college career. His frustration and resentment had all boiled over one frigid day in early January.

It had been an unusually dreary Christmas and New Year's holiday season. David's parents had divorced many years earlier, but the recent death of his mother was the final straw. Sick or well she had been the glue that bound the family together. With her gone,

David and his siblings scattered. With no center, his family had fallen victim to centripetal forces. Clio had traveled to California for her own family gathering, while David attended a sad holiday afternoon with his maternal grandparents, before driving fifty miles to spend the same Christmas evening with the paternal set. With his mother gone there was simply no way the two would celebrate together. Theirs had been a history of barely concealed animosity.

That New Year's Eve he partied with old hometown friends, ultimately spending the night in a drunken tryst with a sad-eyed girl who revealed to David that she had wanted him all through her cheerless high school years. Gratefully, with tears streaming down her cheeks, she stroked and rode him until she finally, through her persistent efforts, extracted what she needed. Until that night David had not realized just how melancholy the sexual act could be. He had left early and awkwardly in the morning, mumbling excuses, saying the appropriate words, both of them knowing he would never call again.

And now, here in Kabul with Reshtina, the situation was all too similar, the difference being that this time he actually cared for the girl as a friend, and that she was an important part of his social network in this foreign place.

On the phone, and hungover the first day of that new year, he had listened to Clio talk about all the fun she was having with her relatives several hundred miles distant. She had invited him to join in the festivities, but

David was too broke and depressed to agree. He had a few days left before Clio got back and winter term classes started. He spent the days reading and walking, and the evenings drinking with the few of his college buddies who still remained in town over the holidays, but his funk grew deeper.

A few days into the new year David walked from his apartment towards campus with the intention of idling for a couple of hours at the Student Union building. He was in a particularly foul mood, and felt the need to get out of the confining three room flat he shared with Clio. He had twenty dollars in his wallet left from the fifty his paternal grandparents had given him for Christmas, and after paying the January rent and electric bill, less than five dollars in his bank account.

This was by no means an unusual situation. For three years he had scrimped and scrounged his way through college, working long hours in the summers and between terms at various menial jobs to finance his education. His present situation was no worse than normal, but for some reason his poverty especially galled David that particular day.

The restaurant was inviting. It was a popular gathering place for professors and the more well-heeled students, but way beyond his budget. An occasional cup of coffee and donut at the student union, or the rare fast food burger was about all he could ever legitimately afford in the way of an epicurean splurge.

Fuck it, he had said to himself that day, and entered the restaurant, determined to spend the remains of his holiday money regardless of future budgetary consequences.

It was well before the noon hour, and the restaurant was nearly empty. The young waitress had raised her eyebrows slightly as he ordered the soup and sandwich special, and a bottle of young but well-reviewed Bordeaux from the fussy menu. He drank the entire bottle of wine and ate the light meal, leaving the restaurant with three dollars in his wallet and a fantastic midmorning buzz.

As he walked on through the mostly empty campus (winter term registration had not yet begun) he imagined his life stretching inexorably out before him: Two more terms at the university, and graduation with a degree in history; marriage to Clio and an entry level job, or perhaps another year of struggle to get his teaching certificate, but regardless, a position making barely more than survival wages. Later, if they lived frugally they might move into a larger apartment or, at best, a small fixer-upper starter home. Inevitably a baby or two; holidays with Clio's family; some new furniture and maybe a nicer used car after a few more years. It all seemed so final—so inexorable, and yet he felt as though he had never consciously chosen any of it.

He knew if he spoke of these thoughts to Clio she would just laugh, and insist their lives would never be that way. She would tell him to stop worrying and to live in the present. They had both agreed early in their relationship to live life day to day, and not make plans or promises while they were both still in school. But he knew she would be terribly hurt to think he might not be willing to accept any future imaginable, so long as it was with her.

After a short walk he arrived at the student union. On the landing were an array of booths, where several organizations promoted their causes and displayed their pamphlets and information. ROTC had a kiosk, as did a local anti-war group. One of the booths had been commandeered by a Peace Corps representative, Vanessa. She was pretty, perky, and personable—the ideal emissary for her recruiting role. Since the semester had not yet commenced, the normally busy area was nearly empty. No students gathered at the recruiting table, and David, still pleasantly buzzed from the wine, struck up a conversation with the lovely liaison. Before he quite knew how it happened he had filled out the application form and given it to the girl.

Somehow in the course of his shameless flirtation with her, he had come to believe that Peace Corps could be the answer to his problem of what to do after graduation. As he filled out the paper work, under the spell of the comely Vanessa and his vinous valet, he gave no thought to the repercussions should he actually be accepted into the organization.

He said nothing to Clio when she returned from her holiday visit. That was the second secret he had withheld from her. Later, he reflected that his one night stand New Year's Eve seemed in some way to have opened the door to this ultimately more serious betrayal. He remained ambivalent. In part he hoped to be accepted, but he was also ashamed of himself for the continued deception, and mostly he hoped nothing would come of it, but he refused to withdraw his application. He had decided to let chance or fate decide the issue.

Life went on as usual for the couple until one day, many weeks later, he received notification that he had been accepted as a Peace Corps Trainee. This he could not hide from her. Clio had been even more devastated by the revelation than he had anticipated, and especially by the fact that he had not consulted her before applying. For several nights he slept in the living room on the couch.

Eventually though, they made up. They even optimistically planned for Clio to join him after he was settled into his post in Kabul—after she saved enough money from her summer job to make the trip. They might trek together through India and Nepal, and even explore Europe if finances allowed, they fantasized in their more lighthearted discussions of future possibilities. But as the time drew nearer for him to leave Clio became moodier. She felt that David had betrayed her and sabotaged their relationship by coming to this decision alone. She cried easily and often.

Their parting scene at the airport burned yet in his memory. As he got on the plane that was to take him half way around the world, it was with the sense that they both understood their relationship would not survive the distance or time. It felt to David like another death in his family, but this time he had been the willing assassin.

Normally it took at least three weeks for a letter to get from the states to Afghanistan. The frequency of Clio's letters had trailed off as time had passed. In her last letter, received three months earlier, she still had not received his own dispatches of the past several months. Apparently letters posting from Kabul were taking even longer to reach their destination than normal, for some unknowable reason. Her most recent letters had been encouraging and positive, but there was no passion in them. He knew her love for him had ended as surely as he knew anything.

David had since comforted himself to a certain extent with several flirtations, and the unfortunate assignation with Reshtina; but the lacuna had affected him more than he could have ever imagined, and though he was careful never to reveal his feelings to even his closest companions here, there were still times, when alone with his regrets, that the enormity of his loss was overwhelming.

CHAPTER 7

Paul Sherman

The hotel phone rang several times before he answered it, rolling over on his side and fumbling sleepily on the night table.

"Good morning, this is your wake-up service. Would you like breakfast this morning, sir?" The voice was masculine, and heavily accented.

"Uh...send me up a bowl of fruit, coffee, and two pieces of toast in about half an hour. Thanks," the man said, sitting up in the bed and rubbing his eyes.

He got up and went into the bathroom. It was modern, luxurious, and more importantly, clean. There was a tiled tub-shower combo, two sinks, heat lamps, lots of towels everywhere, and even a monogrammed bathrobe. Of course his client could afford the best, and the Hotel Intercontinental in Kabul was the best—in fact it was just about the only decent place to stay in the entire country of Afghanistan, by his standards.

He shaved. The face in the mirror was lean, tanned, and by any measure handsome. The reflection displayed a head of closely cropped dark brown hair, a noble forehead over pair of perfectly arched eyebrows, gray eyes set astride a prominent but well-shaped nose, and a boldly masculine jaw line. It was a young looking face—perhaps of a man in his early to mid-thirties—certainly no older. Not many would have guessed he had recently celebrated his fortieth birthday.

He dressed quickly, and picked up his wallet and watch from the night table. His passport lay there too, partially open. It was a well-worn and much-handled document, almost completely filled with customs stamps and official signatures. In fact, this was only the latest in a series of passports the man had owned under several different names. The photo in front was a recent one—a good likeness except that he had shaved the mustache off a week earlier in India.

The name on the passport—his real name on this occasion—was Paul Sherman. The document described a US citizen, born in 1933, height six feet two inches, weight 190. He was dressed simply but expensively; a pair of light khaki slacks; pale blue cotton short-sleeved shirt; a perfectly tailored summer sports jacket; and expensive leather walking shoes, also custom fit. He slipped his Beretta M 1951—an especially reliable early sixties Egyptian version, into the left inside pocket of his jacket. In a special sheath, strapped to the inside of his left leg, was concealed a small short-bladed knife, the blade honed to a razor edge.

More important than the weapons to Paul were the two envelopes stashed in the small leather suitcase (his only baggage), which lay open upon the floor. One of the envelopes contained an official document, embellished with an impressive number of government stamps and signatures of high ranking officials. It requested the cooperation of the governments and police forces of any country he should happen to pass through. The document went on to describe special agent Sherman's mission—an international manhunt.

The quarry was an enlisted navy man, Brian Peccanter: Age 21; height 5' 11;" weight 180; hair, brown; eyes, brown. Identifying marks: Tattoo of mermaid on left upper arm; tattoo of eighteenth century sailing ship with the words 'Property Of US Navy' on right forearm. Wanted for desertion, drug trafficking, assault, and treason. There was a photocopy of the man's military ID photograph.

The other envelope contained a letter from Paul's long time friend and Korean war buddy, Captain Cecil Ramsy. They had grown up together and attended the same high school in California. Cecil had graduated a year before Paul. When Paul graduated they had both enlisted together in the Navy. After Korea their paths had diverged—Cecil continuing on in the military and advancing rapidly through the ranks by virtue of his single minded obsession with all things related to the service, and good timing in being involved in two Southeast Asian conflicts just as many World War II veterans were settling into civilian life. Paul went into Naval intelligence, but did not reenlist when his tour of duty was over, having ultimately found the military life too constrictive for his tastes.

After four years of college and a series of unsatisfying jobs, Paul met up with his old friend again at their ten year high school reunion. Cecil, now advanced to a First Mate position on a Navy cruiser—boozy and boasting of his social connections with certain powerful government officials—suggested he could help Paul find a better a better line of work, having become especially good friends with a high ranking officer of an obscure federal intelligence agency. Drunk he might have been, but Cecil kept his promise, and Paul was once again employed in the espionage trade—this time for a well-funded and top secret spy organization not directly connected to any of the military branches.

This job, lacking the strict trappings and routine of his previous position, had agreed much better with Paul. He excelled at his new station. His status as a confirmed bachelor; his willingness to travel; his intellect; his discretion, and attention to detail had resulted in a great many interesting and important assignments over the years, as well as a few dangerous ones. It was just the sort of life Paul was suited for. He felt privileged and lucky to be one of the few men he knew who had found the perfect employment—work that both interested him and paid well.

He was reminded once again, as he ate his light breakfast in the Kabul hotel, that he ultimately owed his agreeable circumstances to his old friend, the recently promoted, now Captain, Cecil Ramsy.

However, his present assignment was not the sort of duty he was used to. Gathering information in foreign lands while posing as a tourist; monitoring Russ-ian broadcasts from disguised fishing boats; keeping track of suspected enemy agents; or even, on one occa-sion, slipping poison into the meal of a traitorous mole known to have been responsible for the murder of one of their own—these were the kind of assignments he was prepared to carry out. But this mission to track down, and if necessary to kill one of his own country-men, was extraordinary.

This was not, however, an obligation he could refuse, even if he felt so inclined. Cecil, to whom he owed his career, had specifically requested his involve-ment in the case, and through his powerful contacts, had orchestrated Paul's personal participation. During their gin-sodden reunion in Hong Kong a few weeks earlier, his friend of nearly thirty years had described how the young Navy enlisted man, Brian Peccanter, had sold the enemy code secrets, and then somehow es-caped from Viet Nam and the punishment he deserved.

In spite of the three days and nights of drinking and whoring he had spent with his old friend, Paul had not enjoyed the visit. Cecil seemed to have become almost a caricature of himself—a coarser and grosser parody of the man he had known for so many years. Although there was only a year's difference in their ages, Paul had been shocked by how much older Cecil appeared, and by how badly he had let himself deteriorate in the time since they had last seen each other. Cecil's face and body were that of a man easily fifteen or twenty years older than his actual age. He wasn't fat, but he had no muscle tone, and his flesh seemed to hang on him—especially loose around the neck and face—giving him a weak and dissolute appearance. Paul, no teetotaler himself, noticed his friend drank two drinks for every one of his, and continued drinking long after Paul had imbibed more than enough.

His practiced eye also registered other disturbing behaviors. As an intelligence operative Paul had learned over the years to automatically watch for expressions and involuntary movements of people that gave away their true underlying emotional state, especially if the person were lying, tense, or trying to hide something. All during their visit Cecil had displayed many of these signs, especially when they discussed seaman Peccanter. Cecil seemed to be obsessed with the incident, as though he had a personal stake in the capture of the accused traitor. Perhaps, Paul told himself, he did, as Captain Ramsy was considered to be in line ultimately for a promotion to Admiral, and probably felt that this incident, if left unresolved, could affect his chances. Certainly his friend was preoccupied with the desire to advance in rank, but his concern with the escape of the young radar technician seemed to have become an even greater fixation.

"If I wasn't an officer with so many responsibilities, I'd hunt the bastard down myself and put him where he belongs. Why waste the taxpayer's fucking money on a court-martial?" Cecil said on their final night together at a popular Hong Kong bar, where they watched as minimally clothed girls of several nationalities demonstrated their dubious dancing abilities, to the taped music of Tom Jones, Englebert Humperdinck, and The Carpenters.

"I asked the Admiralty for this furlough when I heard he had kidnaped that teenaged girl in Nepal. What kind of animal would drag a young girl through the hell-holes of Asia like that? And that money in his room—more than five grand! Shit, how is an enlisted man on his pay supposed to get his hands on that kind of cash. I'd like to shoot the fucker myself! Bartender! Give us another round! Yeah, make 'em doubles again!"

"Did you ever think maybe he was just selling dope, not secrets," Paul suggested.

He was weary of the whole subject, and the late hours and constant drinking had made him uncharacteristically testy. Paul wanted nothing more than to get a good night's sleep, and to get as far away as possible from the irksome Captain Ramsy. He was both saddened and annoyed by the realization that he was not enjoying his visit with this man, whom he had regarded until that very week as his most trusted and closest friend.

"Hell, they found the code sheets in his room. He's as guilty as a queer in women's underwear!"

"Well anyway Cecil, he's not being accused of kidnaping. The girl's parents are not interested in prosecuting the guy for anything. They say she left a note telling them she was leaving. Her parents are sure she left because she is smitten with the man. Sounds voluntary to me. The parents just want to know that she is safe and her whereabouts. They seem like reasonable people. I got through to the girl's father on the phone this morning, while you were still snoring your ass off," said Paul, increasingly irritated by Cecil's rant.

"Hey! Who's fuckin' side you on anyway? Should I be sorry I requested you for this job? What's wrong—you got no stomach for real work anymore? You must be gettin' too used to that easy duty Washington desk job, and those big titted secretaries, eh?" Cecil said, poking Paul in the ribs conspiratorially.

Sensing even in his intoxicated and disgruntled mood that he had gone too far, Cecil abruptly dropped the subject. Their conversation switched to the more usual topics of military and intelligence community gossip and intrigue, to Paul's relief. For the rest of that final evening in Hong Kong Cecil behaved more like himself, or at least the person Paul was familiar with. Even so, as he waved goodbye to his old friend from the airport tarmac and boarded the plane out of Hong Kong, Paul could not shake the sensation that Cecil was hiding something.

In his room at the Kabul Hotel Intercontinental Paul Sherman finished his light breakfast and pondered the case. The evidence for treason seemed flimsy.The suspect worked with codes on a regular basis in his position as a communications specialist The money could have come from drug sales, or some other sort of covert business. It was common knowledge many of the enlisted men in Viet Nam got high on a regular basis. He did not suppose seaman Peccanter's crew were any different. Maybe the man was one of the dealers who supplied the ship, or perhaps he was the ship's connection to the local sex trade. Da Nang was notably chaotic and corrupt, and it was certainly possible that the young radar technician was involved in illegal smuggling activities. The desertion charge, however, was not circumstantial. Why had he gone AWOL if he wasn't guilty of some crime; and why would he have been so careless as to leave copies of secret information in his quarters?

It's not my job to investigate the case anyway—just to bring in the man, thought Paul, but he felt something was not right, and Paul was a man who normally paid attention to his intuition, which had saved his life on more than one occasion. He had been in Asia less than two weeks, and he was becoming more and more uncomfortable with this assignment.

Agent Sherman went down the stairs and out of the foyer into the bright Kabul morning. He had a near obsession with physical fitness, and never used elevators when on his own. He glanced at his Rolex, noting it was not yet eight o'clock. Paul Sherman was the type of person who always reset his watch to local time on the flight before deplaning at his destination. He was a meticulous man, and he trusted his instincts. Both of these personality characteristics had influenced his decision to travel to Kabul.

After his visit with Captain Ramsy in Hong Kong Paul had flown to Calcutta and Lucknow, then chartered a small plane to Nepalganj, where he had met the Trumans. The conversation with Mr. Truman and his teary-eyed (but very attractive) wife had presented him with an interesting puzzle. The note the girl had left said she and her boyfriend, Brian Peccanter, were heading back to his ship, so that he could turn himself in. But it did not seem to Paul, considering the gravity of the charges against him, that Peccanter intended to return voluntarily, or he would have done so by now. Additionally, the seaman's ship had left Da Nang shortly after his desertion, and the young enlisted man had surely been aware of that event. It was evident to Paul the letter was simply a clumsy attempt to disguise the couple's real intentions.

Paul did not choose to upset the Truman couple any further by spelling out the details of the charges against their daughter's lover. As far as Paul was concerned, it was just as well for the Trumans to think of Karen's boyfriend as simply absent without leave. Paul was not a thoughtless or unkind person. In spite of the fact that the serviceman had apparently enticed their daughter to leave without consulting them, the girl's parents seemed to genuinely like and approve of her boyfriend.

One obvious fact, one hunch, and one clue led Paul to believe the two had not gone east as the letter had suggested.

*The fact: It had been over a month since they had left Nepal, yet his diligent research had come up with no trace of the serviceman or the girl at any location between Nepal and Viet Nam.

*The hunch: It did not seem plausible that the young man, who so far had proven himself to be skilled at evading detection, would be very likely to turn himself in with the likelihood of a long prison residence, or even a possible death sentence as probable outcomes.

*The clue: About a week after the couple left Nepal, the Trumans had received a postcard from their daughter which was postmarked Bara Banki, near Lucknow. While it was true Bara Banki was a convenient stopping place en route from Nepalganj, where the Trumans were based, a quicker route east should have taken them through Faizabad if they were traveling overland.

Paul was sure for a variety of reasons, most especially the young couple's financial limitations, that they would be traveling via surface transportation—buses, trains, taxis or perhaps by catching a ride with one of the young hippie tourists who sometimes traveled through the area. Still, just to be doubly sure, Paul checked flight records at the Lucknow airport, and talked to baggage handlers and taxi drivers in the city. In spite of spending a fair amount on bribes and gifts, he found no evidence the two had ever been in the city or its airport. He had not expected to find anything, but agent Paul Sherman could be thorough to a fault.

Ultimately he followed his instincts and headed west, flying to New Delhi from Lucknow. He spent several days there investigating the airport and train stations. He questioned the bus and taxi drivers, and American tourists and trekkers, as he had at Lucknow. He even checked with the hospitals and the local doctors on the chance that the man may have had another of his bouts of dysentery, the reason he had come into the Truman's lives in the first place. There were no leads in New Delhi either.

His next stop was Lahore, Pakistan. Two more days in that sweltering city left him with no new information and a raging fever, which kept him confined to his hotel room for another two days. When he was feeling better he decided to continue on west to Kabul, the next obvious stopping point besides Peshawar on the overland route west. Of the two cities he was sure the higher altitude and healthier climate of Kabul would be more bearable then the hellish midsummer heat of Peshawar. He did not have much real hope of finding the couple in Kabul, but his intuition was that they had headed west, and perhaps passed through the city.

Although he had not found any evidence of the couple's specific route, he felt sure he was on the right track. His goal was to find them soon, in this part of the world, where an American stood out like a Muslim in a cathedral, and before they could make good their escape to Europe, for he was sure that must be their destination, where they could blend in and lose themselves with any luck and a little common sense.

Paul had a second and even more compelling reason to visit Kabul. His Washington boss had asked him to check in with a contact whose services they had previously engaged. Conrad Slocum was a young American who had been providing some good intelligence to the Agency on a sort of contractual basis. He was one of the few people they had in the country who was completely fluent in Pashtu, and also well placed to gather information on the activities of the local communist parties and their Russian and Chinese contacts. He had been asked by his superior to debrief Slocum and pass any pertinent information on to headquarters when he returned to Washington. Beyond that, Paul's supervisor had urged him to make an effort to recruit the young man as a full-time agent, even encouraging Paul to entice the man with an especially generous starting salary and benefits package if necessary, as an incentive. Paul hoped the young operative might also be of some help in locating the American couple, if they had in fact visited Kabul.

CHAPTER 8

The USAID Bar

Paul Sherman was a confident and persistent man. As he walked the streets of Kabul he mentally reviewed and analyzed the leads and clues—such as they were—of the Peccanter case. The fact that his close friend seemed so adamant that the young miscreant be captured aroused his curiosity to an even higher pitch, and if anything caused him to concentrate even more of his already substantial capabilities on the problem at hand.

All morning, traveling by taxi and on foot, agent Sherman made the rounds of Kabul's modern quarter. He presented his credentials and made inquiries at the British, Canadian, American, French, and German embassies. Paul then paid his respects to the Kabul police chief, leaving his card and an envelope of twenty dollar bills on the chief's desk.

After a late lunch back at the hotel, he took a taxi to the Peace Corps administration office. He did not enjoy dealing with them. From past experience he had found the organization to be generally the least cooperative of all the United States agencies overseas. Perhaps they were sensitive to the accusations made by some that the Corps was a front for American espionage activities. Despite their typical reluctance to offer much in the way of help, he was at least able to get a list of phone numbers and addresses of all the volunteers and employees stationed in Kabul and the nearby communities. He reasoned that if Brian Peccanter and Karen Truman had passed through Kabul, there was at least a chance one or more of the younger Peace Corps personnel had made their acquaintance.

His initial foray had failed to turn up any concrete information on his quarry. Hot and thirsty, he decided to stop in at the bar in the USAID compound. The compound was substantial, with the typical tall enclosing concrete walls topped by an iron railing. It was located on a side street close to Cannon Mountain, a historic fortified prominence overlooking the city, and the location of Kabul's famous 'Noon Guns,' a pair of nineteenth century cannons that had been fired each day for nearly a century.

He acknowledged the uniformed Marine guards, entered through the iron gates, and quickly scanned the compound. Inside were tennis courts—empty this torrid afternoon—the popular swimming pool, which had been commandeered by several rowdy teenaged boys and girls, and a large building which contained the bar, his destination. The low structure was surrounded on two sides by a screened porch. Two young American hippie types were playing ping pong on a table there. An Afghan was watching from a bench close by. Paul noticed the Afghan was drinking a beer—a somewhat unusual sight in this Islam country.

He sat down at the bar and ordered a Schlitz, the only brand of American beer available, he noted. Looking over the room, Paul noticed a couple of amplifiers and a drum set in one corner, a few large potted ferns scattered among the tables, and an old fifties era Wurlitzer jukebox, whose polished metal and glass surfaces clashed with the otherwise understated and muted decor. Two ceiling fans rotated so slowly above that they created no discernible movement of air in the room.

He was immediately disappointed the bartender was not American. Paul had learned over the years that emigre bartenders in exotic locations could often be a great sources of information. But this bartender was a fastidious Indian with an ingratiating smile permanently pasted to his face—the type Paul knew would be deferential without being informative. Paul also noticed he kept a damned fine bar. The place was spotless—not a glass or bottle out of place, nor a speck of dust or drop of liquid on the counter. *Not much business here,* Paul surmised, correctly.

He drained the beer quickly, decided he was still thirsty, and ordered a Bombay and tonic. The two Americans, one with a corona of wild red hair, the other with extremely long brown locks and a full beard, came in from their table tennis game followed by the well-set Afghan. The only other people in the bar were an older American couple in one corner sipping martinis. To

Paul's practiced eye they looked like tourists—sunburned and a little drunk, though it was only mid-afternoon. Periodically the woman burst out with a peal of laughter, a high pitched irritating squeal.

"We need three more beers, if you would, please," said the bearded youth.

In spite of his unkempt appearance, Paul observed he was at least well-mannered. For all his sophistication and percipience Paul was still a man of his generation, with an innate distaste for the beatnik and hippie types, though he certainly did not share the animosity for them many of his fellow agents did. They were young, spoiled, and unrealistic, in Paul's estimation, and would soon grow out of their naiveté.

The bearded man turned his head Paul's way and nodded, acknowledging Paul's presence without assuming he wanted to converse, confirming Paul's first impression of the young man's good breeding.

"Keep the rest," the American said, handing the bartender an Afghan bill.

The three youths found a place at a table slightly behind and to the left of Paul's barstool, but close enough he could make out much of their conversation if he attended closely. The bartender's toothy smile widened even more as he accepted the money and returned to dusting and arranging the already immaculate bottles.

Two more Americans walked in. They were also young, but not nearly so hirsute as the previous two. One of them went over to the esteemed Wurlitzer and made a selection. (No money was required. The coin slot mechanism had been disabled years earlier.) The other newcomer pulled up a chair next to the two ping pong players and their Afghan companion. The one who had made the jukebox selection went to the bar for more beer, before joining the rest of the group. The opening bass guitar line of "Badge" by the rock band Cream issued from the venerable old automaton, but not so loud as to drown out the conversation behind him.

"Are you guys coming to the party?" the bearded one asked the newcomers.

As Paul continued to sip his drink he listened idly to their chatter.

"You can count on me being there! Do you want us to bring anything?" one of the newcomers responded.

"We don't need any more food, for Christ's sake. We've got that covered in spades, but you can bring booze if you want—the more the better. You know the way, right?" The bearded one, David Stuckrath, drew lines on a paper coaster as he described the location of the apartment.

"I remember now. I was out that way a couple of months ago in a cab, and the driver said Peace Corps lived there," the other newcomer said. He dropped the coaster map back on the table, not needing it now that his memory had been refreshed.

"How are things going in Jalalabad?" asked the red haired man, Tony Murphy.

He addressed the first newcomer, whom he was only slightly acquainted with. He knew only that his first name was Bob, that he was a second year PCV near the end of his tour, and that he worked in the Tuberculosis Eradication program in the Jalalabad area, east of Kabul and close to the Pakistan border. Tony remembered fondly the spectacular trip through the Khyber Pass he had made shortly after arriving in Afghanistan, over a year earlier.

"Not so good. We had a malaria outbreak this summer and the clinic is full. We don't have the personnel to deal with it. WHO was supposed to send in some people, but we haven't seen them yet. This place is so screwed up. I'll be glad when my time is up. I will be the first son of a bitch on that jet! No offense intended," he said, acknowledging the Afghan at their table. Ignoring the clean glass in front of him, Bob took a long pull directly from the beer bottle.

The Afghan sitting with them was Shamsher. He smiled at the remark, feigning indifference. Secretly (although he suspected his friend David knew) his burning desire was to someday travel to the United States. It was the reason for his long struggle to learn English, his eagerness to make friends with the foreigners, and his systematic study of the culture and history of the West. There were times when he hated the country of his birth more than this foreigner did. Years earlier, after the death of his father in a pointless, to Shamsher, tribal feud instigated in part by the local mullah, he had secretly renounced his belief in Allah or any God. He despised that same mullah who had compelled him to memorize the Koran with the frequent aid of the willow switch. It pained him to endure his feelings of shame and embarrassment for the superstitiousness and backwardness of most of the people in his country. He felt no anger towards the American, only envy. He wished he could get on the jet with him.

"It sounds like you're getting more than a little burned out. I know just how you feel. There are days when I can't believe I've made it over a year here, and the thought of another year sounds like torture. What kind of a difference are we really making? Should we even be trying to make a difference? You know what amazes me the most, though? It's how guys like Tony manage to stick it out here," David went on, turning abruptly to the red haired man.

"You're one of the most idealistic people I've ever met, yet you're still here—hell you even seem to enjoy this place, and Dennis is the one leaving. He's a lot more of a realist than you are, and he's had a lot easier time with the language."

Tony knew David well enough to realize that much of this bitterness towards their roles in the country was really just disappointment in the imminent loss of his close friend, Dennis—a loss felt all the more because of the feeling of isolation they all shared in this strange country.

"Maybe my expectations are just lower than Dennis'," Tony replied, thoughtfully.

He had a way of deliberating for a moment before speaking if the conversation was serious. That, combined with his serious comportment and Einsteinian hair, caused most people to stop and listen carefully when he spoke. Much of the time, as in this case, he was right on the mark.

Tony was idealistic by temperament—they all were to a certain extent, or they would not have enlisted in Peace Corps in the first place, but Tony's idealism, even more than David's, and especially more than Dennis', was a well grounded optimism buttressed with a good deal of situational pragmatism. His was an idealism firmly rooted in New England traditions of practicality and reticence. He did not expect much in the way of major change in the short term, therefore he was seldom disappointed. His ultimate hopes for Afghanistan, when he could be coaxed into expressing them—usually after several drinks—appeared hopelessly optimistic and impossibly naive to many, but he accumulated small satisfactions, and was gratified in his work with the day to day accretion of small accomplishments. He was just the sort of person who became a successful Peace Corps Volunteer.

"Well, I would agree with you that not having unreasonable expectations can be an advantage in living here—as anywhere," David said. "And maybe Dennis thought he could escape his demons here in Kabul, but if anything they've only been replaced by djinns of worse sort."

"We might not be able to improve the fucking world, but at least we can improve our attitudes, and that is what I intend to do today—all day long! Bartender! Let's have another round for everybody!" the newcomer Bob cried, seeking to lighten the mood.

"That's the spirit—or should I say—spirits! I've been treating this whole bon voyage party for Dennis like a goddamned wake—hell, we are the ones who need the party! He gets to go home, and we're the idiots who are too dumb to catch that plane ourselves!" David agreed.

There was a short silence, not at all uncomfortable for the affable group, while the jukebox searched its mechanical innards for the next selection, and the ever smiling bartender brought more Schlitz.

"As long as you make even one friend here, you have made for a success," Shamsher interjected into the conversational lacuna.

"Well said! I think that is something we can all drink to," Bob exclaimed, raising his beer. "To friends everywhere!" There was a spirited clinking of beer bottles and glasses.

"I hope there are some western women at this party," said the other newcomer, whose name was Frank. He had just returned from three months in a small rural Afghan community, where he had assisted in a clinic operated by a German veterinarian.

"I haven't seen anything but sheep and chadarees for months!"

They all laughed at this. Afghanistan was difficult for these young men in many ways, and the shortage of liberated women was not the least of their hardships.

"Well, you'd better come to the party then. Just wait until you see this gorgeous redhead," offered David. "She's got the body of a playboy model, and the face of an angel—only one problem—she already has a boyfriend. He seems like a nice enough guy—ex-Navy I gather from the look of his tattoos. But damn! It will make your day just looking at her. Besides, there will be plenty of other women there, mostly PCVs, but maybe a few tourists too, if we're lucky."

At the description of the redheaded girl, Paul, who had stopped consciously listening to their conversation, began to pay attention again—and at the mention of the word "tattoo" he nearly dropped his drink. This was the lucky break he had not dared to hope for. Obviously they were the couple he was seeking. It all fit. The picture the Truman's had given him of their daughter, Karen, showed a striking young women—a girl certainly capable of turning the heads of lonely young American men stuck in a Moslem country where most of the women, when seen at all, appeared publicly dressed in full length veils with only their feet and hands exposed.

Paul listened discreetly to the rest of their conversation, but learned nothing else about the couple. The group discussed their Peace Corps duties and Bob's recent trip to Pakistan and India. They groused generally about the conditions of their employment in Afghanistan. He stayed at the bar, hoping vainly for any additional information on the couple. He made a trip to the bathroom, and slowly nursed a third drink until the four Americans and the Afghan finally left. As soon as they were out the door, Paul paid the bartender and exited quickly, deftly pocketing the crude coaster map on his way out, before the fussy attendant could clear the table.

Outside, in the brilliant afternoon sunlight, Paul could see from the hastily drawn diagram that the location of the party was on the fringes of the so-called New City, or Shari Nau, across town and north of his present location. He hailed a nearby cab. It would be nice to get back to the hotel and have a good meal and shower, he thought, as the taxi driver tediously threaded his way through the confusion of men, animals, and machines.

This was one party he would not miss—invitation or not—but first he had one more stop to make. He needed to make contact with Conrad Slocum—the other reason for this Asian expedition, and he hoped the young Agency contact might be induced to help him apprehend seaman Peccanter. Paul knew little of the Pashtun language, but he had acquired an adequate, if not quite fluent command of the so-called 'trade language' or lingua franca of Afghanistan, the Farsi or Dari tongue. It was particularly useful here, as it was understood by all of the taxi drivers and shopkeepers. Using a map of Kabul, he was able to direct the driver to Slocum's apartment.

CHAPTER 9

Conrad Slocum

"Jesus Christ I'm coming!" Conrad yelled, wondering who could be knocking.

It was mid-afternoon and he was not expecting anyone. He left the chain lock attached, and opened the door slightly. The unfamiliar man stood well back from the door in the full sunlight so that he could be easily seen. The stranger was only slightly shorter than Conrad, well dressed, clean-cut, and fit looking.

"So who the hell are you?" Conrad asked.

Paul Sherman introduced himself and showed his identification. Conrad had no doubt the man was legitimate, but he decided to hassle him some just the same.

"How do I know your ID isn't fake?" he retorted.

"Cut the crap. It's been a long day. I don't think you want all your neighbors to listen in, do you?"

Conrad opened the door and ushered the stranger into his living room. Paul Sherman studied the space appreciatively, noticing the high quality of the carpets and the few but tasteful furnishings.

"It looks like you are doing all right here. Nice place. You must have a good paying job."

"Now who's the bullshitter? I guess you must know how I pay my bills if you are who you say you are. I haven't seen your face around town, so I would bet that you're not stationed here. What, if I may ask, brings you to Kabul?"

Without preamble Paul explained his mission and described Brian Peccanter and Karen Truman. While Conrad listened without comment, Paul spelled out the details of seaman Peccanter's crimes. As he listened, Conrad made the decision to hide his knowledge of the couple from the agent.

Conrad had a natural tendency to extract more information in conversation than he gave out—a tendency that had served him well so far in Kabul as elsewhere in life, but Paul was even more experienced, and was more than a match for him in that capacity. Just as Conrad instinctively held back his knowledge of the couple, Paul for his part did not divulge what he had overheard at the bar a short time earlier. Paul was sure the couple would be at the party and he could intercept them there. Any information Conrad might add could be helpful, but was not critical to the accomplishment of his task. His main reason for this meeting with Conrad was unrelated to the question of Brian Peccanter's whereabouts anyway.

"I was hoping you could help me find them of course, and perhaps save me some effort and leg work. Aside from that, and more importantly, I have been authorized by my supervisors to offer you a permanent position with the Agency. I mean a real full-time position with all the perks that come with it, not the casual sort of relationship you now have. Nice pay, travel expenses, health and retirement benefits, and more. As you might expect, it won't be just another nine to five grind, but of course there will be more demands made on your time and energy than under the present arrangement."

This was only partially true. In fact Paul had been recently promoted, and although he had been careful to run the idea of offering Conrad this new position past his superior, he actually had full authority to authorize the position without further formalities. Paul preferred as few people as necessary in Kabul knew of his true position in the Agency hierarchy—including even some of his fellow operatives.

"Maybe I should have checked your credentials closer after all. You sound more like a salesman than a spook. I'll have to think about your job offer. It is tempting, but I wonder just how much extra official crap I will have to put up with. I'm pretty happy with the way things stand. As for finding this couple—what's in it for me if I do help? From what you say it seems to me it's the Navy's problem, and I have got absolutely no beef with anyone who goes AWOL from that idiotic war."

"I am well aware of your objections to the Viet Nam conflict. You have certainly made no secret of your opinions, and I can say that your attitude has caused some in the Agency to doubt whether you should be offered this important position, and even to question your loyalty, but your vocal criticism of the war has not been as big a problem as your family history of activism and certain other irregularities in your background."

"Look, Mr. Sherman—let me make something perfectly clear—as our president, Dick Nixon, is so fond of saying. I do not give a shit what the Agency or anyone else thinks about my political opinions, family history, loyalty, or anything else, and I don't have any illusions about my role here. I'm only in this game for the money. I'm no fucking patriot. I do not believe in the superiority of capitalism, the American Way, Christianity, or any of the claptrap the conservative bigots presently in control of our country love to blather about. You can find someone else to do the job if you want—no skin off my back. I can get along just fine without your cloak and dagger games. Furthermore, as you obviously know from perusing my dossier; my mother was a card carrying communist, and my grandmother—perhaps the woman I admire most in the world—a vocal and radical Wobbly. Although I do not profess to have any more faith in those political ideas than I do in religion or capitalism, I'm extremely sympathetic to their views and to those who share similar views. You might say I have at least an emotional, if not a genetic attachment to any group which espouses equal rights for all, and a leveling of the economic differences between classes."

"Understood, and I for one appreciate your candor, and have no problem with your point of view, as long as you can provide us with the intelligence we need. But as you and I are perfectly aware, even if some in the Agency refuse to admit it—you negotiate from a position of some strength—at least for the time being. Vanishingly few American citizens have your command of the Pashtu language, or your connections in Kabul, as you well know. Realistically, the Agency cannot afford to give up the access to information you provide, as long as you are willing to provide it. Enjoy your circumstances while you can, Mr. Slocum, but things can and do change. Your situation could become more tenuous, and you might find you need someone you can trust—someone who is more sympathetic to your unique circumstances than others in the Agency might be. The relationship you now have with our division will change in time one way or the other. The current administration has greatly increased funding to the entire intelligence community, and departments are being reorganized and duties redistributed."

Although Conrad's answers had been calculated to provoke, Paul refused to take the bait. He sensed the younger man's attitude might be some sort of diversion, and in any case he really could use an ally here, or at least a trustworthy Pashtun language translator. Additionally, he saw a hint of his own youthful impudence in Conrad's insolent responses, and rather than angering Paul, it brought on a transient feeling of nostalgia.

"In other words, I might get fired? And that sympathetic someone might be you? Why not just have Burke or one of his idiot underlings do your dirty work. It's obvious you have my files at your disposal, but I've never heard your name before, so please forgive me if I seem hesitant to embrace you or your friendly overtures at our first encounter."

This was only partially true. Conrad had indeed heard of Paul Sherman, and was somewhat aware of his reputation, though this was their first meeting.

Paul knew that Conrad was not alone in his detestation of the notorious Terrence Burke, the self-styled agent 007 who had arrested Timothy Leary at the Kabul airport some months earlier, and had become a celebrity of sorts when a feature about him had come out in Rolling Stone magazine. American narcotic officers were practically tripping over each other that year in Kabul, in a virtual drug-busting frenzy, while swarms of intelligence agents scoured the city for any bits of information that could be gleaned about the intentions of the Russians and Afghan communists. The Soviets and Chinese were not to be outdone in the contest for information and influence. Paranoia was rife, and reasonable. The twentieth century version of 'The Great Game' or 'The Tournament of Shadows' continued.

It was also common knowledge in the local intelligence community that Slocum and Burke had actually gotten into a shoving match at one drunken gathering at the infamous Hotel One. Burke had lost face with his cronies when he drew his sidearm and Conrad instantly slapped the gun out of his hand and walked out of the party in disgust. For all his posturing and braggadocio, among the few long time Agency insiders who had some knowledge of Conrad's intelligence gathering activities, the feeling was that Slocum was more than a match for Burke in just about any capacity. It was even whispered in certain circles that Burke's supposed fluent command of Pashtu was an exaggeration, and his high visibility and flamboyant reputation made him too much of a risk for serious intelligence work. Whether or not this was the case, it was a fact that Burke was now primarily involved in matters related to drug smuggling, and was not as engaged in the more traditional and respectable types of intelligence work, where a lower profile was essential.

"Okay then, fair enough. I can certainly understand some of your reticence. I agree with you about Terrence for the most part, but whether we like him and his kind or not, they are the people we have to work with here—at least for a while longer. I too share your distaste for both the man and some of his methods. In any case he is far more interested in stopping drug traffickers and making high profile arrests, like his recent one of Dr. Leary, than in ferreting out the sort of information that we hope you can provide us with. I doubt you will have much reason for contact with him or his cohorts in the future—at least professionally—and from what I have heard you don't have much reason for further social contact either. As I suppose you already know by now, more and more money is being channeled into drug interdiction these days, and agents like Burke and his ilk who are hungry for advancement will follow that money trail. In case you change your mind about helping me with the AWOL case, or the Agency offer, you can leave a message for me at the Hotel Intercontinental. Here are my room and phone numbers." He wrote the numbers on a hotel card and offered it to Conrad.

"It sounds like I picked the wrong team if I want to become financially independent. From what you say I should just embrace the narc squad—it looks like that is where the smart money is. I wonder sometimes why I am helping you spy on the local communists, since they are the only political group in this country that seems to give a damn about the plight of the poor working people, and the women. I can't say either that I am very happy about our policy of snuggling up to the Muslim Youth Movement students at Kabul University—a bunch of sick bastards in my opinion. It seems to me that could backfire down the road—and I most certainly don't agree with that gang's misogynistic and medieval goals for Afghanistan," Conrad said, accepting Paul's card and ushering him to the door.

"I understand your reasoning, though I see things differently; but in spite of those sentiments I certainly hope you give this offer the serious attention it deserves. I don't think your duties will be too onerous, and I believe you will find that your new status will have benefits which more than make up for the increased demands on your time and independence," Agent Sherman responded, in a last effort to recruit Slocum.

Conrad sensed that Paul might actually be more sympathetic to his viewpoint than any of the others in the intelligence community he had so far come into contact with, and too, some of his bluster was a diversionary tactic. He wanted to steer the discussion away from the subject of Brian and Karen.

Conrad's intuition about Paul Sherman was partially correct, but Paul had manipulated Conrad to a certain extent by agreeing with him about Burke, and suggesting that he was somewhat well-disposed to Conrad's point of view. Paul was perfectly mindful that he too was being sounded out, and aware that Conrad would not automatically accept the Agency offer. Although he had said the only thing that mattered was the money, it was clear to Paul and his superiors that Conrad Slocum was a maverick who must be carefully courted. The troublesome truth was that some of the best operatives in the Agency were like Conrad—men who were fiercely independent and notoriously difficult to control.

Paul himself, though somewhat more circumspect in his youth than Conrad, had butted heads more than once with other agents and superiors over the course of his career. Although he had mellowed some with age, he had been passed over more than once for promotion due to his outspoken opinions and lack of cooperation in some matters, especially with respect to civil rights and apartheid, where his ideals and scruples had clashed at times with Agency goals and operations.

Like Conrad, Paul was also slow to anger but extremely dangerous if he felt sufficiently threatened. Conrad was perfectly correct in suggesting that Paul had the advantage of having read the Agency files on him. If he had been granted the same access, Conrad might have been more cautious in his initial aggressive approach to the older man. A decade earlier Paul Sherman had spent some months in prison for killing another intelligence agent during a confrontation. Only the combination of an immediate need for his skills in the field, and the intercession of a congressman on his behalf (brought to his aid by his old friend Cecil Ramsy) had led to Paul's eventual release and reinstatement.

The fact that he might still be in prison but for Cecil's efforts weighed heavily in Paul's inability to refuse his old friend's request for help, even though he found the manhunt assignment distasteful. Moreover, by killing the other agent Paul had effectively bound himself in servitude to the Agency for as long as they wished. It was a way of life he fortunately mostly enjoyed, but it did not change the fact that he was not free to leave at will without repercussions. But none of this would be known to Conrad for some time yet.

After agent Sherman left, Conrad thought about his options in light of this new development. At Karen's insistence Brian had told him of his true situation—the reason he was on the run—and Conrad had seen no reason to doubt his tragic tale. Before the appearance of agent Sherman Conrad had reasoned that the couple had a decent chance of making good their escape, and that perhaps he could help them with a little money, some useful contacts, and some general advice on the route they should take when they were ready at last to head west to Europe. But with an experienced agent like

Paul Sherman now involved and present in Kabul, the matter was more urgent than he had supposed.

One thing was certain: Conrad had no intention of helping Paul or anyone else apprehend the couple regardless of how it would affect his future relationship with the Agency. Agent Sherman was right about one thing; they would be hard pressed to replace Conrad in Kabul, so neither he nor anyone else in the Agency really had any way to compel Conrad to help in the search, or for that matter to do anything else he did not agree to. In fact, it was his intention to warn the couple of this new development, but he would have to do that without blowing his cover, and without interfering in any obvious manner with the Sherman. All of his friends and acquaintances, even his closest associates, believed he was simply an expatriate part-time carpet dealer and occasional English language teacher with a weakness for opium, who periodically left Kabul on business trips. It was a facade he had carefully constructed and maintained. Certainly no more than half a dozen people, all save one in the employment of one or another of the various intelligence agencies in Kabul, knew of his relationship to the Agency, and to a certain extent his very survival depended on that. The Pashtuns in general had a reputation for handling such matters quickly and effectively, and the Pashtun communists were known to be even more ruthless.

As he pondered his options, Conrad thought of the un-likely train of events that had brought him to Kabul and his present situation.

After graduating from high school in Seattle and two terms of college, he had found himself by the spring of 1968 at loose ends. He had no idea what he wanted to do, except that he needed a break from the university and the academic routine. He had a little money in the bank, put away for spring term, and a battle scarred but mechanically sound 1953 Buick Roadmaster. The highway beckoned. He had no particular destination in mind —just somewhere a little dryer and warmer than the Puget Sound.

After a time of wandering the back roads of Eastern Washington, Oregon, and northern Nevada, camping out or sleeping in the old Buick for the most part, he had made his way at last to San Francisco. At first he was taken with the city; its climate, energy, and bohemian society; the music, parties, and the girls; and of course, the drugs. He found it interesting at first, but it certainly did not live up to the popular hype, and in the end he began to feel more like an anthropologist studying some exotic tribe than an actual member of any community. The dark side was evident, and as the summer wore on he became restless again.

Conrad, with his background in the martial arts, and the habits of mental and physical self-discipline which he had developed over so many years under the tutelage of a unique group of exceptional instructors in the course of a very untraditional education, was not the sort to be diverted for long by the superficial attractions of hedonism the 'City By The Bay' seemed to offer to some. Chalking the experience up as another chapter in his education, he once again took to the road, spending a week exploring highway 101 all the way south to Los Angeles.

One night in a Santa Monica bar he struck up a conversation with a somewhat older wanderer. The trekker had just hiked the portion of the Pacific Crest Trail from Yosemite to the Mexican border. Before the night had ended Conrad had set for himself the goal of traveling the entire route from north to south—from the Canadian border to Mexico.

By the following week he had sold the steadfast and well-used Buick, bought a sturdy backpack and some good hiking boots, and was on his way north by train. However he had made too late a start from the British Columbian border. Winter was upon him before he finished with the Oregon section of the trail, and he had grown weary of the constant loneliness and discomfort. So Conrad had decided to take a break and pick up the trail again in the spring.

That winter he roomed with a college friend in Seattle, spending the infrequent dry days sailing Puget Sound, and his nights revisiting the old familiar haunts with companions from his school days. But he was stir-crazy and impatient with his friends, who still seemed so content with their old comfortable routines. He began following the news again, which he had ignored for so many weeks in the isolation of the forested slopes of the Cascades.

The war in Viet Nam dominated the thoughts of all the men in his age group, and Conrad realized it was only a matter of time before his refusal to register for the draft would lead to legal problems. He had no intention to serve and perhaps die in a war he considered utterly pointless. Unlike many of his generation, Conrad had no specific moral objection to this particular war. He considered it no different in general than any number of previous conflicts, declared or otherwise; he simply saw no reason to risk his life, health, or youth on an activity that did not interest him, and patriotism was not one of Conrad's virtues.

While he considered his options, an opportunity suddenly appeared in the form of a small inheritance from a distant relative. Within a few weeks he was on a plane bound for Paris. Southern Europe, Morocco, Egypt, and Turkey beckoned. He spent a month sailing the Aegean as a crew member on a wealthy Italian magnate's yacht. A conversation with fellow travelers in an Istanbul hostel led to an overland trip to Afghanistan in the company of Australian wanderers. Although he had made several side trips to Pakistan, India, Nepal, and back again to the Mediterranean, Kabul had been his home base since the summer of 1969.

Naturally gifted at languages, Conrad had no problem mastering Farsi or Dari, the common trade language used by the various Afghan tribes, Iranians, Indians, and Pakistanis in this part of the world. But his rapid mastery of the tongue of the dominant Pashtun tribes was his real accomplishment, and the key to his special status in Kabul. With his command of Pashtu allowing him to bargain like a native tribesman, and by investing some of his inheritance, he was able to establish himself as a small-time trader, expediting the sale of local carpets, jewelry, and clothing to several importers stateside.

The business activities did not take up much of his time or energy. They provided him with enough money for the basics; an apartment, food and other staples, and his limited domestic help. To his dismay, he had still needed to rely at times on his fast dwindling inheritance, and part-time work teaching English classes. His trading activities, however, gave him far more access than most foreigners into Kabul society. Conrad was a frequent guest at the homes of several politically well-connected Kabul businessmen. It was these connections which ultimately led to more reliable income.

He had not been in Kabul much more than a year when he was approached by a be-spectacled middle-aged stranger one afternoon as he browsed the periodical section in the USIS library. It was his habit to visit this small library at least once a week to catch up on events in the outside world. The man, whom he remembered seeing there some weeks previously, had the appearance of a professor or researcher, and introduced himself as 'Bill Green,' asking if he might have a word in private with Conrad.

The stranger—who had never named the exact agency he worked for, only that he was employed by an 'intelligence gathering department of the US government'—offered Conrad a substantial 'token of appreciation' to be deposited at his bank of choice back home, as well as a monthly Afghan stipend for as long as he was willing to supply him with certain information. All this was fine with Conrad, who had no aversion to money, and at that moment happened to be unusually short on funds, having recently lost a distressing amount of cash on an unprofitable business transaction. The mysterious Mr. Green had offered interesting work, decent pay, and most crucially—immunity to the draft for the present and in the future—as long as he provided the information requested.

"What makes you so sure I would ever want to go back to the States?" he had asked agent Green at the time.

"Oh, you will—you will. Nobody stays here long, and things are happening that will make it damned uncomfortable for us around here in the very near future."

Bill Green was perhaps the most influential and well-connected American agent in Kabul. He was rumored to be a close friend of congressman Charlie Wilson. Although he was a quiet and inconspicuous man, with wire-rimmed glasses and a self-effacing manner, who looked very much like he would be more at home in the stacks of a university library than as a secret agent in Asia, he was perhaps the deadliest killer in the Agency, known for his cold-blooded ruthlessness in certain sensitive matters. Later, Conrad would have cause to respect his expertise in that line of work.

"Why me, in particular?" Conrad had queried.

"As you have probably guessed by now, we—that is the Agency—have been observing you for some time, and we think your attributes and abilities seem a perfect fit to the tasks we have in mind."

"So you've been watching me, eh?" he felt the hair rise on the nape of his neck at the thought.

"Oh no—not tailing you or spying on your private life—nothing like that, of course. I meant to say we know through interviews with a few people you have done business with here in Kabul, that you seem to be the type of person who might be very useful to our organization."

It was obvious to Conrad the man was equivocating, and that he had in fact, been under close observation for some time here. That early realization was reinforced by what he learned in later years working for the Agency. Ultimately he had been persuaded to accept the work, which mostly involved getting to know members of the local communist party and reporting on their activities, especially their interactions with Russian officials.

Conrad had been chosen for this work because of his age, ability to speak the Pashtun vernacular, his close social connections to several local party members, and his ability to mix with students at Kabul University—a hotbed of political and revolutionary activity.

The communist party of Afghanistan had been founded in 1965 as the "People's Democratic Party of Afghanistan" (PDPA). By 1967 it had broken into two main factions; the radical "Khalq" faction headed by Taraki, and the more moderate and urban "Parchem" faction with Karmal at the helm. Conrad had two friends at the university who were active members of the Parchem faction, and he often did business with a Pashtun trader who was a vocal member of the Khalq group. Specifically, agent Green and his superiors hoped Conrad might be able to supply more detailed information about the PDPA's connections with the Russians, and additional names of members, especially those in government positions and the military, or with special access to influential Afghan leaders.

Conrad had enjoyed the financial benefits of this relationship for nearly three years, pleased to note the increasing balance in the bank account he had opened back in Seattle, for he did indeed have plans to eventually return to his childhood home at some point, especially now that he had nothing to fear from the draft board. He had long dreamed of owning a sailboat capable of ocean voyaging, and hoped someday to explore the South Pacific or perhaps even circumnavigate in his own vessel.

Although Conrad recognized that he was inexorably becoming ensnared by, and to a large degree dependent on this association, the fact was the life he wished to live required a certain amount of money and free time to explore his varied interests. Since he had to earn a living, he reasoned he might as well do something interesting, and which allowed him plenty of schedule flexibility, as well as good pay and benefits. Perhaps more to the point, Conrad realized he was ill-suited by nature for any sort of more traditional employment, or to spending long years in a classroom setting.

As he considered this new offer by agent Sherman and pondered his options, Conrad realized the question of whether or not to accept this new position had more to do with how much longer he wanted to stay in Kabul than anything else. The last winter had been particularly tedious, and Conrad did not look forward to another. He had not been out of the country for many months. He was not sure if he just needed a temporary change of scenery, or if it was really time to move on.

His travels before arriving in Afghanistan had been at least partially motivated by his desire to avoid registering for military service. That problem had been solved by the immunity he had been granted when he had been recruited by Mr. Green. The Viet Nam conflict was now officially over and military draft had ended in June. There was nothing to prevent Conrad from returning home or traveling to any destination he chose.

Like the renowned explorer and scholar Aurel Stein, Conrad fantasized of retracing the footsteps of Alexander The Great from Macedonia to the extreme borders of that ancient empire. He had already explored the ruins of two of the ancient cities founded by the great conqueror; Alexandria on the Caucasos, some forty miles north of Kabul near present day Charikar, and Alexandria on the Oxus, in northern Afghanistan, and that taste of the region's fascinating history had only whetted his appetite for more adventure. Still, a few more months in Kabul would do much to increase his boat fund savings account—especially at the increased pay he would receive as a full-fledged agent, and it might also give him the cover and excuse to explore more of this region before he returned home, effectively killing two birds with one stone.

In spite of the impression of ambivalence he had affected during his interview with Paul Sherman, Conrad had all but decided to accept the agent's offer by the time the man's taxi cab had pulled away from it's parking place on the street below his apartment.

CHAPTER 10

An Eventful Party

A rare summer rain fell on Friday, July 13. Afterwards the omnipresent haze from the thousands of kerosene lamps, charcoal heated samovars and braziers, and the hundreds of neighborhood naan ovens was briefly washed away, and for a few precious hours the all-too-human smells of the filth-ridden ditches vanished, or were at least moderated. Even the haggling in the bazaars seemed more relaxed and friendlier, and the horses and donkeys perked up, needing the flick of the whip less often to urge them down the crowded streets.

In mid-afternoon, the day of the bon voyage party for Dennis, the rain began. Less than a half hour later the showers gave way to a surreal patchy cloud cover through which now and then a shaft of biblical sunlight pierced, illuminating for a moment a certain section of the city, or even a single building. Except for the occasional sound of an automobile horn, David could almost imagine himself transported back a thousand years, to the time of Mahmud The Great, when Afghanistan had been the center of a vast empire stretching north beyond the Oxus and east into present day India. Periodic sheet lightening lit up the sky and the surrounding mountains. The evening was warm and unusually humid. The air felt almost tropical, a refreshing change from the typical mid-summer dusty dryness of the city.

At first David had worried his plans for the roof top party would have to be changed, so he was relieved when the rain quit early enough for the landing to be swept and flogged dry with time to spare for the food, carpets, and cushions to be laid out before the first guests arrived. The party was to start at six. The elevated setting would become even more dramatic after dark, as periodic bursts of lightening continued to flash in the night sky and illuminate the outlines of the nearby buildings for hours after the rain storm had passed.

The apartment occupied by David Stuckrath, Dennis Butler, and John Mesmer was one of three which made up the second floor of the building. Above them, on the third and topmost floor, were two more flats. A narrow exterior iron-railed walkway provided access to the stairs leading to the two third floor apartments, and also opened onto the large landing, which was just the flat roof over the outer most second floor apartment unit. The party was held on the landing some twenty feet above street level. The adjoining apartments served as staging areas and provided kitchen and bathroom facilities.

The three second floor units were occupied by Peace Corps volunteers and trainees—all male. A mixing of males and females in the apartments would have been scandalous without the contract of marriage even here in Kabul, the most cosmopolitan and modern of Afghan cities. One of the third floor apartments was rented by two young women, Dorothy and Aletheia, also Peace Corps volunteers. A young American couple employed by the United States Information Service (USIS), who had only been in the country a few weeks, and would be moving out when their house was ready, were temporarily encamped in the other third floor apartment, their belongings still packed in boxes scattered about the four room flat. In the meantime they were living somewhat below their station.

Not that the apartments were so bad by local standards. In fact, for Kabul they were rather nice. Each unit had a large picture window with opening screened side-lights in the great room, and a door leading out to a small balcony on the street side overlooking the busy bazaar below. More exceptionally, each apartment had electricity (240 volt European style), and a bathroom with a shower, sink, and toilet. A western style kitchen with sink and cold running water, and a small refrigerator and electric range was also provided. The cold showers took some getting used to, but were a major improvement over the lot of many Afghans, who were often forced to use outdoor public faucets for their needs, or worse yet, the Kabul river, not much more than a dirty trickle this time of year.

In preparation for the event David had organized the entire apartment complex. He had retained two of the domestics for the evening. All the PCVs had pitched in money for their overtime pay, amounting to two hundred afghanis, roughly four dollars US. Even pennies mattered here where a Peace Corps volunteer's wages were about one hundred dollars a month, and the average Afghan made far less than that.

The party preparations were impressive and elaborate, considering their financial resources. Several large carpets completely covered the roof top landing—loaned for the occasion by Conrad Slocum. In the center were tablecloths, spread Afghan style directly upon the carpets. The deck itself had been meticulously swept and scrubbed clean by the domestics. The well-timed rain had made their work far easier, for which they gave thanks to Allah. Strewn about the area lay an assortment of cushions; some borrowed from the other apartment denizens, and some rented for a nominal cost from one of the shop keepers in the bazaar below.

As the guests started to arrive the two domestics, Samot and his helper, began setting out vast quantities of traditional Afghan foods. The table cloths were loaded with bowls of steaming Kabuli Palau, the local pilaf, and other mutton, beef and chicken dishes. A good selection of fresh produce complimented the entrees. Figs, dates, grapes, nuts, slices of 'kharbuza' (melons), and several varieties of vegetables—most harvested that very day from the many acres of farmland immediately surrounding the city, or within a few hours journey by farm truck or donkey cart—were all in abundance. Kabobs of beef, chicken, and lamb sizzled over two portable charcoal braziers. The usual pots of black and green tea and the ever-present stacks of fresh naan were strategically located about the freshly starched and ironed cloths.

The occupants of the second floor apartments had contributed a dozen bottles of the local Afghan wine (sold only to infidels), produced in nearby Charikar, and quite agreeable to the unsophisticated palates of the young imbibers. Other guests brought beer and more wine. One English embassy worker was nearly mobbed when he arrived with a rare and expensive treasure—a bottle of good scotch whisky.

In one corner of the landing the traditional band Shamsher had helped David hire began tuning up their instruments. The little gathering of celebrants on the roof was an isolated pool of light and noise in the twilight above the otherwise tranquil purlieu. Clusters of people talked, laughed, drank, and attacked the food.

A few guests stood and admired the view under the fading sunlight, which cast weakening rays over the patchwork of grain and hay fields that began only a few blocks away from the apartment building, located near the edge of the sprawling city.

The scene to the south and west changed abruptly from urban residential to a pattern of alternating yellow, brown, and green fields—each with its own collection of buildings contained within the tan mud-brick walls encircling the property. A farmer in the distance cut hay by the fading light, his scythe swinging with an easy and practiced rhythm. Children played king of the mountain on a nearby haystack. Directly north the view was interrupted by a hill of perhaps seven or eight hundred feet in height, upon which young boys could be seen watching over a herd of sheep. David and Dennis often walked the few blocks to its base and climbed to the grassy summit, the better to take in the sweeping vistas of the city and surrounding countryside.

From the vantage point of the rooftop one could also see down into the walled courtyards of the nearby homes, with the clothing hanging out to dry, the back-yard wells, and wisps of smoke drifting up from the outdoor braziers often used for cooking during the warmer months. Many of the homes had screened sleeping porches, also convenient on the hot summer evenings. To the southeast the third floor apartments rose and blocked out the sights and sounds of the bazaar on the street below.

Old Kabul, convoluted, mysterious, and ageless stretched eastwards across the valley floor and onto the lower slopes of the foothills. In the distance were the great brooding flanks of the Sher Darwazi Mountains, purple-black in the fading sunlight, and the jagged angular ridge underpinning the fifteen century old Hephthalite stone walls crumbling back into the rocks that were their foundation. Most of Kabul's several hundred thousand people settled down for the night, while on the roof the party was just beginning to get lively.

By some unspoken consensus the dopers had gathered in Dennis' apartment. Several smokers stoked up the 'nargile,' or water pipe, and soon the pungent smell of hashish smoke pervaded the room. Meanwhile, John Mesmer held a long stemmed pipe to his lips while David Stuckrath heated a bubbling black mass of opium in the bowl with a wooden match.

"I thought you only smoked hash—not opium," said Aletheia teasingly as she watched the ritual.

She was short and pudgy, with close cropped brown hair cut bowl fashion which did nothing to compliment her plain face, with its oversize mouth, and crooked teeth. But her eyes were lively, and she had an adventurous and gregarious nature which made her very popular with the other PCVs and trainees. She was one of the few Peace Corps women who had spent much time outside the major cities of Afghanistan. Aletheia had been working most recently in the Jalalabad area in the Tuberculosis eradication program. She was temporarily staying with her sometime roommate, Dorothy, in the upstairs apartment, taking a two week respite from her medical duties.

"I never used to, but I sure like it a lot better than Lomatil. I only uses it for medicinal purposes," John joked, exaggerating his Carolina drawl for Aletheia's amusement. She laughed and took the pipe he offered.

"Hey, I finally found a house to rent," said Tony, from a cushion near the window. Although he got on well with the other apartment denizens, he had been trying to find more private lodgings for some weeks.

"Where is it?" Aletheia asked, passing the pipe to David, industriously engaged in cutting another slice from the rectangular block of opium.

"It's just off Chicken Street—only a couple of blocks from the Pashtoon Hotel. It's not real big, just one floor, but it has running water, electricity, and even an electric water heater that works! You can come over for hot showers." He gave Aletheia a teasing wink.

"I just might take you up on that, but I'll probably have to wait in line. When are you moving?" she asked.

"Next month, Allah willing," he replied, poking gentle fun at the local convention.

"Sounds like the perfect occasion for another party," remarked David, relighting the pipe. "But damn, this place is going to feel pretty empty—Dennis leaving Sunday and you in a couple of weeks. I'll have to find another roommate."

"Like I said before—you are welcome to move in. There are two bedrooms, and with both of us it would be almost as cheap as this place," Tony replied.

They had already had this conversation earlier. Tony had made it clear he had no desire to take over Dennis' room in David and John Mesmer's apartment unit, in spite of their friendship. Tony wanted a quieter place, and David would not agree to the house rules Tony wished to impose at the new residence. There was too much activity in the busy apartment complex over the active bazaar for his more introverted tastes.

Tony had grown up an only child in a family where both parents worked, and was used to having his own space and privacy. Kabul suited him fine, with its walled homes and architectural emphasis on domestic seclusion. Tony was uncomfortable with what he perceived as the unruly mixing of the private and public spheres. In David's apartment one never knew from day to day who might be showing up for dinner, or staying on for breakfast the next morning. There was a constant stream of visitors coming and going from the flat, and all too many of them ended up spending the night in a drug or alcohol induced stupor for Tony's taste.

David, on the other hand, had grown up in a family with four other siblings, spent his poverty plagued college years in semi-communal squalor (until he and Clio had found their own lodgings) with nomadic droves of students and camp followers. Rarely less than four or five persons, and often many more had occupied the same often cramped lodgings throughout his first three years at the university. Although David insisted on his own bedroom, his need for solitude seemed to end at the door to his sleeping quarters. The apartment suited David just fine. He liked the location, the convenience of the bazaar below, and the camaraderie that existed with all five units generally housing young PCVs or employees of other foreign institutions in Kabul. As long as he had his own reasonably secure place to sleep and store his limited possessions, it was privacy enough.

Their quiet smoking ritual was interrupted by shouts and commotion from outside the apartment.

"That must be Dennis and Conrad," said David, carefully setting the pipe down. They all filed out to the rooftop to rejoin the party.

On the landing Conrad and Dennis were quickly surrounded by revelers, many already beginning to show the effects of the alcohol and other intoxicating substances. If Dennis had known about the surprise party, he certainly did not let on, appearing genuinely surprised and pleased.

The group of people on the landing had by now grown to more than thirty guests. It included most of the first year volunteers who still remained in Kabul, many second year veterans, some new trainees, and a smattering of Peace Corps 'brass,' as well as a few other American functionaries from the sparsely staffed USIS and embassy offices. Several tourists whom David knew casually from chance encounters at his favorite Kabul restaurants had also accepted his invitations. Most of the guests were Americans or Europeans.

Only nine Afghans were present, including the two domestics, and the four musicians. The other three sat together talking, while they shared a bottle of Charikar wine. Shamsher had arrived early, and had been engaged for some time in conversation with the two other Afghan guests, both language teachers at the Peace Corps training center. Reshtina, the only Afghan woman in the entire group, besides tutoring Peace Corps Volunteers, also worked a second part-time job as a nurses aid in the American dispensary. She was one of only a tiny minority of Afghan women even in this, for Afghanistan, most liberal of times and cities, who would have dared to attend such a gathering unescorted.

Reshtina, it was common knowledge, had a crush on David. It was a very intense crush, bordering on an obsession. She was the youngest of the Afghan teachers employed by the Peace Corps to train the volunteers in the languages and customs of the country. Reshtina was short and rather swarthy, with coke bottle thick glasses—the result of a childhood infection which had left her nearly blind. Though not in any conventional sense pretty, she did have a generous bosom, flawless skin, and a sort of glowing health and outgoing friendliness that made up for her otherwise plain face and lack of conventional allure.

Reshtina was especially well educated for an Afghan woman—the result of a domineering and imperious mother who had insisted that both her children (she had a younger brother, Khalid) be educated in the modern manner—to be the intellectual equals of the western infidels with which her mother's family often consorted. Reshtina's father, though himself the nominal headman of a once prominent Pashtun tribe, could not claim either the prestige, ancestry, or wealth, let alone the moral authority of his spouse, for he was a hesitant and anxious man who had married above his station. Unfortunately for Reshtina, her mother had died earlier that year, and though Reshtina continued to teach at the foreign school, her father and other family members had begun to challenge her way of life openly, something they would never have dared while her mother lived.

Her father's brother had suggested it was not right that a young unmarried woman should go about in western clothing and unchaperoned in the streets of Kabul, or live with her younger brother in a city apartment (owned by her mother's family) in a section of Kabul commonly frequented by the infidel westerners. Her father's mullah, a radical conservative who advocated a return to the strictest and most repressive form of Islam, had recently put forth his own son as a marriage match—a union he would never have proposed while her mother lived, knowing how little regard she had for traditional Islam in general and the role it assigned to women in particular. Through her mother Reshtina was related to the present king himself, Zahir Shah, and part of the ancient and powerful Durrani royal family. While she was alive Reshtina's mother had found many opportunities to remind her husband and the mullah of that kinship.

Reshtina's infatuation with David was not entirely her own fault. In spite of her mother's progressive ideals, she had neglected to educate her daughter properly on matters of love and sex. Two months previously, at a drunken party, David—horny beyond any sort of self-control or conscience—had lured the naive and inexperienced girl, spinning drunk herself, into his apartment bedroom. An intense session on his charpoy ensued, followed by regret on his side and an inevitable fixation on hers.

For Reshtina—already morbidly attracted to the young American with whom she had become so comfortable during the many hours of language classes—the culmination of those pent-up and barely repressed concupiscent dreams combined with the novel feelings of her newly discovered sexuality—for he was her first and only lover—added an incendiary fuel to her smoldering fervor. This first sexual experience with a man, added to her general fascination with all things foreign and exotic in such a manner as to completely break down any of her remaining decorum, diffidence, and reserve.

This state of affairs was much to David's chagrin, for he had no real physical attraction to her—at least when sober, and only a general friendly attachment as a result of so much time spent with her in the classroom setting and at casual gatherings with mutual friends. After that night she became very possessive, clinging to him in public, and even speaking to several of their mutual friends of the romantic connection, and a possible future wedding. But to David that evening had been no more than a regrettable indiscretion, enabled by too much alcohol and a moral lapse on his part. Back in the States it would have only registered as a dating mishap, slightly shameful and somewhat embarrassing, but of little real consequence.

Unfortunately for David, Reshtina could not or would not understand. She proprietarily tracked his every movement when they were in public together, even though he had been careful afterwards to avoid a repetition of that encounter, and had managed so far to put off any sort of private assignation with her. David hoped that she would eventually give up her infatuation if he simply ducked any sort of intimacy for long enough.

The Afghan quartet began to play in one corner of the terrace. Most of the guests had gathered around the starched white cloths, sitting cross-legged on the colorful carpets, or lounging on the cushions. They settled down to the daunting but pleasant task of consuming the cornucopia of food and drink.

Except for his slight discomfort regarding Reshtina, David was happy. Things were going well. Dennis looked as though he was enjoying himself, making the rounds, much of his late habitual reticence gone, though he still sported the faint remnants of a black eye and some bruising from his adventures at the Fourth of July party nine days previously. David speculated that perhaps the events on Independence Day had been a necessary catharsis, or maybe Dennis was just happy that his departure, only days away, was so close. Even his other roommate, John, was looking better, although he still had not regained much of his former weight, and was now undergoing antibiotic treatment for his dysentery.

The only people missing from the party were a handful of higher ranking American officials of American agencies who had been invited, more out of politeness than a hope that they would actually attend. The thought went through David's mind that it was for the better, as they might have put a damper on what looked to be a most enjoyable and relaxed gathering. Most of the senior officials frowned on the younger generation's use of hashish and opium. They most certainly would not have approved of the open smoking of hash-laced cigarettes that the Afghan band shared with some of the guests during their breaks, or the water pipe which had moved from inside the apartment out into a dark corner of the rooftop.

If David was mildly disappointed there were no 'society' people at his party and slightly inhibited by the proximity of Reshtina, this was more than made up for by the presence of the young couple he had met a few days earlier at the Pashtoon Hotel—Brian Peccanter and Karen Truman. As on his first encounter, David felt a rush of intense attraction for the red-headed beauty. Looking for a good way to insinuate himself into the conversation with the attractive couple, he noticed Dennis conversing with a small group of friends and went over to him.

"Hey, there are a couple of people here I want you to meet," he said, nudging his friend's arm. They picked their way through the crowd.

"Karen! Brian!—I'm glad you decided to make it! You missed a great Fourth of July party though. Here's the guy who started all the fun," David said, nodding to Dennis.

David was not one to be shy, even around new acquaintances. If anything, the circumstances seemed to make introductions and new friendships easier to make. There were so few Americans in Afghanistan, and they were all of interest to each other.

Dennis blushed and looked awkward. He was embarrassed about the reference to July 4. He wanted to forget the whole incident. David, already high and oblivious to Dennis' discomfort, continued with his introductions.

"This is also the man who has provided us with a reason to party—not that we really needed one—my good friend, Dennis Butler. Dennis, meet Karen and Brian—sorry, I'm not very good with last names." Actually, he recalled as he spoke, the couple had never given their last names.

"They haven't been in Kabul long. These are the two Conrad introduced me to a few days ago," David elaborated.

"Glad to meet you," was all Dennis managed.

"So this is your going away party—don't you like it here?" Karen asked.

"It's a long story," Dennis managed in reply.

"My friend is a man of few words, but much wisdom," David said, attempting a rescue.

"How do you feel about taking a little ride across town? I could use some company, and you might enjoy coming along. Have you ever ridden in a 'gaaddie' at night? It's fantastic! I'm supposed to pick up a friend and bring her to the party. She expects me at 8:30, and I see it's already after eight," David explained, looking at his watch. "Why don't we all go together? It's a great night for it," he urged.

"Sure, why not," replied Brian, "but can I take my glass with me?"

"Glass hell, we'll take a couple of bottles!" David replied.

He commandeered two unopened bottles of Pakistani wine and led the way to the stairs. They stopped several times on the way so David could introduce the couple and describe their mission.

"Don't anyone go anywhere, and leave a little food and drink for us!" he called as they headed down the stairs. "We'll be back soon!"

"Don't expect any booze to be left when you get back!" someone yelled back.

Downstairs on the street the bazaar had pretty well closed down for the night. All of the merchants but one on the south side of the street had moved their tables of merchandise back into the tiny shops and locked up for the evening. They would be back all too early, David thought, usually by 4:30 AM or so, before their morning Fajr prayers. The front of their apartment building on the north side of the street had been divided into a number of these small shops. One of them, owned by their building manager, Bagnur, was still open. He sold a variety of Afghan and imported goods, including the tasty karbuzeh and other fruits, transistor radios and batteries—and of course, toilet paper.

"Why are you still open? Come join the party." David spoke to him in his halting but serviceable Pashtu.

Bagnur was amazed and pleased with David's progress in the difficult language, for which no completely comprehensive English to Pashtu dictionary existed, though the language was ancient and spoken by perhaps fifty million people in central Asia. David liked the fact that Bagnur was always prompt in responding to any problems with the apartment (usually related to plumbing or electricity), and had gone out of his way on one occasion to find him a European made overstuffed armchair for a good price. He also gave the apartment dwellers the lowest prices on toilet paper without haggling. In return David and his friends bought all their hashish from Bagnur, who never let them down in quality, and had a reputation (according to both Conrad and Shamsher), for being discrete in such matters.

"I am waiting yet for one more customer. Then will I certainly come to your party. I am very sad to see Mr. Dennis leave Kabul."

Bagnur's lopsided grin and the deep smile lines around his eyes always suggested a sort of friendly sarcasm. He was something of an embarrassment to the Peace Corps supervisors, as he made no attempt to hide his reddened eyes, or his habit of smoking the hash laced cigarettes which often filled his shop with their pungent fumes. But Bagnur could afford to do as he wished. For an Afghan, he was very well off. He was one-third owner with two of his brothers of the apartment building, and could have easily afforded to hire someone to run his shop full-time (he sometimes left the business with a teenaged nephew when other duties called), or done without the shop revenues entirely. But Bagnur loved people. He loved the gossip, noise, and energy of the bazaar. He loved the haggling, the crowds of shoppers, and the excitement when some new western or Japanese gadget would arouse the curiosity of the customers. He also enjoyed observing the comings and goings of the foreigners and being privy to some of their secrets, and it was common knowledge that the Americans paid the highest rents—higher even than the Russians, English, French or Germans—the other major nationalities with a substantial presence in Kabul. He smiled at the young Americans and watched as they walked to the end of the street where the taxis usually waited. They were after all, 'his Americans.'

There was usually at least one taxi or horse-drawn carriage waiting at the intersection this time of night, as the presence of the westerners made it a lucrative corner to work. Tonight, because of the extra activity of the party, they had their choice of two carriages and a tattered Toyota taxi. David chose the gaaddie pulled by the healthiest looking animal, and after five minutes of haggling with the driver, they were off.

"Where are we headed?" asked Brian, settling onto the unpadded wooden seat of the gaaddie, with one arm around Karen's shoulders and a bottle of wine cradled in his lap.

The two benches of the vehicle were arranged back to back, with a low backrest between. Dennis sat forward with the driver while David, Karen, and Brian were snugly packed onto the rear facing bench.

"Just a mile or so across town," David said. "We're picking up Cindi Webster. Her father is a bigwig at the USIS, but he and his wife are out of town, and Cindi and her older brother are on their own while they are away. I think you will like her, Karen, she's younger than you but she's been here three years and really knows the place. She speaks better Farsi than any American in Kabul except maybe Conrad, and I think she even knows more Farsi swear words than he does!"

The horse trotted along the darkened streets at a leisurely pace. The only sounds were the clip-clop of the animal's hooves and their own voices. The flashes of lightening lit up the mountain ridges in the distance, and washed out for that instant the light of the stars, otherwise sharp and brilliant in the thinner highland air. The frequent flashes created a strobe-like effect on the buildings as the cart swayed and creaked down the street.

Karen sat between Brian and David. David felt the warmth of her leg next to his through her thin faded Levis. He could smell her and feel her breathing. He took a drink from the wine bottle she offered and passed it over the seat back to Dennis. He wasn't sure if it was the presence of the girl, the combination of wine and opium, the magic of the warm night air and lightening, the hypnotic motion of the gaaddie, or the ambiance of this ancient city—or the combination of it all —but he felt blissfully high, and acutely aware of the sublime moment. Surely it was the unique combination of all those things, but whatever the reason, he knew this was a time he would never forget—a moment when life seemed wonderful, strange, and full of potential. David was aware that every moment of existence was just as unique, just as remarkable as this particular ecstatic instant, but only rarely does one attain the altered mental state necessary to apprehend such precious slices of time as they occur.

The others experienced some of the same bliss. They spoke very little during the trip, but their silences were not at all uncomfortable. Brian and Karen did not seem to want to discuss the specifics of their past or reasons for their presence in Kabul, as gentle questioning from David quickly revealed, and he was not inclined on this numinous night to pry.

All too soon they arrived at Cindi Webster's home. She was just sixteen, and her parents were not overly excited about her spending time with the older PCVs, some of whom were notorious for their drinking and drug use. David knew she would attend the party one way or the other with her parents out of town, and he felt in some sense responsible for her safety. Her parents preferred she limited her social activities to school functions, but there was far more mixing of age groups here than would have occurred back home, due to the small number of Americans in Kabul.

David was glad her parents were not home, as he always felt a bit uncomfortable around them. He was aware she had a crush on him, as were her parents, so even though he was not particularly attracted to her, and thought of her more as a little sister, he always felt vaguely uncomfortable and defensive. In fact, it was partly his discomfort over his relationship with Cindi that had led to his unfortunate tryst with the equally innocent but older Reshtina. Cindi's teenaged infatuation had reminded David—no paragon of the arts of love, but still experienced enough to long for something at least slightly closer to what he had grown accustomed to in his college years—of what was missing in his otherwise pleasant enough routine—a relationship unfettered by the subterfuges and maneuvers of associating with young women who did not have the freedom to do as they (or he) wished.

For the last few weeks he had seen less of Cindi. She was beginning to drink too much in David's estimation—not that he had much room to talk. He found her especially irritating and strident when drunk, although she seemed years older when sober, mostly because of her amazing facility with the local language and self-confident ability to navigate both the city and the expatriate community residing there. She also seemed to be more friendly with Dennis lately, or maybe it was just because Dennis was leaving soon; they were, after all, good friends. Perhaps she had shifted her affections from him to Dennis. He hoped so. Maybe, he mused, if

Dennis had a girlfriend he might change his mind about leaving.

Reshtina was somewhat jealous of his friendship with Cindi, but assumed she had displaced the other girl in David's mind and heart, now that they were, in her mind at least, lovers. Both would have been astonished at the force of his attraction to the new American girl, Karen, who had become, on the basis of just two meetings, the exclusive object of his desires and fantasies.

Cindi met them at the door, ready to go.

"You are twenty minutes late," she pouted. She had already been drinking. She was small—just over five feet, and slightly built, with deep brown eyes and incredibly thick long black hair which, as was the case tonight, she usually wore in a sort of loose bun, "...to keep my neck cool," she had explained once when David had asked her why she never wore it long.

"So who's keeping track of the time?" David said, teasingly.

David really liked and enjoyed Cindi as a friend, and he found it somewhat odd that he was not more attracted to her sexually, but he dismissed it as simply a lack of the proper chemistry and her age and inexperience.

"Oh, Steve's on his 'big brother' kick again. He says if I'm not home by one he will tell mom and dad when they get back."

As if on cue, her brother appeared at the doorway.

"Hey, what's the idea Cindi? What am I supposed to tell dad when he notices this—and he will!" Steve held up a half empty bottle of vodka.

"Tell him you and Khalid drank it!" she answered, laughing as he chased her down the entrance steps.

The truth was Cindi had the leverage and power in their relationship, in spite of being the younger sibling. One afternoon several weeks earlier she had burst into her brother's room unannounced to find him in bed with the Afghan boy, Khalid, brother to Reshtina, and scion of the well-connected Pashtun family. Although they had never discussed the matter openly afterwards, Cindi had been quick to use the knowledge to her advantage, as she did now. She stopped at the bottom of the steps and offered her cheek, which he dutifully kissed, tacitly admitting defeat. He looked at the bottle in his hand and shrugged his shoulders.

"I guess I could add some water."

"Hey Steve, are you gonna come to my wake?" Dennis asked.

"Yeah, I'll come over a little later. I'm waiting for a friend to stop by." Cindi rolled her eyes at him. At nineteen he was three years older than his sister, tall and gangly, with the thick dark hair and deep brown eyes which he and his sister had both inherited from their mother.

David introduced Karen and Brian to the siblings, and they exchanged brief greetings. Cindi got in the front seat of the gaaddie with the driver and Dennis.

"Remember, one o'clock—and watch the booze!" yelled Steve, as the carriage pulled away.

"It's bad enough having overprotective parents, and now Steve thinks he's got to be one too," Cindi complained.

"At least you have a brother. I always wanted one," Karen said handing Cindi the remnants of the first bottle of wine.

She guzzled the remainder quickly, and tossed the empty bottle into the roadside ditch with a flourish.

"I guess he's a pretty good brother most of the time, just not when he is playing parent."

David opened the second bottle of wine.

Karen was eager to make friends with Cindi, the first American girl near her age she had met since leaving the States for Nepal with her parents more than a year earlier. She eagerly questioned Cindi about her life in Kabul as the horse trotted down the dark streets. Soon they were talking like old friends. The three young men shared a bowl of hashish, passed the wine bottle around, and listened to the girls, only occasionally speaking themselves, content to enjoy the leisurely ride. The Afghan driver silently urged the horse on with deft movements of the reins, thinking happily of the large fare and tip he could expect from the young foreigners.

CHAPTER 11

Captured

A few blocks north of them, on a parallel street, but moving at three times their speed, Paul Sherman sat in the back seat of a taxi. He looked forward to the resolution of his mission, and with any luck, the prospect of a speedy return to the States. Tonight, in addition to his usual Beretta and knife, he also carried a pair of handcuffs. He had already made arrangements with the Kabul Chief of Police for a temporary jail cell for his prospective prisoner. There were some things about this country he appreciated. As in certain countries in Latin America, it was relatively easy to arrange for the transportation out of the country of a prisoner, without the hassle and red tape of notifying the higher authorities or immigration. All it took in this case was his letter of introduction and a few well placed greenbacks. Additionally, and for only ten dollars more, he was able to arrange for the help of two local police officers who, if his luck held, should already be waiting for him at the end of the block where the Peace Corps apartments were located.

It irritated him only slightly that the local Agency contact, Conrad Slocum, had not appeared at the time and place he had named, but he felt confident he could handle the situation without him. Slocum had, after all, made it clear he had no interest in helping him out in the manhunt. Paul was used to working solo in any case.

Earlier in the day, while pretending to shop in the bazaar, he had cased out the place, noticing the single stairway up to the apartments. It would be difficult for seaman Peccanter to elude him even if he were for some reason forewarned, with no other exits to the apartment complex and one of the Afghan policemen stationed at the base of the stairs. If all went as planned he would have the cuffs on before Peccanter even knew what was happening. Once he had his man, he was sure the girl would be no problem. He should be able to persuade her to go home to her worried parents in Nepal. However, Paul Sherman was a thorough and adroit agent, and he knew from experience things rarely ever went exactly as planned. That was why he had hired the extra police help.

Paul had also sent a telegram to Captain Cecil Ramsy, US Navy. It read: "Located our man Kabul Stop. Paul" That was enough. He had no doubt Cecil would be on the next available plane.

Bagnur sighed and looked again at his watch. He realized he had been dozing the last quarter hour and more.

It seemed his expected late customer was not coming after all. He relit his omnipresent hashish laced Turkish tobacco cigarette, and began putting away his merchandise and closing up the small shop. This time of night, after nine o'clock, the bazaar was usually closed and abandoned. The only people present would normally be the taxi and gaaddie drivers, who often hung around until midnight or later, smoking, talking, and listening to the radio on Japanese transistor radios, waiting hopefully for one last fare. On many nights they were successful, as the young Americans often came and went at odd hours, especially on weekends.

Tonight, besides the usual drivers with whom Bagnur was acquainted, there were two other men, Afghans in shabby western clothing, who stood at the intersection smoking and talking quietly. They seemed to be waiting for someone. One of the men checked his watch frequently. Bagnur did not recognize the men, but he felt sure they must be police officers.

He was not worried about the large supply of contraband he kept hidden in his shop. Although it was strictly speaking against the law to use or sell hashish or opium in Afghanistan, in practice these regulations were rarely enforced, and in many of the Chaikhannas the patrons smoked openly. Under the law it was a much more serious offense for a Moslem to be caught drinking alcohol, for the prophet had specifically forbade its consumption, while making no specific injunction against the other substances. In any case, a little baksheesh in the right hands could always solve any problem, and Bagnur was known to be very generous in such matters. Only a month previously he had made a substantial contribution for the purchase of new police uniforms. Bagnur had received a special note of thanks from the chief of police himself, which he had framed, and proudly displayed in a position of honor directly under a photograph of King Zahir, so that any customer could not fail to recognize his merits as a good citizen of Kabul.

Bagnur suspected the presence of the police had something to do with the party upstairs and decided to inform Shamsher, whom he knew had experienced previous difficulties with the law, about the two strangers on the corner. Bagnur liked Shamsher. He had brought him much business over the last several years, helping the young foreigners find him in a virtual sea of willing hashish and opium peddlers. The business had brought in a lot of valuable dollars, marks, francs, and pounds, nicely augmenting his income from the apartments and the shop. He padlocked the shop shutters and went upstairs.

"There are some strange men waiting outside. They have been there for a long time now. I thought you might want to know," Bagnur told Shamsher discreetly, after the usual Pashtun greetings and pleasantries.

Having warned Shamsher, Bagnur turned and began making the rounds, helping himself to the remnants of remaining food, and in his pleasant manner striking up conversations in his heavily accented but adequate English with several of the young renters and guests. Shamsher went into David's apartment and looked down onto the street. One of the men stood smoking under the street light, and the other paced nervously on the opposite corner of the intersection.

"What's going on Shamsher?" asked Tony, returning from a trip to the bathroom and noticing his friend at the window.

"Maybe I will have some trouble," Shamsher said, without shifting his gaze from the men below.

"What do you mean?" Tony pulled the curtain open wider and followed Shamsher's gaze. "Do you know those men?"

"Yes, I recognize one of these men. He is a policeman. When I was in the Tolkif jail, he was the one who hurt me. The one smoking. I can never forget that one's face." Shamsher spoke quietly and deliberately, but Tony could feel the tension in his voice.

"What could they want here? You're not in trouble, are you?" Tony asked.

"No—wait, there is someone else!" Shamsher declared.

A taxi had pulled up at the corner under the pool of light, and a tall, neatly dressed man stepped out. The man paid the driver and immediately began speaking with the pair of poorly disguised policemen. After a few minutes one of the policeman walked away from the intersection and was lost to view in the shadows of the street below the apartment.

"Oh shit, the tall one looks American! I wonder if he is here to hassle Dennis about the Fourth of July fiasco. We had better warn him!" Tony exclaimed.

"Dennis went with the others to get Cindi. They no longer have returned," Shamsher replied, his grammar betraying his unease.

"Maybe we could walk up the street a few blocks towards Cindi's place and warn them before they get here."

But it was already too late. As they descended the stairs the gaaddie crossed the intersection and drew to a stop in front of Bagnur's shop.

It had been a magical ride back to the apartment. The lightening flashes had continued, though less frequently. The horses hooves beat against the pavement with a primal rhythm older even than the ancient city. They finished the second bottle of wine. The hash pipe went around a second and third time. Cindi talked and laughed with her new friend, and flirted with Dennis. Brian told dirty jokes he had learned on board the Navy cruiser, holding back the crudest ones for a time when the girls were not around. When the gaaddie arrived back at the apartment they were singing, drunkenly and a little off key, the refrain to 'Hey Jude.' None of them noticed the strangers waiting in the intersection adjacent to the apartments.

Paul watched as the cart approached, passing directly under the single street light that lit up the intersection. He noticed the thick, long red hair on one of the two girls. One of the men sitting beside her had a long hair and a beard—the man he had seen at the AID bar—the other matched the description and photograph he had been given of his quarry. Paul motioned the two Afghan police to follow him. Neither of them spoke much English, but they had been instructed previously on what to expect by an interpreter at the police station. Paul allowed the bearded one, David, to settle the fare before approaching the group.

"Just hold it right there for a minute—all of you." He spoke quietly, but with authority. In his right hand the Beretta spoke even more forcefully.

The five young Americans turned towards him.

"You," he said, pointing the gun at Brian. "Take off your jacket and show me your arms."

A grim expression came over Brian's face, but he slowly removed his Levi jacket. The tattoos were obvious even in the low light.

"All right Mr. Peccanter, just get down slowly and put your hands against that wall and spread your legs—that's right—just the way they do it in the movies. Miss Truman, please stay where you are. The rest of you go about your business, your friends will be accompanying me from here on. This business has nothing to do with the rest of you."

One of the Afghan police patted down Brian as Paul spoke, finding only his wallet and the Swiss Army knife which he always carried. The other checked Karen's purse.

"Hey, what the fuck is going on here! Just who the hell do you think you are?" said Dennis, recovering his voice if not his judgement.

"What does it matter—I've got the gun kid—but if you must know, I'm a United States government agent acting with the full cooperation of the Afghan authorities." He flashed his ID at Dennis. "Your friend, Mr. Peccanter is wanted for a variety of criminal charges. Miss Truman is wanted by her parents."

Dennis and David both looked at Paul's identification card. It certainly looked official. The officer checking Karen's purse found a small bundle of hashish which he handed over to Paul. The other Afghan officer stood nervously by. Paul looked briefly at the contraband, dropped it on the street, and ground it contemptuously under his foot without comment.

"This thing could be forged. You got any other ID?" asked Dennis insolently.

A surge of anger at the young punk wasting his time caught Paul. He stepped over, and with a quick movement hit him in the solar plexus, not hard enough to do any permanent damage, but enough, he hoped, to put him in his place and discourage the young Americans from further interference. Dennis collapsed in pain, gasping for breath.

"That's all the identification you will get from me," he said, "but if you're still curious as to my legitimacy you may enquire at the embassy. They won't tell you much, but they will confirm that I am a bonafide United States agent, and most certainly they will tell you to mind your own business. Anyone else have questions?" Paul took a step towards David, who quickly backed away.

At that moment Shamsher and Tony came stealthily out of the stairwell and onto the street. Paul, with his back to them, did not notice their approach. Dennis saw his friends emerge from the doorway as he crouched in the street, gasping for breath, and glaring at Paul. Shamsher raised his index finger to his lips. Neither Cindi, bending over to comfort Dennis, nor David, still partially in shock, noticed their arrival on the scene.

Without hesitation, to Tony's astonishment, Shamsher produced a large knife from the inside of his jacket and rushed forward. With one hand he twisted one of the Afghan officer's arm behind his back while he drove the point of his knife under the man's chin just hard enough to draw a trickle of blood. The man's eyes went wide with fear. As Paul turned to the commotion, his feet were suddenly knocked out from under him. As he went down Paul kicked out quickly with his right foot and felt a satisfying thud followed by a yelp of pain. He quickly stood up again, gun still in hand, and surveyed the situation.

"That was a stupid move," Paul said, gesturing with the gun in the direction of Dennis, who clutched his bleeding face.

"It looks like I still have the advantage, and I don't think killing that officer will help your cause any," he declared, turning to face Shamsher and the petrified Afghan policeman.

"I don't know if you understand English, but one should never bring a knife to a gun fight."

Paul reached in his pocket with his free hand and gave the handcuffs to the other Afghan officer as he spoke. The officer cuffed Karen and Brian together. Shamsher, with the knife pressed to the hostage policeman's throat backed slowly away. Tony and David did the same.

"I'm taking these two, and there is nothing you can do about it. Try any more stunts like the last one and I will not hesitate to shoot. I suggest you let the officer go before you get into any more trouble," he said. "And get your friend here to a doctor. Come on now! Into the taxi!" he ordered, motioning to Karen and Brian with the gun.

The Afghan officer pushed the couple into the back of the car and climbed in after them. Paul Sherman took the front seat next to the driver.

When the cab had vanished, Shamsher, still holding his knife to the policeman's throat, spoke to David.

"Please go up and find Conrad. I am thinking now we will need his help."

"I'll take Dennis to the dispensary," volunteered Tony, recovering somewhat from his shock.

"I'll go with you," said Cindi, herself pale and shaking with fear.

Dennis swore incomprehensibly through mangled lips, but he managed to get on his feet with help from his two friends. He staggered to one of the waiting gaaddies, whose driver along with the other taxi owner, had retreated to a safer distance when the gun had made its appearance.

Shamsher questioned the two gaaddie drivers, but either they genuinely did not know the taxi driver who had brought the American (which seemed to him to be unlikely), or they were not willing to tell for the amount of baksheesh he was offering.

In any case Shamsher thought grimly, *the information as to where they were taking Brian could be extracted from the policeman—one way or another.*

Conrad came quickly down the stairs with David. Because of the music of the Afghan folk ensemble and the general noise of the party, no one had heard the commotion below, and the third floor apartments blocked the view of that part of the street from the second floor landing, where the party was still in full swing.

"I told him what happened," David said, slightly breathless from his run up and down the stairs.

"Look's like you got yourself in a big fucking mess, Shamsher. Why don't you just let the good officer go?" Conrad remarked causticly.

Shamsher smiled and jerked the policeman's arm up roughly. The officer yelped in pain.

"I have some bad memories from this man, and I would like for him to have some from me too."

"What good will that do us or Brian? You are just going to bring more cops down on us when his buddies at the station start to miss him, and that won't take long."

While Conrad tried to persuade Shamsher to come to his senses, the gaaddie with Dennis, Tony, and Cindi receded down the dark street, on the way to the Peace Corps doctor's house.

"I think this man will know where we can find Karen and Brian," Shamsher replied.

"We don't need him to get that information," retorted Conrad. "There are only a couple of reasonable possibilities, obviously. He has got to keep Brian from escaping until he can get him out of the country, and he needs to contact the girl's parents."

Of course Conrad knew exactly what agent Sherman had in mind, but he had to hide that knowledge from his friends and somehow keep from getting tangled up in the affair, if at all possible.

"But how can what he says be true about Brian?" David interjected.

"A while back I had a long talk with Brian and Karen, and here is the situation as I understand it," Conrad replied.

He went on to give David and Shamsher a quick outline of Brian and Karen's recent history and circumstances, and filled them in on the particulars of Brian's unfortunate witnessing of the captain's horrible atrocities.

David was too shocked and sickened by the description to respond immediately.

"You have not told us where we can find this American, or your reasons for being so, how should I say, confidence?" said Shamsher, when Conrad had finished.

"The word is 'confident.' Think about it. There are only two places a man like that would stay in Kabul; the Hotel Intercontinental, or with friends. I'm betting he is the type who likes his privacy, so that leaves only the one possibility. So you see, there's really no point in keeping this good public servant here any longer," Conrad finished, nodding towards the frightened officer in Shamsher's grip.

Of course Conrad knew exactly where Paul Sherman was lodging, but it was critical to his cover and perhaps even to his very survival that as few people as possible know about his connection to Paul Sherman or the Agency.

"I think I will keep him a while longer all the same," Shamsher insisted, forcing a groan from the man with another twist of his arm.

"They will not miss him until tomorrow, and I think we have much work tonight. We will still find maybe some good use for him, okay?" Shamsher smiled —a smile that telegraphed more menace than amiability.

"But I will need some small amount of rope," he added.

Conrad shrugged in acquiescence. It was evident Shamsher would not be persuaded, and Conrad, though worried about the repercussions for his relationship to the Agency he was nominally employed by, was hopeful he might yet find a way to resolve the situation without blowing his cover. He was also fairly certain that Shamsher was one of the few people in the city who knew or suspected something of his secret intelligence gathering activities. Regardless, Conrad would have bet his life on Shamsher's discretion and loyalty to their friendship, such as it was. Shamsher and Conrad were by no means close friends or confidants in the usual sense—they were both too secretive by nature, but they shared a mutual respect and trust that in some ways went beyond the more common limits of most friendships, and until now Conrad had found no reason to doubt Shamsher's normally sound judgement.

"Wait a minute! What are you planning? Are you crazy? That guy is armed, and he has official papers—and definitely the backing of the Kabul police at the very least. This isn't something we should be sticking our noses into!" David interrupted.

He could not believe the turn of events. Only a few minutes ago David had been happily enjoying the company of his friends and what should have been a very pleasant if somewhat bittersweet evening, and now he was apparently about to be involved in interfering with an international manhunt. David did not like confrontation of any sort, and so far in his life had managed to avoid any contact with police other than a couple of minor traffic tickets.

"Don't kid yourself about the rule of law any-where, but especially here. The police in Kabul are not the only owners of guns, and the unwritten law here supports those who understand how to use bribery, blackmail, and force majeure to their best advantage. There are certain advantages to such a system, once you accept that it exists. In the United States the myth of the power and sanctity of the law is accepted by the common citizens. Those who really hold power ensure that the illusion is believed by the populace, but the wealthy and powerful do much as they wish where it really counts, while the lower classes are mislead and kept well entertained. Here the stark reality is plain for all to see, and those who wish to exercise their will do so without excuses or moralizing."

After his surprising monologue Conrad looked from David to Shamsher, then continued.

"What kind of a chance do you think Brian will have if he is returned to his captain? I wonder if he is even supposed to make it back to the states alive? I must say I agree with Shamsher on this point, though I don't necessarily think we need to kidnap this officer."

Shamsher nodded, but said nothing. He did not let go his hold on the police officer. David thought for a moment before answering.

"It does seem suspicious to me that some man claiming to be a United States government agent appears in the middle of the night to haul the two of them off. I don't consider myself much of a man of action, but I would like to know what is really in store for Brian.

For all we know the guy could be someone Brian's captain hired to shut him up if Brian's story is true," David said at last.

"My guess is the man is for real, and he will take our unfortunate AWOL sailor to the Tolkif jail tonight and put him on a plane tomorrow," Conrad replied.

Of course this was more than speculation. He could not reveal his relationship to agent Paul Sherman without exposing himself, and the same logic applied to Paul. Conrad did not want to think about what might have ensued had he been on the street when agent Sherman appeared to arrest seaman Peccanter. Young and relatively inexperienced as he was, he knew the Agency would not tolerate lack of cooperation in its employees—especially low status for hire informants such as himself.

Some of the same characteristics that made Conrad such a good catch for the Agency—his situational awareness, powers of observation, resourcefulness, skepticism, and mental agility—also tended to make him hard to control and totally immune to propaganda. His relationship to the Agency would never be entirely comfortable.

"He's not going to take Brian to the hotel with him. That would be risky and it would be too easy for Brian to cause a disturbance. No, he will put him in a cell at least overnight. Karen I'm not so sure about. My guess is he will take her to the embassy or the hotel. In any case we need a plan," Conrad said.

"I think this officer could help us if we go to the jail. I have seen this same policeman at that jail when I was put in there," Shamsher replied.

"Okay then," said Conrad. "You could be right. He might prove to be useful after all. We should tie him up and gag him if we must take him along. But we will need to wait a little while to make sure things have settled down at the prison, and the American has gone back to his hotel, or wherever. If we don't find Brian at the prison, then we will have to go to the Hotel Intercontinental."

Conrad actually had no intention of going anywhere near the hotel, and he wanted to be sure enough time passed that he stood no chance of encountering agent Sherman at the prison.

"What about Karen?" David asked. He realized somewhat guiltily that his concern was more for her than her boyfriend. He was entirely smitten.

After a short pause Conrad responded.

"I don't think she is in any danger. The man said she was wanted by her parents. That means he has been in contact with her parents or a go-between, and maybe he will get some kind of reward if he finds her. I am fairly sure the reward will be greater if she gets back home in one piece! I think we can leave her for now and concentrate on Brian's situation. We should stay here for another hour or so. Shamsher, you are going to have to hide that officer before somebody from the party sees him and starts asking awkward questions."

David ran quickly up the stairs and retrieved a length of clothesline from his apartment, while Shamsher and Conrad waited below with the captive Afghan policeman. Fortunately all the partygoers were out on the landing, and they were able to smuggle the bound and gagged police officer up the stairs and into David's bedroom without being seen. David had a quick glass of wine to calm his nerves and stifle the panicky feelings that threatened to overwhelm him, but his hands still shook.

"We might as well enjoy the party for a while longer while we wait, although I would advise staying reasonably sober," Conrad said, looking pointedly at David, "But I suppose Shamsher will have to stay in here to keep an eye on his old friend."

"I do not mind to do it. You must enjoy your friends on this night, and I will be content to pass the time with this man who treated me so badly when I was his prisoner. Perhaps I can show him a truer hospitality!" Shamsher grinned widely and flourished his bright blade in the Afghan officer's face.

"Well, you are responsible for clean up if he pisses himself or worse, so I'd go easy on him, Shamsher,"Conrad suggested.

CHAPTER 12

In Custody

It was a short trip through the deserted streets across town from the apartment complex to the Tolkif Prison. Karen sat tight-lipped in the back seat, her wrist cuffed tightly to her boyfriend's. Her confusion and shock had by now distilled into a mixture of anger at her powerlessness mixed with despair over Brian's situation. At the prison money was exchanged and Paul, with the help of the remaining officer and the papers he had procured earlier—signed by the chief of police himself—had no problem convincing the guard in charge he needed a secure and reasonably clean cell for his prisoner.

"Don't worry babe, I'll get out of this somehow," Brian called to her as Paul and the guard led him away to his cell.

Karen found she had nothing to say to his pitiful attempt at reassuring her. Tears welled in her eyes. There was not even an opportunity for a last embrace.

Paul was efficient and methodical, and at times even officious, but he was not cruel. Once in the cell, Paul removed Brian's handcuffs.

"You are so considerate," the seaman said sarcastically, rubbing his wrists.

"Look, I've got nothing personal against you. I'm just doing my job, and it will be a court's place to find out whether you are guilty or not, and your punishment if you are."

"You've got it all wrong asshole! This is as personal as it gets!" Brian yelled through the bars as Paul and the guard walked away. "I won't even get to see the inside of a courtroom, and you know that is the truth!"

When he returned to the taxi Paul handed the officer who had helped him some Afghan banknotes and thanked him. The officer returned to the jail, presumably to tell his fellows about the night's adventures and to organize the rescue of his unfortunate partner.

The taxi motored slowly through the dark and empty streets towards the Hotel Intercontinental. Paul gave little thought to the officer he had left captive in the hands of the knife-wielding man at the apartment complex earlier. He assumed the poor fellow would be rescued, if he had not been killed by now. How this would go down with seaman Peccanter's young friends likewise was not his problem. His only real concern was that Brian Peccanter, Karen Truman, and he were on the next available Ariana flight to Peshawar. There he would meet the girl's parents and get rid of one responsibility. Then it was on to Hong Kong where he would turn his other charge over to the military police.

Paul imagined that if Cecil Ramsy did not show up in person before he flew out of Kabul, having read the telegram Paul had sent earlier, his old friend would certainly be in contact very soon. Regardless, once they arrived in Hong Kong he could forget this whole distasteful assignment, and take a much earned vacation some place where the women wore bikinis not burqas, and the men preferred straw hats to turbans.

On the way from the prison to the hotel Karen wept quietly for a short time, but surprisingly soon she had her emotions under control. Paul was relieved to find she was not the hysterical type.

"He won't be mistreated, and we will all be on a plane out of here soon."

He felt the need for some reason to explain his actions to her. The girl, like her mother, he could not help noticing, was especially pretty, even with her face streaked with tears. Paul found himself taking an immediate liking to the young woman, and uncharacteristically feeling a little sorry for her unfortunate boyfriend. Usually he did not get emotionally involved in his cases, but this was certainly not a normal case.

More typically, his domain was the collection of information. In the situations where he dealt with people directly, they were agents of the 'enemy' and thus depersonalized for him. It occurred to him he could never have been a cop in the states. There were far too many gray areas in that line of work. His first impression was that seaman Brian Peccanter did not appear to be the kind of monster Cecil had described to him. He seemed too young and unsophisticated to have been involved in the kind of treasonous activity he was accused of, and Cecil's claim that he had kidnaped the girl or somehow coerced her was plainly false. It was obvious from the couple's parting scene and Karen's behavior at the prison that she was Peccanter's more than willing traveling companion and lover.

The truth is for some jury to decide—my job is just to deliver the goods, he reassured himself, repeating in thought what he had told the others, but the repetition felt strangely hollow.

"Where are you taking me now?" Karen asked, after she had regained her composure.

"Your accommodations will be quite a bit better than your boyfriend's. You are certainly not a prisoner in the same way, but you are still my charge and responsibility until I can get you to your parents, where you belong."

"What do you know about where I belong? Besides, I'm eighteen now and I can legally do what I want," she retorted bitterly. "Maybe I don't want to see my family just now."

Paul said nothing, but his sympathies were more for the girl's worried parents. They seemed like such intelligent, pleasant, and understanding people. The thought flashed through his mind that he had not seen his own parents for several years now. His mother thought he sold life insurance, but his father he was sure suspected that was not the case. He must wonder why his son had never tried to sell him a policy.

The taxi pulled up to the hotel. Paul paid the driver, tipping him generously to ensure he would be available for hire in the morning.

"Shall I put these on, or will you come with me on your own?" Paul asked, showing Karen the handcuffs before opening the car door.

The girl hesitated, started to speak, and instead looked intently into Paul's face. The exterior hotel lights framed their faces through the taxi windows. Something unspoken passed between them at that moment. They became instantly alive to each other, and aware that the other sensed this heightened sensitivity as well. Later Paul reflected that their brief eye contact in that taxi had as much to do with his attitude change toward seaman Peccanter's case as everything else that followed.

Karen said simply: "You don't need to handcuff me. I won't run."

He put the cuffs in his jacket pocket and they got out of the car.

Where is she going to go at this hour?—and she knows she can't help her boyfriend anyway, Paul thought, ringing the doorman and showing his room key as identification.

"It's not that I don't care about my parents," Karen continued as they climbed the stairs to his room. "I'm old enough now to make my own choices. If I was back home in the states they would not have even tried to stop me. My older sister left home at seventeen and they only asked that she call them once a week."

He could feel her frustration and anger. They stopped in the hall at his room on the fourth floor.

"Don't you think the concerns of your parents are at least somewhat justified? This is one hell of a different situation than leaving home in the states! And did your sister run off with an accused criminal? How often have you called home since you left?"

He tried to sound indignant, but his heart was not in it. She was simply too attractive and mature to scold, and it was not a role he was familiar with, having never had children himself.

"Brian is not a criminal," she said as they entered the room.

"What do you mean? He was all but caught red-handed. They found the codes in his room, and the money in his mattress. Even if he is not guilty of spying, he sure as hell is guilty of dealing dope, desertion, and assaulting the guard that tried to stop him from getting away. Hell, the poor guy got a pretty serious concussion. It seems your boyfriend knows how to land a punch."

"Well, what would you do?" Karen pleaded. "They execute traitors sometimes, don't they? Besides, he wasn't spying. He told me the whole story. He was framed by that horrible captain. I'm sure Brian felt bad about hitting the guard, and he'll admit that he used pot and even sold some to friends, but he is not a spy or a traitor. He would have stayed and proved it if he thought he had any chance." She paused and blushed slightly, uncomfortable at the thought of the anxiety she was obviously causing her parents.

"You are right about my mom and dad, though. It's not like back home, and I know they must be worried, but I couldn't risk contacting them until we were in a safer place."

"What do you mean, he was framed?" asked Paul.

Before responding to Paul's question Karen looked over the well-appointed suite. The main room held a couch flanked by mahogany end tables, and two overstuffed chairs. On opposite sides of a short hall doors led to a comfortable bedroom and a spacious bathroom. The suite was furnished like many of the others in the hotel chain. It was nearly devoid of any local flavor except for a large Afghan rug over the wall to wall carpet in the living room, and photos of bucolic Afghan locales on the walls.

"Oh, you probably wouldn't believe his story anyway. It's his word against the captain's."

"Do I need to put a chair in front of the door or something—just so you don't get any silly ideas?" Paul said, bolting the door and feeling a little over-dramatic and foolish even as he spoke.

"Like I said earlier—you don't have to worry. I won't try to escape. I might get my face kicked in, or shot in the back," she retorted, glaring at him.

"Well, I had not intended that anyone get hurt, but in my line of work it is always a possibility. I hope your friend has no permanent damage to his face. He should not have attacked me."

"I had only just met Dennis—the guy you kicked. He's not a friend, but I still feel bad that he got hurt because of us."

"He didn't have to interfere. He was warned," Conrad countered.

"Hey, this is a pretty nice place," she said, in an effort to change the subject. She suddenly realized there was no point in arguing with this commanding and handsome man, who in any case held all the cards.

Beyond that, she intuitively felt there was a chance of persuading him at least to question Brian's guilt and the official accusations. It was more than just his movie star good looks that Karen found appealing. There was something else—a feeling that she was dealing with a man who was at heart ethical and fair, though he was obviously capable of violence.

She rose and inspected the bedroom and bathroom, becoming in the process uncomfortably conscious in these surroundings of how grubby she must look after weeks of traveling in the same clothing, infrequent showers—usually cold—and living in seedy rooms. She suddenly felt an intense desire to use the opulent shower facilities.

"What did you two think you were going to do anyway—go back to the States? And what did Mr. Peccanter intend to do about his family when they no longer could rely on his military income? If he is such a great guy, as you contend, he must have some plan for them as well."

"You mean his ex? I know he had a wife, but he hasn't told me too much about her."

"Then I guess 'Mr. Honest Abe' did not think you needed to know that he is still married and has a two year old son to provide for."

Karen's already pale skin turned positively alabaster. She appeared to recover her composure quickly, but Paul noticed she now leaned for support against the hallway wall, and all traces of her former flippancy had vanished.

"Why didn't he tell me?" she murmured. Her question was not addressed to Paul.

"I admit it is a shock. I thought... I just assumed he was divorced, I guess. He always called her his 'ex.' I'm not sure how much difference it would have made if he had told me right from the beginning anyway, and I suppose the longer he went without telling me about his family the harder it was for him," Karen continued.

She realized even as she spoke that she was simply making excuses for her lover. She felt as though the very floor beneath her might drop away, and she might plunge straight down at any moment.

"You seem very perceptive for your age and experience, Karen," Paul replied.

He was surprised to find he now regretted his words, or at least his sarcastic tone, and once again he was impressed with Karen's self-control and maturity.

"This is what I am aware of, in any case. I can tell you he is not legally divorced. I have no idea whether they are separated or estranged, or what sort of emotional attachment he might have," he replied, attempting to assuage the impact of his previous words.

He felt now he at least owed her the facts as he knew them, as it was unlikely she would ever have the chance to hear the particulars from her boyfriend himself, or even that she would ever see him again after Cecil took over custody. Paul imagined once the man was tried and imprisoned, Karen, being so young and appealing, would soon find another relationship and forget about her dishonest lover.

Karen did not reply, but walked slowly back to the couch and sat down. She felt utterly deflated. It was all too much to comprehend at once, and she did not have a clear idea of her real feelings. There was on the one hand, the emotional reactions she thought she should be experiencing, but for reasons she had yet to sort out, she was not affected in the way she would have predicted for herself. She thought perhaps too much had happened too quickly for her to have the so-called 'normal' responses to all that had occurred in the last few hours. She just felt numb, tired, and drained of emotion.

"Tell me what your boyfriend told you about what happened in Viet Nam—you have no idea what I might or might not believe," Paul queried, returning to the subject of their earlier conversation. "You were saying that he claimed he was being framed by Captain Ramsy."

Somewhat reluctantly, but hopefully she repeated what she remembered of Brian's story of his Viet Nam experiences to Paul. When she had finished she stared down at the geometric patterns of the Afghan carpet, not wanting to see the patronizing look which she imagined must be on Paul Sherman's face.

It was Paul's turn to be shaken by new revelations about someone whom he had imagined he knew well. The story sounded fantastic, but Paul remembered the dissipation of Cecil in Hong Kong, and his feeling that something was not quite right about the captain's obsession with the seaman's case. As much as it pained him to think of it, he could not quell the disturbing thought that the girl could be telling the truth, and it might be his old friend Cecil who was the deceiver.

"What makes you so certain your boyfriend is telling the truth, other than your love for him?"

"Mostly the dreams. He would not tell me at first, but he finally did just a few nights ago. Almost every night while we were traveling, and while we have been here in Kabul he has had these terrible nightmares. He moans and cries in his sleep and wakes up covered in sweat. Finally he told me he was dreaming about the captain killing those poor people. I believe him. How could he make up such a horrible story?"

Again she gazed at Paul with her unwavering green eyes. She wished desperately that she could somehow convince him.

She did not realize how close to persuading him she actually was. There was the ring of truth in the tone of her voice and directness of her gaze. Paul was sure she was telling him what she believed to be the truth, but whether her boyfriend had told her the real facts was, of course, another question. After all, he had not been honest with Karen about his marital status or the fact that he was a father. In Paul's profession the truth was rarely obvious. Deception and duplicity were expected and more the rule. From his point of view, this was a truer reflection of the reality of the human condition than most religious, political, or philosophical apologists provided.

"Whatever the facts of the case are, he cannot prove his innocence by running away. I can promise you that I will help him get a good lawyer and a fair trial when we get back to the states. Now, it has been a rough night and tomorrow will be a busy day. You can have the bedroom. I will be comfortable on the couch, and the bathroom is yours now if you want, I've got a phone call to make."

While Karen luxuriated in the shower he placed a call to Cecil Ramsy, still on leave in Hong Kong.

"I got your telegram. Great job Paul! I knew you wouldn't let me down! I will be there as soon as I can. I'll call you when I get my flight booked."

Cecil's voice was thick with drink, and the phone connection was bad, but Paul could sense the excitement and something else—*relief?*—in Cecil's voice.

After hanging up the phone, he realized he regretted making the call.

Before settling down to sleep on the couch Paul slipped his gun under his pillow, as was his habit when on assignment. He listened to the sounds of Karen showering and getting ready for bed in the next room. He had a difficult time calming his thoughts, and it took longer than usual to fall into an uneasy and restless sleep.

CHAPTER 13

Brian And Reshtina

The Tolkif jail was an odd mixture of architectural styles—a product of many hasty additions as the prison population had increased over time. Paul had given the officer in charge money to be sure Brian's cell was not located in the worst part of the prison—a hideous dungeon-like affair where only the poorest captives or the insane were left to die—a fate which usually found them in a few weeks or months at the most. Still, his cell was small and dirty, and there was no plumbing. The bed was so filthy he could not bring himself to lie on it, tired as he was, and Brian was not overly fastidious in such matters. He sat instead on the only other piece of furniture in the cell, a rickety and battered chair with one leg that fell off whenever it was moved. The only other item in the concrete floored cell was a dented metal bucket apparently intended for his latrine.

There were twenty cells in this wing of the prison, ten on a side facing each other across a narrow corridor, about eighty feet in length. Bare light bulbs glared unblinkingly down from the peeling ceiling, ensuring that the prisoners could be observed easily even at night by the guards. The cells on the other side of the hall were even less pleasant, Brian noted, as their rear walls formed one side of a solid interior wall. At least Brian's cell, and the other nine on his side of the wing, had small heavily barred unglazed window openings high up on the outside wall, which Brian imagined must let in some sunlight during the day. However the windows were set too high to allow the prisoners to see anything of the outside world but the open sky.

Eight of the twenty cells were occupied. In one of them, across the corridor and one cell down from Brian's, was a Dutch student whose vacation had come to an abrupt end. He had extraordinarily long hair, and was dressed in a ludicrous and filthy fringed leather outfit, looking like a sort of squalid Hollywood cowboy. As Brian soon discovered, he spoke fluent English.

"How long have you been in here?" Brian asked him, after they had exchanged greetings and explained to one another the reasons for their present predicament. His new confidant had been caught smuggling hashish at the airport.

"Three days and two nights," the Dutchman explained. "I will be getting out of this place tomorrow, God willing." He smiled, showing teeth that certainly had not felt a toothbrush for the entire stay.

"I thought the penalty for smuggling was a lot worse."

Brian was grateful to find another westerner in the cell block. He did not think he would be able to sleep this night, and it was comforting to have someone to talk with. The other prisoners, as far as he could tell, were all Afghans. In any case, no one else had spoken.

"It depends somewhat on the nature of the crime, somewhat on who makes the arrest, and a lot on who you know and how much money you have. For murder or theft it is fairly expensive I hear, but for other crimes not so much. In my case it was a large amount of hashish and I was caught by airport officials, so quite a few people are involved. Each has his price, and the prison guards are the least expensive. Altogether now it will have cost me—let's see…maybe five hundred dollars American," he said after some mental computation. "But I have heard of others getting out for as little as twenty dollars for lesser crimes."

"Unfortunately," he went on, "in your case it might be very expensive. It sounds complicated to me. Since the man who arrested you is some sort of American official, and has the cooperation of the Kabul police, it might not be so easy to bribe your way out of here. Jobs may be at stake if you were to escape. But there are always ways around such things if enough money can be found," he went on more cheerfully.

Or enough time, Brian thought.

"That's not much help," he said, realizing there was no one to rely on for help but Karen, and she herself was still a captive as far as he knew. As for baksheesh, they had no more than four hundred dollars between them, and that was all back at the Pashtoon Hotel where neither of them could get to it now.

Brian jumped at a sudden noise, then relaxed as he watched the animal run across the floor of his cell. The rodent squeezed under the metal-barred door, and scuttled down the corridor.

Even the rats are deserting me, Brian thought dejectedly.

"What the hell happened to him?" the sleepy young American doctor said, opening the door to the trio, after several minutes of knocking had finally roused him.

Tony and Cindi stood arm and arm with Dennis, whose once handsome features were swollen and bloody from the kick he had received from Paul Sherman.

"Too much booze—he fell in the stairway," replied Tony, holding to the story they had all agreed to on the ride there.

"Can we come in? He needs help."

"That's obvious as hell! Of course—come right in, sorry it took me so long to get out of bed."

The doctor was a little grumpy, having just nodded off into a deep sleep after a late night of reading. His name was Robert Demming. He was a serious, competent man in his late thirties, who specialized in so-called third world diseases and had spent time previously in Africa before coming to Afghanistan six months earlier to replace the ailing and homesick doctor who preceded him. Most of his practice involved treating dysentery, malaria, and the other common afflictions westerners often came down with in this part of the world. Stitching up gashes, and attending to contusions was a little less common in his regular line of work, but he was reasonably skilled if not particularly quick at such patch-up tasks, and Brian was ultimately put to rights.

"Well, it's not as bad as it looks," the doctor said after he had finished dressing the wounds.

"He may end up losing a couple of his teeth at worst, and he will have a nice scar on his cheek that hopefully will remind all of you in the future of the hazards of your boozing. I just cannot understand why so many of you insist on drinking to excess, even when you see the results of it," he lectured the group.

Dr. Demming was a pious man, and a confirmed teetotaler.

After the doctor had done his work, and despite her protests, Tony and Dennis dropped Cindi off at her house before returning to the apartments.

Conrad greeted them at the bottom of the stairway.

"Is everything okay?" he asked, looking closely at Dennis' bandaged face.

"I'll live," mumbled Dennis through swollen lips.

"Demming says he might loose a tooth, but otherwise no broken bones or permanent damage," Tony added. "Has the party broken up yet?"

"Mostly—there are still a few diehards, and several so wasted I imagine they'll be crashing here tonight. David has his hands full with Reshtina. She's attached to him like a leech, and won't let him out of her sight. She's drunk, sentimental, and completely shameless. I can't imagine how he will get rid of her."

"So what about Shamsher and that police officer? Any news on Karen and Brian?" Tony asked.

"Let's go on upstairs and talk. No use standing out here in the street gabbing. We should get Dennis comfortable, and we can discuss things up in the apartment," Conrad replied and led the way up the stairway.

They helped Dennis, who was feeling the effects of the painkillers the doctor had given him, up the stairs. Shamsher and the Afghan police officer were still in David's bedroom. The officer lay bound and gagged on David's bed. His eyes widened in fear when the others entered the room.

"As I said earlier, Shamsher and I agree Brian is most likely in the Tolkif jail," Conrad said.

"It is a very, very bad place. We must get Brian out right away soon," Shamsher insisted, recalling his own unpleasant stay there.

"Are you crazy? That man—the one that took them away—is some sort of a special agent or international cop, and he's got a gun! You are only going to put us all in danger and make a bad situation even worse—forget it! I'm staying put!" Tony exclaimed.

"Sometimes things must get much worse before they can get better," replied Shamsher philosophically.

Dennis, despite his condition, stood shakily and raised his fist defiantly.

"You are even more fucking insane than Shamsher!" Tony declared.

"While you were getting stitched up, Dennis, Shamsher and I came up with a plan that just might have a chance, but it would work best with three people. I'm afraid you're just too wasted on morphine or whatever I imagine Demming gave you to be very useful, so that just leaves you, Tony," Conrad continued nonchalantly, ignoring Tony's protests.

Tony started to speak, but Conrad cut him off.

"Look, before you object again... David is obviously occupied and probably drunk by now, and Dennis will soon be completely zonked out. We need someone with a clear head and good judgment. If it looks too dangerous or impossible we will abort. Shamsher and I do not intend to put our lives at risk for Brian, but if we can spring him without too much trouble why not make the effort? What if one of us were in a similar fix?" Conrad explained.

"So in for a penny in for a pound I guess. But I am telling you right now—if I think it looks even slightly too risky I'll be out of there, and that's the end of it! Even so, I'm still not sure why the hell I am letting you talk me into this," Tony answered.

The three friends, with Shamsher urging the police officer before them with dire threats, emerged from the apartment. Dennis found David on the rooftop landing and diverted his attention while Shamsher, Conrad, and Tony hustled their bound and gagged hostage down the apartment stairs. Providentially Reshtina had detached from David on a kitchen errand (she fancied herself David's cohost for the party) just long enough for Dennis to inform him privately of the latest developments.

"Man, you look terrible," David said.

"At least this is a bon voyage party I'm not likely to forget," Dennis replied.

"Well, it certainly didn't turn out anything like I planned," David reflected, morosely.

"Not to worry—like I said—it has been a memorable night. You put on one hell of party, but I'm sorry to say that I'm almost asleep on my feet due to the effects of the good Dr. Demming's fine pharmaceuticals. I'm off to bed and I leave you to clean up the mess. It looks like you've got a good little helper there at least," Dennis said at Reshtina's approach, enjoying the jest at his friend's expense.

"Poor Dennis! What happened to you?" Reshtina said, weaving slightly as she drew near the two, and extending her small hand tenderly to Dennis's gauzed visage.

"Never mind him—just a slight accident—he will be fine. I need to make sure everybody still here makes it home safe, or at least gets a blanket if they decide to crash here instead," David said, ushering Reshtina away. The only way to keep her from drinking any more was to encourage her to continue in her hostess role, David knew.

David and Reshtina made the rounds of the landing and apartments. Most of the revelers had left earlier, but the few who did remain were well beyond the limits of moderate inebriation. David managed to arrange a taxi for two pickled Peace Corps Trainees, but several more wassailers, including a blasted brace of Australian trekkers, and a trio of soused second year PCV veterans on holiday from fieldwork in the hinterlands, who had not had a drop of alcohol in months and were completely incapacitated, were given blankets where they lay, or shown to more sheltered sleeping areas.

Reshtina was a separate and far more difficult problem. She refused to take a taxi home, and when David tried to insist she began to sob and accused him of being heartless. Worse, she continued to drink, becoming more pitiable with every sip. David resigned himself to his fate. She would spend the night. He knew it would only make matters worse, whether or not they had sex, but she simply would not go without a scene, which he was not able or willing to endure. He was at least sensitive enough to see that sex itself was not the real issue for Reshtina, but he could not comprehend all that their relationship meant to her.

What he thought was mere possessiveness and puppy love was for her nothing less than a chance to live—really live, in a world that she desperately desired and had experienced a small taste of as a teacher of Peace Corps Trainees and the lover of David Stuckrath. She sensed that David was her one chance to escape a life she had come to see as far too constraining, and a future she dreaded. A constricting world that, since the death of her mother, she could feel extending its minacious tendrils inexorably towards her. A future which for her could mean only a shadowy existence as a chador-shrouded servant of an omnipotent husband, and breeding stock with which to get sons to carry on his name and tribal identity. There would be no more teaching of foreigners; no joining in their carefree laughter; no more dancing or Hollywood movies; the end of the coruscating conversations and exciting nightlife she had become accustomed to since moving into her own apartment. Just the eternal monotony of cooking, cleaning, and raising children, with the occasional beating or conjugal rape as the only diversion, until finally, old before her time, she would be tossed aside for a younger wife and relegated to mere scullion status until she became too old to be of any use whatsoever.

No wonder Reshtina held so tightly to David and protested so forlornly when David suggested it was time for her to go! She was not too drunk to see that he and all he represented was slipping from her grasp, but her judgment was far enough gone that she still felt another night might be enough to change his mind. With no real experience of the social and sexual revolution that the young westerners took so much for granted, but had little relevancy in her world, she read far more importance into the sexual act than did David. Moreover, having come from a household with (until her recent death) a dominant mother as a role model, Reshtina fancied she could have things her way with David if only she exerted her will sufficiently.

She had not told David of the recent considerable pressures she had come under. She had revealed nothing and would not. Reshtina would not use that kind of leverage on him. It was beneath her, and at any rate she really did believe she was in love, and that because she was, he must be too, or would be in due course if only he could be shown the depth of her feelings. She would not tell him of the stern reproaches of her father, grown suddenly far more authoritative and self-assured since the death of his wife, or the threats of her uncle; or worst of all—the promise her father had made to the mullah's son, Sartor—that she would marry him and give up her life in Kabul—give up exciting cosmopolitan Kabul for a life in a desolate and moribund sheep herding community that lacked even electricity—never!

In the bedroom, alone at last with David on his narrow bed, she took off her thick glasses and smiled invitingly, waiting for his touch. She was well aware from her contact with Americans, and from watching Hollywood movies, that modern women were supposed to enjoy sex, and her first experience with David, though not fully satisfactory, had certainly had its moments of pleasure.

In turn David, seeing the inevitable, decided to make the best of the situation. He really was quite fond of Reshtina as a friend, and did not wish to hurt her feelings; moreover, he was just drunk and titillated

enough to take advantage of the opportunity that presented itself once again. Although David found Reshtina
passive and inept at lovemaking, in her favor she had
fine generous breasts, and flawless skin. At any rate he
could think of no way to dismiss her that would not be
cruel in the extreme. He dreaded the scene that he
knew must ensue in the morning, and the others that
would follow after that. There was no avoiding the fact
that he would have to break off the relationship, and the
sooner the better, but he was in no state of mind to do
so this night.

Shamsher instructed the taxi driver to stop a block away
from the prison. It was after two in the morning and the
streets were completely deserted. After they parked,
Tony, Conrad, Shamsher, and the Afghan policeman,
still bound with the clothes line, continued on foot.
Conrad had paid the cab driver several times the usual
fare, and promised more yet if he would keep station
until they returned. He was a driver Conrad knew from
previous experience could be relied upon for his discretion.

The Afghan officer walked before them, gagged
with his hands bound at his back while Shamsher kept
pace directly behind, knife at the ready. Shamsher knew
the prison well, both from having been an inmate himself, and from visiting others there. He knew one of the
wings was generally used for foreigners, or prisoners it
was expected might have access to significant amounts

of money. This wing had its own separate access, and Shamsher remembered, two sentries, one inside the prison and another outside in a small guard house a few yards before the entrance.

Getting past the guard house turned out to be easy. The sentry was fast asleep in his chair, snoring rhythmically. They walked quietly by and up a short concrete walkway to the heavy steel entrance door. On the way Shamsher spoke quickly to their hostage in Pashtu.

"I will take off your gag and the rope which binds you. You must do exactly as I say, or by Allah you will feel the bite of my knife in your back!" He flashed the knife in the man's face.

"You must make the guard inside let us in, and do not arouse his suspicion, or you are a dead man! If you do as I say you will go free I swear on the grave of my father!"

The policeman shakily pushed the small button which rang a buzzer in the building. A drowsy looking guard in a dirty ill-fitting uniform, who obviously had not benefited from Bagnur's donation to the police uniform fund, appeared at the small barred window. Recognizing his fellow officer, who in any case slightly outranked him, he opened the door to the other's command. Shamsher quickly pushed his way inside and relieved the sleepy sentry of his stout billy club and keys. Tony, Conrad, and the captive officer followed directly, and the heavy door swung shut behind them. The dull metallic clank woke several of the prisoners, including Brian, who had finally nodded off in his chair.

"What the fuck is going on?" came the sleepy voice from his cell.

"It sounds like we're in the right place," Tony said.

At that instant, while Shamsher's attention was focused more on the prison guard, whom he planned to lock into one of the cells along with the officer they had taken hostage earlier that evening, the hostage made his move. He lunged for control of the knife Shamsher now held in his left hand. The prison guard sprang quickly to his aid—but not quite swiftly enough. Shamsher reacted even faster, bringing the truncheon in his right hand down with terrible force to land just behind the ear of the guard The gaoler's forward momentum carried him into Shamsher, and all three fell to the floor. The full weight of the guard and Shamsher drove the knife deep into the hapless hostage.

Shamsher shook himself free and stood up. The long blade was buried to the hilt just under the ribs of the ill-starred police officer. He took some time to die, his liver spilling its dark blood onto the bare concrete. The guard lay still next to the hostage, senseless from the blow of his own baton.

"I spit upon you! Your own stupidity has resulted in your pointless death!" Shamsher spoke in Pashtu to the prone form of the dying officer.

The unfortunate man's eyes, focused elsewhere or nowhere, betrayed no trace of understanding.

"We must hurry!" Shamsher then declared in English.

For once that night, Tony, shocked to his core by the violent scene, felt no need to argue. They tied the wrists of unconscious guard with the line they had previously used on the now lifeless hostage, and drug the insensible prison guard unceremoniously down the hall to Brian Peccanter's cell. There, with Brian's help they laid the guard out on the filthy bed and locked him into the room with his own keys.

"Let me out too!" came a cry from the Dutchman's cubicle. "I will be forever in your debt!"

Shamsher shrugged and looked to Conrad for a decision.

"I think it might be best to let all of the prisoners out, as they have seen us now anyway. If we free them it will cause more confusion, and we might have more time to get Brian out of Kabul," Conrad suggested.

Shamsher instructed the prisoners to remain silent and to stay together until all were well away from the prison, and unlocked each of the occupied cells. The group walked quietly down the driveway past the still snoring officer in the guardhouse. The Afghan prisoners waved their gratitude to their unlikely liberators as they scattered into the city's darkness. The Dutchman continued on with Tony, Shamsher, Brian, and Conrad to the waiting Taxi, whose driver smiled and silently thanked Allah for the good providence of a month's worth of fares for the work of a single night.

"I owe you, should we ever meet again. Good luck to all of you!" the Dutchman exclaimed, and he too vanished into the night.

CHAPTER 14

Shamsher And Brian

"So what now?" Tony asked, as they got into the cab. "You know as soon as they get descriptions of us from that guard the cops will head straight to the apartments, if they are not already waiting there."

"If that guard ever regains consciousness—you hit him pretty hard, Shamsher," Conrad commented.

"I think Brian and I must leave Afghanistan as we have planned," Shamsher replied thoughtfully.

"I would not worry too much for yourself, Tony," Conrad continued. "I doubt that guard got much of a look at us in the dim light before Shamsher clubbed him. Beyond Shamsher himself, I doubt he could identify any of us positively. Who knows what he will be able to remember when he comes to—if he does—and the other officer certainly isn't going to be talking."

"To the Pashtoon Hotel!" he ordered the driver in Farsi.

"The people of my tribe will hide me in Pashtunistan, and Brian also if he wishes. He is a friend of mine, therefore he must be granted the Nanawatai—asylum from his enemies. My relatives there still strictly follow the Pastunwali. We will be safe. There is much talk of revolution. It is said the general Sardar Daoud Khan will return and free Afghanistan from the greed and corruption of Zahir Shah. Perhaps when this has come to pass I will be free to return to Kabul," Shamsher explained as the Taxi wound through the streets.

Tony slouched back into the taxi seat. He stared straight ahead into the cone of illumination the headlights shed on the abandoned streets, numbed by all the night's events. He felt drained and exhausted, and longed only to forget everything in sleep.

Brian too was lost in his own private thoughts. At least Karen would be safe. He would miss her, but it was better that she return to her parents. He had always supposed that at some point he would have to leave her anyway. His future could only be a life of hiding and staying constantly on the move. He felt a pang of regret that a man had died in the process of his rescue, but, he rationalized, it was his own fault for attacking Shamsher. He wondered what Shamsher's motive was in freeing him, and how he could ever repay the debt.

No point in worrying about that now. I'm not out of danger yet, he realized.

"We will borrow my uncle's car at the hotel," Shamsher continued. "That man who died was the policeman who treated me badly before when I was in that jail. In the morning they will have known who I am and where to find me. By then we must be some little ways into the mountains. My uncle has also a gun and money he will loan to us."

When they arrived at the Pashtoon Hotel Tony, Brian, and Conrad waited while Shamsher and his uncle, Mahmud, discussed the situation. Although they were in an adjacent room the strident voices carried through the office door, and it was evident things were not going well for Shamsher.

"Christ, what have I gotten you all into," Brian finally spoke.

"Don't worry about us, we'll be fine. It's you and Shamsher who have a problem, judging by what I'm hearing," Conrad replied, nodding toward the kitchen door.

"My only real hope is to somehow prove I'm innocent and see that the captain gets what he deserves."

"It seems like that madman's brutality and insanity has sucked us all into some awful vortex—violence and suffering breeding more of the same!" Tony spoke as much to himself as to his friends.

"Yeah, I know what you mean. It's like some kind of whirlpool that just keeps growing, pulling in everyone who befriends me. Sometimes I think it would have been better if he would have killed me, or maybe I should have stayed and gone through the court-martial," replied Brian morosely.

"No, I don't agree with that," Tony countered. "This Captain Ramsy must be stopped somehow. A man like that will never quit preying on people. I agree with Conrad that the best way to stop him is to make sure you stay alive and free to tell your story. In the meantime we have simply got to trust that Shamsher can get you safely out of Kabul. We don't have much of a choice, considering the situation."

"Maybe you're right, but this American agent, whoever he is, is the wild card. He doesn't seem like the kind to give up easily."

Conrad listened but made no comment. From the bits of conversation he was able to pick up from the other room he could tell Shamsher's uncle was not in any hurry to loan out his car, or help out his nephew.

At last Shamsher and Mahmud emerged from the kitchen. The uncle looked angry, and Shamsher no longer displayed his usual easy smile.

"He will let us borrow the car and some little can of gasoline, and too my uncle's old rifle. Unfortunately I was not able to make certain to Mahmud that I will soon pay him such monies as he wants for his car. My uncle insists he must have eight thousand afghanis in his hand before we may have the keys."

Tony checked his wallet and found he had four hundred and fifty afghanis, roughly nine dollars, a fair amount of money in a country where even the best cuts of beef went for twenty-five cents a pound, and a loaf of fresh naan could be bought for about five cents, or even cheaper by the locals, but far short of what Shamsher's uncle was asking.

In the meantime Brian went to the room he and Karen had shared and got his pack. Besides his clothing it contained all their traveling money. Hurriedly he split the money, nearly four hundred dollars, and placed Karen's half along with a hastily scribbled note into her pack. The cost of the car came to about one hundred sixty US dollars, and with the addition of Tony's contribution he would have some extra for fuel and food on the road, but it was little enough, and he would have to depend on Shamsher rather than bribery or baksheesh if they were challenged.

"I am sorry to borrow these monies, but we will need them to arrive safe in Pashtunistan," Shamsher said, accepting Tony's small sum.

"Forget it Shamsher. I wish I had more on me. For that matter I wish I was leaving Kabul myself. I have a feeling it's going to be a little hot around here the next few days."

"We must be hurrying," Shamsher said, shaking Tony and Conrad's hands in the western manner he had adopted.

"I will call you when we are arrived in safety. You maybe can get a message to us through Mahmud, though I regret to say it will cost you some few more afghanis." Shamsher indicated his uncle with a disapproving scowl.

The uncle shrugged his shoulders and smiled slightly. He feared there was a good chance he would never see his treasured automobile again, or that it might be returned damaged, and in fact they both knew the eight thousand was more than fair given the potential financial risk. Mahmud was fond of his dead brother's son, who had brought much business to the hotel. But he was wary of this latest whim of Shamsher's, which seemed to carry too much risk.

Although Shamsher had paid off the debt he had incurred when Mahmud had rescued him from the Tolkif jail several years earlier, and his nephew seemed to have matured and outgrown some of his earlier lapses in judgment, the fact was he did not completely trust Shamsher's discernment in some matters, nor did he approve of his adoption of the modern western style of dress, or of Shamsher's constant consorting with infidels. It was one thing to do business with people of their ilk—and when it came to money, only the Hindu merchants could compete with Mahmud in sophistication and the unprejudiced and tolerant acceptance of nationalities, races, and religions—but it was quite another to adopt their habits, or to keep company with foreigners to the exclusion of one's own kind.

When they had finally settled with Mahmud he ceremoniously gave the keys over to Shamsher, exhorting him to take special care of the vehicle. The men shook hands, bowed, and parted with the customary polite exchanges. Shamsher and Brian got into the car—a dull black, much dented, and rust-eaten 1953 Chevy model 210. Tony observed, as the two drove away, that at least the tires looked good and the engine fired up on the first try. He hoped their luck held. Conrad and Tony took the taxi back to their respective apartments. Conrad advised Tony to call him if the police contacted him.

Winding through the streets of Kabul, Shamsher headed south, intending to follow the main road as far as

Gardeyz. A rough but serviceable dirt road led from there to an obscure village in the Paktia district where he had family connections. Once there the two could slip across the border on foot and make their way to Quetta, Pakistan, and Brian could continue his travels westward to Iran via the road to Zahedan. Beyond that Brian felt his best chance to avoid detection was to travel to Turkey and lose himself in the throngs of Istanbul, or move on to Cairo, or some other Mediterranean city where an American would not stand out so obviously as in this part of the world. Shamsher would be safe with relatives in Paktia among the fierce tribesmen of the area.

After leaving the outskirts of Kabul they continued through the surrounding farmland and began their ascent up the pass through the rugged Hindu Kush. Some time later, a few miles from the town of Khowst, they came around a blind corner straight into a road block. Two men in shabby uniforms aimed AK-47s at their car. A third man, armed with a pistol and wearing a bandolier over his shoulder, approached the driver's side as they stopped. Shamsher opened the window.

"Salam alaikum" was the only phrase Brian understood in the rapid exchange which took place between the two Afghans, but he noticed with relief that both Shamsher and the man smiled and nodded to each other, and he relaxed some.

"Our plans must change for a while, I think," Shamsher said to Brian as their interrogator walked back the other soldiers.

"What's up? Can't we go on?" asked Brian.

"These men are followers of general Daoud Khan, who has promised to overthrow the corrupt Zahir Shah. They have need for our car, and have asked me to join them when they gather in Kabul very soon to make the revolution."

"So I guess we're stuck here then?"

"You alone may stay in Khowst until after the fighting, where you will be safe, or return with us to Kabul, if you choose. In much confusion which follows the overthrow of the Shah I do not think anyone will be wanting to look for you. These men are of my tribe, and I must go with them to rid Afghanistan of Zahir and his very bad rule. When Daoud Khan left the ten years ago, he promised to return if things did not get better for Afghanistan. Now is the time come, and I am very much excited to be a part of this revolution."

Brian quickly made his decision. "I'm with you, then. I know a little something about radios and communication from my time in the Navy, so maybe I can help out. I'm not too eager to strike out on my own through these mountains anyway."

Brian gazed up at the formidable peaks on both sides of the valley and the narrow dirt road which led up through the pass. He thought again of Karen and the possibility he might be able to figure out a way to get her out of the American agent's clutches in the turmoil and confusion that he imagined would accompany the coup attempt.

"Good! We wait here for the rest of Daoud's soldiers to come. We will have good beds and plenty to eat, and you will be safe here."

Any port in a storm, Brian thought. *But what if their coup attempt fails? In any case I can't go on alone through these mountains. It seems my fate is tied up with the fate of this Daoud Khan, whoever he is.*

They parked the old Chevy near the small hovel beside the road, and joined the soldiers inside.

CHAPTER 15

Paul And Karen

Paul was awakened early the next morning by the telephone. An interpreter from the Kabul prison headquarters informed him of Brian's escape and the murder of one of their policemen. Paul swore as he hung up the phone.

"What is it? Is it about Brian?" Karen asked sleepily from the hotel bedroom doorway.

"Your boyfriend has really screwed things up now. He somehow escaped last night and a cop is dead. Whatever he may or may not have done in Viet Nam, he has only compounded his difficulties now."

"I don't believe it! Brian would never kill anyone!" Karen exclaimed.

"Well, you might be right at that. Apparently he had help from an Afghan man escaping—probably the same man I saw with your group in the street last night. You can bet the local authorities will be after them both, and around here I understand they shoot first and ask questions later. Your boyfriend's only chance now is if I can find him and get him out of this country before the Afghans catch up with him. So if you've got any ideas about where he might have gone, you might want to tell me now, so I can get to him before they do."

"Why would I want to tell you anything even if I did know? If Shamsher is with him then he is safe, and that is his best chance to get away. Besides, I heard you on the telephone last night and I know you called Brian's captain. Even if I did trust you, which I'm still not sure about, I definitely don't trust him."

As Karen spoke she moved from the bedroom doorway to the couch where Paul sat undressed but for his boxer shorts. The sheet and blanket were partially wrapped around his waist and in disarray from his sudden fumbling to answer the phone. Karen's thick auburn hair was tousled from sleep. He became aware of her smell, her bare legs and feet, and the exposed skin of her neck and chest where the oversized hotel bathrobe hung open slightly. It was obvious she had thrown the bathrobe on in a rush, and that she wore nothing under it.

Paul had a sudden urge to touch her. The sensation was fleeting, but intensely compelling while it lasted. Along with the feeling came a sudden tumescence, and he was grateful the blanket still covered him.

"All right, maybe your boyfriend is not a killer, but I think you are wrong that his best chances are with that Afghan. We can talk more over breakfast. You can have the bathroom first," he said suppressing his fantasy with some difficulty.

Though young, Karen was in no way naive. She was well aware of the effect she could have on men. She noticed Paul's eyes as they quickly scanned her, and she made no effort to pull the bathrobe lapels closer together. If her allure could help to make him more sympathetic to her cause she was not above using this age old strategy, and Karen was smart and sophisticated enough even at eighteen not to overplay her hand. If she let the bathrobe fall open slightly more as she turned to walk to the bathroom so that Paul caught a fleeting glimpse of her briefly exposed breast, it could certainly be blamed on the combined effects of the ill-fitting robe, and her sudden motion in turning to go, or just a sleepy lack of awareness on her part.

It was a delicate game though, for she was sure Paul would not fall for any obvious manipulation on her part. She was aware that only her youth allowed her to even attempt such an appeal. She was right to sense Paul would have immediately suspected such a gambit by a more mature woman. If it came down to it, Karen was not even sure how far she would go on the chance that it might help Brian's cause, though she had to admit to herself that she was quite physically attracted to Paul's masculine yet elegant appearance, and she could imagine far worse sacrifices. She rebuked herself for the admission, which made her wonder if her love for Brian was really all she had thought it was, or just a temporary infatuation.

They had breakfast downstairs in the least formal of the hotel dining areas.

"I will have to call your parents today and let them know I have found you," Paul said between bites.

"So I'm still your prisoner, then?" she said contemptuously.

"Does it seem like that? We're just sitting here eating our breakfast like two civilized people. I know you are angry with me over locking up Brian, but that is water under the bridge, and we have a bigger problem now. Should I just ignore the situation and let the police find him? He is free at the moment, but if I don't get to him first somebody else will, and they won't be nearly as sympathetic. I know it's difficult, but try not to take it too personally. I answer to others above me, and I must do as I am ordered."

Paul immediately regretted his last words, which he knew sounded callous and trite, though there was some truth to them. Although Captain Ramsy did not work for the Agency, and was not technically his superior, he had powerful contacts, who had prevailed upon Paul's boss to give him this assignment.

"Look, now that Brian has escaped I admit I have no real reason to hold you. You are free to do what you want. I was asked to find you and to find out if you were still with Mr. Peccanter, and to report your whereabouts. I was not directed to arrest you, or even to escort you back to your parents."

"You don't have to call my parents. I will call them myself. Do you believe what I said about Brian?"

The abruptness of her question caught him off guard. Paul hesitated and avoided her direct gaze.

"I believe that you believe what he told you," he replied at last.

"That's not exactly what I asked."

"Well, I'm not sure I have enough information to know what to think about the whole thing right now. Let's just say I am keeping an open mind for the time being. I've got another suggestion too. We should agree to stay in touch. I promise I will tell you anything I find out about Brian if you will do the same with me. Simple, you see. You help me, I help you."

"Like I said before—why should I trust you at all?" she replied, eyes flashing.

"I do see your point," Paul said. He thought a few seconds before replying.

"I don't know exactly when Cecil will arrive in Kabul, but he is supposed to call me before he boards his plane. You know where I'm staying now. You can come by or call, and I will let you know what time he is arriving as soon as I find out. While you are at it you can call your parents on my dime. Fair enough?"

"Okay, but I want you to promise one more thing —that you will not leave him alone with that captain if you do find Brian."

"I promise, Scouts honor," he said, thinking to himself it was a reasonable request, given what Karen believed about Cecil's character.

"I bet you were a good Boy Scout," she said.

Was she flirting with him?

"And I bet you were never in the Girl Scouts," Paul replied.

"You might be surprised. In school back home I was considered to be one of the good girls," she said, smiling demurely.

"I did not mean to infer that you were anything else," Paul said.

Their eyes locked for a second longer than was comfortable for either of them. In that instant Paul gave up any effort to keep a professional emotional distance

"Where were you planning on staying? That flea-bag hotel might not be your best choice by yourself," Paul said, with real concern.

"I will have to go back to the Pashtoon Hotel and get my things, but you're right—I won't stay there by myself. I'm sure I can stay with one of the Peace Corps friends we met at the party you crashed."

"Hey, I'm sorry about how that came down, and that one of your friends got hurt, but he should not have interfered."

Paul's limited apology was so obviously sincere and unpremeditated, even with its qualification, that Karen was moved.

"You don't have to apologize about that. Of course Dennis was out of line from your point of view. I guess another man in your position might have done worse, or even killed him."

She reached across the table and put her hand on his forearm in a move that took him by surprise with its sudden intimacy, and she once again challenged him with her direct gaze.

"I know you will help see that Brian gets a fair trial. I don't exactly know why I trust you about this, but I do."

Even as she spoke she realized she would have a hard time explaining this to her new Kabul friends, but she reasoned that if she could be persuaded the others could too, if only they could have the opportunity to talk with Paul as she had.

They finished their meal. Paul paid the tab and called a taxi.

"You could stay here. I'm pretty sure the hotel has other rooms vacant—at my expense of course."

"That is tempting, for the shower alone, but I have a lot to do in town, and I'm sure I can stay with one of my friends there. I would feel too isolated up here in this hotel, but thanks. I will take you up on that offer to use your phone later on, and I promise to let you know then if I find out anything about Brian today."

Although she had known her Kabul acquaintances for only a few days, Karen was certain one of them would provide for her temporary housing needs. She did not want to put herself completely in debt to Paul. Karen was sure that David—whose attraction to her was obvious—would help her, and she was equally confident that both Conrad and Cindi could be depended on. She had no idea how much longer she would stay in Kabul, but if there was no news of Brian soon she had every intention of moving on, though as yet she had no particular destination in mind.

"How about seven this evening? My parents should be home then."

"I will be here, just have the front desk ring me," Paul said, as he ushered her to the waiting cab.

He watched the taxi wind its way down the hill. From the top of the prominence the Hotel Intercontinental, modern in every way and built just four years earlier in 1969 by Juan Trippe's corporation, Pan American, commanded a spectacular view of the city and the surrounding mountains.

After a moment Paul looked at his watch and remembered he had an early lunch appointment with an intelligence contact scheduled. He went back inside to arrange for his own transportation downtown, hoping that his contact might also have some useful advice as to how and where to begin this new search for the resourceful Mr. Peccanter.

CHAPTER 16

Karen And Cindi

Karen gave the driver directions to David's apartment. She did not want to go alone to the Pashtoon Hotel, and felt sure one of the friends she had met at the party would help her find a place to stay. That much of what she had told Paul was true at least, but beyond moving out of the hotel and trying to find out what had become of Brian, she had no idea what she really wanted to do next. Although she had promised to call her parents and intended to do so, she had no intention of returning home now that she had tasted the freedom of life on her own, or (she corrected herself mentally) at least life outside of her parent's home.

David was up when she knocked, but his room-mates still slept, recovering from their adventures of the previous night.

"Come in, Karen. How did you get away? We all thought you were a prisoner of that man—but I have good news! Brian is out of jail!"

David was completely mystified by her presence at his apartment. She looked fresh and radiant and even more beautiful than ever.

"I know about Brian. I found out from Paul—that's his name—the government agent. How is Dennis?" she asked.

"Oh, his face will heal okay thanks to Dr. Demming, but I'm not so sure about his pride. Everyone here will be dying to know how you managed to get away from that man, whoever he is," David insisted.

"He just let me go," she said evasively. "He was mostly hunting for Brian, not me. I just had to promise I would contact my parents. How did Brian get out of jail? Do you know where he is?" she asked eagerly.

"I had nothing to do with it. It was Shamsher's idea, and Conrad and Tony helped. As far as I know he and Shamsher left the country. I guess they must be somewhere in Pashtunistan by now—that no-man's-land beyond the border."

David filled her in on what Tony had told him about the jail break.

"Oh, but I'm sorry. I'm not being a very good host. Do you want anything to eat—or maybe some tea?"

They had been standing in the doorway. David ushered her into the main room.

"No thanks, I just had breakfast with Paul," she answered.

"Well, maybe you could tell me what the hell is going on with this Paul character, then. Is he friend or foe? We're all in pretty deep here—a cop is dead for Christ's sake!"

"I promise I will tell you everything I know, but I need to ask you for a favor."

"I'll do my best," David said.

"I need a place to stay for a few days—just until I figure out what to do, or until I hear from Brian. I've got a little money, and I can help with food and chores, of course."

"Hey, don't worry about that. If all else fails you might be able to stay here, but it would cause a serious scandal with the locals and the Peace Corps brass. I think it would work out better if we talked to Cindi Webster."

"Yeah, Cindi—the girl I met at the party! I like her. Do you really think I could stay with her?"

"I'm sure you can, at least for a few days, especially since it is just her and her brother at the house while their parents are away. You could probably stay at least until her folks get back. Let's give her a call."

David dialed Cindi Webster from the phone downstairs in Bagnur's shop. (They could not afford one in the apartment on their limited pay.) He brought her up to date on Brian's escape and explained Karen's predicament, before handing the phone over to Karen.

"Of course you can stay here as long as you want. That's crazy about your boyfriend. So no one has heard from him yet?" Cindi asked.

"Not so far, and I don't expect to find out anything until they get somewhere safe and far away from Kabul. Hey—I've got to go to the Pashtoon Hotel to get my things, and I thought I would get lunch at the Khyber Restaurant or maybe Salim's. How would you like to join me?"

"That sounds great! What time? "Cindi replied.

They made the arrangements. Karen hung up and they thanked Bagnur for the use of his phone.

"You might as well hang out here until it's time for you to meet Cindi. You were going to tell me about this 'Paul' guy—the American secret agent or whatever he is," David reminded her.

Karen followed him back up the stairs to the apartment. She had nowhere to go until her rendezvous with Cindi, and she did not want to wander Kabul alone. Although the residents were used to seeing uncovered western women in the commercial areas, an unaccompanied woman could still be subject to verbal harassment in many parts of the city.

"He is some sort of a government agent, though he hasn't said which agency—and it is true he came here to find Brian and me. But he was only supposed to find out if I was safe and let my parents know. I was never really his prisoner," Karen replied.

David went into the kitchen and started water boiling for tea. There was a knock on the door and Tony entered. Tony explained the adventures of the previous night at the prison in more detail. Karen was shocked by his description of the death of the policeman. Soon Dennis and John, awakened by the noise, joined them in the living room. It was necessary for both Tony and Karen to rehash the events of the previous evening once again for their benefit. Dennis' face was swollen and discolored, and a gauze bandage covered part of one cheek.

"Man, I was so wiped out on that morphine Dr. Demming gave me I don't remember much after that," Dennis said.

"Reshtina and I had to practically carry you to your room," John said. "And I don't think I was in much better shape than you were—but at least my face looks better!"

"Ah yes....Reshtina... Is she still here too?" Tony asked, mischievously.

"She left a little while ago," David said, blushing bright red. He was especially embarrassed because of the presence of Karen in the room.

"Karen is going to stay with Cindi for a few days —at least until we find out where Brian is," David said, by way of changing the subject.

"Well, for a while anyway. I'm not sure how long I can stay there, or even how long I will be in Kabul."

"I've got an idea, Karen," Tony offered. "If you end up staying here longer and the Webster's place doesn't work out, I just rented a house. I could use another roommate to help split the costs—quite a bit of privacy and room—even a nice courtyard and hot water."

"Thanks for the offer Tony. Who knows how long I'll be here. I don't know what I'm doing at all yet, but you are all such great friends!"

David realized he was not the only man here attracted to the lovely Karen. He had to give Tony credit for his timing and tact.

After more tea and talk they all left the apartment together—the men accompanying Karen part way to her lunch date with Cindi, before splitting off on their individual errands.

The Khyber Restaurant in Pashtunistan Square was an establishment popular with westerners because one could eat there without fear of contracting dysentery as a general rule, and besides the restaurant at the Hotel Intercontinental, it was one of the few establishments in Kabul to serve American style meals. The milk products were pasteurized, the water distilled, and the foods prepared to 'modern standards of hygiene' for the most part. Two bearded German tourists at an adjacent table looked the two young women over appreciatively as they seated themselves, and a few other customers took advantage of the less crowded time between the breakfast and lunch rushes, but otherwise they had the room nearly to themselves.

"I know this menu by heart, I've eaten here so many times," Cindi said.

"What's good?" Karen asked.

"Oh, you really can't go wrong with anything, but it's the only place in Kabul, and probably the whole country where you can get a pizza."

They decided to split a medium pizza and ordered two cokes.

"It seems really odd to be eating like this here," Karen commented.

"It's not all that unusual for me. Our cook at home knows lots of American dishes. My brother is the only one in our family who really likes to eat like the locals. In fact, I wouldn't even be surprised if he became a Moslem," Cindi said between sips of her drink.

"Would he really?"

"I wouldn't put it past him. He might convert just to bug mom and dad."

Karen happened at that moment to look past Cindi through the windows of the restaurant. She saw Paul Sherman outside in conversation with another man, American or European by the looks of him. Cindi followed her gaze.

"Isn't that the man we saw last night? The one who took Brian away?" she asked.

As they watched, the two men resumed their walk, disappearing from view.

"That's him—Paul," she said, blushing slightly. She wondered if he had followed her, or if his presence was just a coincidence.

"Now that it's light and I can see him better, I think he looks like a movie star, even if he is a bad guy. I wonder if he is following you, thinking you might know where Brian is," Cindi whispered, leaning forward conspiratorially, echoing Karen's own thoughts.

"Dad says Kabul is filled with all kinds of spies and secret agents," she continued, picking up a second piece of pizza.

"The problem is, I don't really think he is a bad guy, even though he did kidnap Brian and hurt Dennis."

"What do you mean?"

Karen explained Brian's situation to Cindi, and told her what Paul had promised her about helping to make sure Brian got a fair trial in spite of Captain Ramsy's allegations.

"I don't know what the best thing to do is, but I am sure Paul is no monster."

"Well, he did let you go, I guess," Cindi replied, when she had recovered somewhat from the impact of Karen's story.

"What do you mean?"

"I think he didn't have to let you go this morning. He could have taken you to the embassy or locked you up somewhere until your parents got here. You say he hasn't even called your parents yet. It seems like he trusts you quite a bit for someone he just met." Cindi slurped the last of her coke.

"I wish I knew what to do. I only know I don't want to go back to live with mom and dad."

Karen did not reveal to her new friend the other disturbing things she had learned from Paul about Brian's wife and child back in the states, or the fact that she was beginning to have doubts about Brian herself—not about his story, but about her real feelings for him.

"Stop worrying! For now you can stay with me at least. Let's go get your things, and after that we can hang out at my place for a while. I just got some new records we can listen to, and Dad had a new stereo imported a few weeks ago for mom's birthday."

At the Pashtoon Hotel they found Mahmud to be in a fowl mood. He insisted on collecting a full week's worth of rent on the room for what he claimed was "all his trouble."

"The police have been here twice already, and I only just managed to hide your belongings from their curious eyes," he told the American girls.

Cindi, with her facile command of the Farsi language translated for Karen, but she was not able to bargain with Mahmud, and Karen was forced to pay him the rent he wanted in order to retrieve her things. After some badgering Cindi determined he had no new information on Brian and Shamsher. He went on for some time about all the difficulties they had caused for him. They were finally able to extricate themselves, feeling relieved they had managed to get Karen's possessions, including her passport and her half of the money which Brian had left in the pack, for what amounted to a few American dollars.

In the cool and luxurious interior of the Webster house they spent the afternoon listening to Cindi's new copies of "Exile On Main Street," "Harvest," "Ziggy Stardust," and "The Harder They Come," while they raided the Webster's diminishing liquor cabinet.

"Do you have any grass?" Karen asked, flushed and mellow from two tall glasses of wine, as the weird strains of "Star Man" issued from the speakers.

"Are you kidding? I wish I could get some. You can get all the hash you want for peanuts in this place, but try to find some leaf—forget it!"

"I'd settle for a hit or two of hash, then." Karen replied.

"I don't have any, but I know where Steve keeps his—even though he thinks it's well hidden. He gets it from his boyfriend," Cindi said suggestively.

She went down the hall and returned moments later with a pipe and a large slab of pungent hashish.

"Man, this stuff is strong," Cindi said, after a fit of hacking. "How do you manage to inhale without coughing?"

"I guess I just got used to it after smoking so much with Brian. He likes to smoke everyday, and when you're with him..." she trailed off, remembering the way he liked to fondle her as they lay languorously together after they had consumed his favorite combination of red wine and hashish.

"You know what I miss most about the states?" Cindi said, after they had let the pipe go out.

"Hamburgers and chocolate milkshakes?" Karen suggested.

"Well, they are pretty high on my list, but mostly I miss dancing. Before I came here our school back home had dances, and sometimes my brother would have parties, and his friends would put music on and we'd dance. I used to watch American Bandstand and dance in front of the TV."

"So, let's dance then!" Karen said taking Cindi's hands and pulling her up from the couch.

"All right, I'll turn it up!" Cindi said.

They moved the coffee table and chairs back against the wall. Cindi cranked up "Suffragette City" and they danced around the living room.

"Don't you just love Bowie," Cindi shouted over the pounding music.

"I think he's sexy, in a strange kind of way," Karen replied, as her supple body swayed to the music.

When Bowie finished Cindi put on "The Harder They Come."

"What's that?" Karen asked, hearing the music for the first time.

"It's an album my brother ordered. He said it's called reggae music. It's from Jamaica. Do you like it?"

"So far I do. It has a cool beat for dancing, but different from rock."

The girls danced for much of the album, finally pausing to refill their glasses and have another pipe.

"Wow, I'm really stoned," Cindi said, as they sat together on the carpet catching their breath.

"I'm not tired at all. Let's dance some more," Karen said a few minutes later. She put on the Neil Young album.

"I'm too stoned now," Cindi protested.

"Never too stoned to dance," Karen insisted, pulling Cindi to her feet.

Delicately Karen put her hands on Cindi's small waist. Cindi raised her own hands to Karen's shoulders and they danced a while this way, swaying gently to the beat, Karen taller and older, taking the lead.

"Closer, Cindi said," after a short while, pulling Karen towards her. They moved together and Cindi put her head against Karen's shoulder while the romantic music played on.

"What is it like—I mean, with a guy?" Cindi asked, enjoying the warmth and the pliant feel of her new friend's body next to hers.

"Well, most guys don't dance nearly as well as you do," she said teasingly.

"You know what I mean," Cindi said, snuggling closer.

"You mean sex? Haven't you ever gone out with any guys? You're sixteen now aren't you?"

"Yeah, but I've been here for almost three years. All the guys I know are either too ugly, too weird, or they just act like little boys."

"You mean to tell me you're sweet sixteen and have never been kissed?" Karen said, genuinely astonished. "The guys here must be stupid as well!"

"Not really kissed," Cindi replied. "Just—you know—kid stuff."

"Ah, what a shame—you're so pretty!"

"Do you think so—really?" They stopped dancing and Cindi stepped back so Karen could look at her.

"You're a knockout, Cindi! Don't you ever look at yourself in the mirror? You are gorgeous! Look at your skin, your hair. You have a fantastic figure." Karen cupped Cindi's face in her hands and gently pinched her smooth flushed cheeks.

"But I'm so short and my breasts are too big," she complained, though obviously pleased by Karen's evaluation.

"Don't be silly. All men love big boobs, and tall girls just intimidate guys who aren't tall themselves."

They danced again.

"What does it feel like when Brian kisses you?" Cindi ventured.

"I can't describe it. He is so urgent. Sometimes he is tender, and other times I think I can sense a kind of violence—like a wild animal inside his human skin."

"Show me," Cindi whispered dreamily, her head still pressed against Karen's shoulder. They floated together in their common cocoon of intoxication. As Karen spoke of Brian's kisses Cindi felt the older girl's nipples harden against her own chest. Karen wore no bra under her light cotton blouse.

"I can't show you, I'm not a man," Karen said, laughing, but continued to hold Cindi closely while the music played on.

"I'm serious. I want to know how it feels."

They stopped dancing, but the room seemed to pulse slowly to the beat of the music. The afternoon light streaming through the window caught the dust particles suspended in the air, muting the colors of the carpet, furniture, and potted plants, and diffusing the light to a soft focus.

"You really do mean it, I can see," Karen said softly, pulling away slightly, but continuing to hold Cindi lightly.

Tentatively, she kissed Cindi quickly but firmly on the mouth.

"That's how my mother kisses me," Cindi insisted. "You can do better than that!"

This time Karen held Cindi close to her and kissed her at length. To her surprise, the experience was pleasant and arousing. Certainly not the same as with Brian or her earlier boyfriends, but erotic in a more playful sense. As she pulled away she realized she wanted to kiss the girl again.

"That's better," Cindi said catching her breath. "But I bet that isn't all there is too it."

"Guys are more insistent, and they use their hands more—like this..." She kissed Cindi again, this time lightly touching the inside of the girl's upper lip with her tongue and slipping her hands under Cindi's blouse to explore her breasts.

"I like it. It makes me feel shaky and warm. Is it the same with you?"

"Shhh, be still, and I'll show you more," Karen said as she removed her blouse.

"You're so beautiful," Cindi said, almost reverently.

Karen helped Cindi remove her shirt and bra.

"There's more too—the best part," Karen said and she pressed her hand between Cindi's legs and gently stroked her through the material of her jeans as they reclined on the carpet.

"I bet I can guess what comes next," Cindi giggled and shivered slightly from Karen's touch.

"What's it like—I mean his dick?"

"Haven't you ever seen your brother or Dad naked?"

"Sure, and pictures, but I mean when it's hard."

"It's kind of funny looking, and guys are so proud of themselves. It's like all the blood leaves their brains when it fills up their dicks. But once it's inside you, you forget all about how funny and silly it all is, believe me."

They lay side by side. Karen continued to stroke Cindi's shoulders, neck, and breasts as they talked. The music from the phonograph had stopped. In the quiet Cindi heard the entrance gate of the house's high-walled yard slam shut.

"Quick—my bedroom! My brother must be getting home," Cindi insisted.

They ran laughing down the hallway, and quickly dressed in Cindi's room. They heard her brother shut the front door, then the sounds of his rummaging in the kitchen.

"You have to distract him while I put his pipe and hash back in his room before he finds out we used them, Karen!"

"Okay, but it is getting late, and I need to get up to the Hotel Intercontinental to see if Paul has any news of Brian for me, and to call my parents. I told him I would meet him at seven. Could you call a taxi for me?"

"Sure I will, but you have to do something for me too," Cindi replied, smiling coquettishly.

"Sure, what ever you want," Karen said.

"Kiss me again."

"Why, you greedy little thing!" Karen tickled Cindi and dodged her lips, laughing. "...and I suppose you will want me to sleep in your room tonight too, right?"

"Don't tease me. You will won't you?"

"Of course I will. Best friends, right?"

Karen held her briefly, and quickly kissed her once again before they left the bedroom. Karen struck up a conversation with Steven Webster while his sister returned the pipe and hashish to their hiding place, but Steven noticed the empty bottle of wine.

"You'd better replace the booze you're guzzling before mom and dad get home, Cindi."

"Look who's talking! Don't worry about it, we've still got another week. I'll make sure the liquor cabinet looks just like it did before they left, but you have to replace what you and Tariq drank too," she replied, irritated by his nagging.

"By the way, Karen's going to be staying here for a few days until she figures out what happened to her boyfriend—all right with you?"

"I don't mind. Do you cook?" he said turning to Karen and carefully looking her over, as though he was evaluating her fitness or usefulness.

Karen found it uncomfortable to be studied so closely by a young man who was so obviously not in the least bit sexually attracted to her. At that moment Karen would not have been surprised had he asked to see her teeth or looked in her ears and eyes, much as a veterinarian professionally evaluated the health of animal patients. The irony of her relationship to the sister and brother did not escape her.

"Damn it, Steve! She's not one of the hired help —she is my guest! You asshole!" Cindi aimed a punch at her brother who easily deflected the blow.

"Hey! I didn't mean anything by it. It would just be cool if she knew how to make a couple of new dishes we could try," he said.

"All you ever think about is food. Look at you stuff your face! You'll be fat as a pig when you stop growing!" Cindi said.

"Yeah, well at least I don't have a fat ass like you," he taunted, and blocked another of Cindi's blows.

"Hey, I didn't mean to cause a family feud," Karen said. "I can stay somewhere else."

At this they stopped their tussle, and turned to Karen.

"You really are welcome here, and I'm sure our parents would say the same if they were home," Steven said, more concerned that Karen might think him uncouth than actually solicitous of her welfare.

"Don't mind him, he really has no manners at all, though he pretends to. You absolutely must stay here, and as long as you like," Cindi said.

Steve shrugged and turned back to the kitchen counter where he was assembling a multilayered sandwich from the leftovers in the refrigerator. The two girls went outside to wait for the taxi. When it appeared Cindi negotiated the fee to the Hotel Intercontinental. In spite of Karen's protests she insisted on paying the fare.

"I'll see you later," Cindi called out hopefully after the cab.

CHAPTER 17

Karen And Paul

I must look like hell, Karen thought, and dug into her backpack for her small mirror and makeup kit. She brushed her hair and did the best she could with her cosmetics while the taxi, its suspension far gone, plunged and swayed over the rough streets. The worn out Toyota Corona rocked like a boat in rough seas as it wound its way up the hill to the Hotel Intercontinental.

It was not until she stepped out of the taxi that Karen realized just how stoned she was. She felt slightly dizzy and disoriented. She hesitated on the sidewalk in front the hotel for a few seconds before entering.

"I do have a little news for you. But first—are you hungry?" Paul Sherman said, by way of greeting.

He had appeared in the lobby before she could ring his room, as though he had been waiting for her, even though she had arrived fifteen minutes early. He looked sophisticated and comfortable in his light cotton short-sleeved shirt, khaki slacks, and loafers. By contrast, she felt dumpy and self-conscious in her more casual outfit of jeans and a blouse, wrinkled and slightly soiled from two days of wear in the heat of the Kabul summer. At his question she became aware that she was in fact famished.

"Sure, I could eat something," she replied, trying to pretend it was of no great importance.

She found she did not mind his benevolent hand on her arm as he guided her into the hotel restaurant. Over their meal Paul discussed what he had found out of Brian's whereabouts, which was little enough. His information mostly consisted of a list of places where Brian was not, and some conjectures about which routes he may have taken out of Kabul if indeed he had left the city.

"I also found out something else that might interest you," Paul finally said, saving his most exciting news until last.

Karen had to make an effort to eat slowly and deliberately. The food tasted fantastic.

"I made a phone calls and managed to get a hold of the man who claims to have gone with Mr. Peccanter on the day he was AWOL in Viet Nam. He just finished his tour of duty a couple of weeks ago. His story jibes with what your boyfriend told you as far as it goes. He says he did go with him that day and fell asleep after they had been drinking heavily. He says Peccanter appeared really shaken the next time he saw him. He also says he cannot believe that your boyfriend could have done any of the things he is accused of."

"Does this mean he can be a witness for Brian in court?" Karen said, putting down her fork with an effort of will.

"He was asleep for a couple of hours that afternoon, and has no factual knowledge of what your boyfriend was up to, so he cannot provide any kind of corroboration for that time period. But he is a character witness for him, and he can at least testify that your boyfriend was not with him for a certain period of time that day. If any evidence at all could be found that Captain Ramsy committed those murders, the friend's testimony would be very important in placing Peccanter in the area during that time, and more importantly, it would certainly indicate a motive for the frame-up that your boyfriend insists occurred."

Paul paused and had another sip of his gin and tonic.

"So there might be some hope for Brian at a trial, then?" Karen asked.

He looked at her closely. She fidgeted in her chair. *Can he tell that I'm high?* she wondered, still feeling the influence of the hashish and wine, though the effects were beginning to wear off at last.

"It is a start, but he will need more. We need concrete evidence. It's time I told you that Cecil Ramsy, the captain, is an old friend of mine. I have known him most of my life, and up until now I have never thought him to be anything more than a dedicated career soldier. I owe my job to him in more than one sense. He has helped me out several times over the years, and he has some pretty influential contacts. It is pretty hard for me to believe he would do something like what you have described, yet I can see that you do believe your boyfriend's story, and I have done enough of a background check on Mr. Peccanter to know he does not have any kind of criminal record, or any seriously bad character references in his files before these recent accusations—though he was certainly less than honest with you about his marital status."

"Did the captain call today?" Karen asked him, picking up her fork again. She did not want to think about Brian's wife and child.

"Yes, I told him Brian had escaped and there was no point in coming to Kabul now, but he insisted on coming anyway. He will be here tomorrow. It will be an awkward situation for me. I'm not looking forward to it."

"Awkward because you don't believe Brian is guilty, or for some other reason?"

"That is part of it. Let's just say I have some serious doubts now. Also, because although I'm in charge of this investigation for—for the government agency that employs me, Captain Ramsy is still technically seaman Peccanter's superior officer. I'm not exactly sure who will be legally in charge once the captain arrives. It's complicated because we are not in the states. To a very large extent I am on my own here when it comes to this case. If Ramsy decides to take your boyfriend into his custody, I'm not sure I can legally oppose him."

"Well, then I will just have to hope no one finds him here, and that he has gotten safely out of the country."

"Don't misunderstand me. I intend to keep your boyfriend under my protection if we do manage to find him, regardless of what Cecil wants—if I find him first. That's why you and your friends need to tell me where he is if you know. If what your boyfriend told you is true, as much as I hate to believe such a thing, my old friend might be capable of anything."

They finished their meal. Paul offered dessert and after dinner drinks but Karen declined both. Now that her hunger was sated, she was ready to speak to her parents, and wished to be reasonably straight and sober for the call. On the way up they passed a flyer in the display outside the bar advertising music by "The Esquire Set."

"What's this? Kabul has a rock band?"

"Apparently so. Like some sort of new strain of influenza, it appears this plague has even penetrated the Hindu Kush," Paul quipped.

Paul's tastes ran more along the lines of Cole Porter, Ella Fitzgerald, and Frank Sinatra, but he could see Karen was excited by the idea.

"I am told they are from Sri Lanka, imported by the management for the diversion of the younger guests. I'm afraid you already missed this week's performance, though. They don't play on Sundays."

Paul allowed Karen to use the more private telephone in the bedroom of his suite. She was relieved to find only her father at home to take her call. It was always easier to deal with her parents individually. She said nothing about Brian's predicament or his capture and escape from prison, answering evasively when he asked about her boyfriend. She reassured her father that she was healthy and safe, and enjoying the attractions of Kabul. When he volunteered to wire her money she gladly accepted. Before hanging up she promised to call in two days, when her mother was scheduled to return from a European excursion.

"Everything all right?" Paul asked, when Karen had finished her call.

"Yeah, okay—and thanks again for letting me use your phone."

"Now that we have got the chores of the day out of the way, and there doesn't seem to be much of anything else we can do but wait—what do you say to that dessert and drink?" Paul asked.

He hoped she would stay a while longer. Paul led a largely solitary and sometimes lonely life, rarely staying in one place for long. He had no friends in Kabul, only his few contacts through the Agency. The idea of seduction had crossed his mind, but he was even more motivated by the simple desire of encouraging a closer relationship of any kind. Karen's mere presence was for him a great pleasure, and something he wanted to prolong.

"Sure, something sweet sounds good. I wonder if they have baklava here."

"I'm pretty sure they do. Shall I call room service or do you want to go back down to the restaurant?"

"It's nice here, and I'm really not dressed for being seen in public here."

"What sounds good besides baklava? The bar can make nearly anything."

"Something refreshing, I guess. Surprise me!"

Paul called room service. Minutes later the dessert, a mojito, and a gin and tonic were delivered. Karen was delighted with the unfamiliar drink.

"What did you call it again? It tastes great!"

"I thought you'd like it. The mojito was invented in Cuba they say. Rum, lime juice, mint, soda water, and sweetener. But of course the trick is getting the proportions right—and good rum, naturally. I was once at the Bodeguita del Medio, Havana, where some say the drink was invented."

"When were you there?"

"A couple of times back in the late fifties. Before it became off limits for Americans."

"I wish I could have seen it then. The Hemingways, Castro, Spencer Tracy, revolution in the air... It must have been exciting!"

"I once had a drink with Hemingway."

"A mojito?"

"No, actually it was a daiquiri, and at a different bar where that drink was perfected—the equally famous El Floridita. Papa Hemingway bought a round for the house, and I had the good luck and timing to be there."

"Did you actually speak with him?" Karen had read many of the author's works, and was an unabashed fan.

"It wasn't much of a conversation. I thanked him for the drink, and he nodded and said I was welcome, and hoped I was enjoying my visit to Havana. He did not look well. It was shortly before he left Cuba for good, and went to Idaho, where he died."

Paul called room service for drinks twice more. Karen found herself enjoying her conversation with the handsome agent. Besides his physical attractiveness, he radiated a kind of understated urbanity that made her feel secure and comfortable in his presence. The subject of Brian had not come up again, nor that of Captain Ramsy.

"I almost forgot—I told Cindi I would be back to spend the night later. I should be going," Karen said, finishing her third mojito, and rising, a bit unsteadily to her feet.

"Well, if you must go, I will see you to the taxi. I could use the walk," Paul said, getting up from the couch.

She had been sitting for some time cross-legged on the carpet next to a small end table beside the couch, where she placed her empty drink as she stood. Karen's left leg had grown slightly numb from so long in one position, and she stumbled slightly as she got up. Paul caught her and held her gently. They kissed, at first tentatively, and then once again for a far longer time. Karen spoke no more of leaving that night.

CHAPTER 18

Reshtina's Dilemma

Reshtina walked slowly up the stairs to the second floor apartment she shared with her younger brother, Tariq. She was hungover, out of sorts, and just as confused about her relationship with David as she had been before the evening of the party. He had been amorous enough during the night, but obviously in a hurry to get rid of her that morning. They had spoken little over a hurried breakfast, and when she left he had not suggested another assignation.

Most distressingly for Reshtina, the subject that must be spoken of very soon, and which had occupied her thoughts for the past several weeks, had not been raised. There simply had not been an opportunity, for after their boozy coupling the night before, David had fallen immediately and soundly to sleep, and had risen before her that morning. This was not a topic she could bring up during breakfast and tea—with the chance that one of his roommates might overhear them from their adjacent bedrooms. So she had left David after their breakfast with the important words unspoken.

She opened her own apartment door and was surprised to see her uncle, Khalid, and the man her father had promised her to, Sartor, in heated discussion with her brother.

"What are you doing in my house, Sartor? I have told you to stay away from me!" she exclaimed.

"Ah… I am so happy to see you, my lovely flower! I have come with your dear uncle to take you back to our home. Our wedding date draws closer, and we must meet with the mullah," Sartor replied, smiling and bowing deeply.

He was a massive sweaty man of nearly three hundred pounds, with a swart greasy complexion. Sartor was more than twice Reshtina's age, nearly three times her weight, and already possessed two wives closer to his own age, with a half dozen children between them. His ancient father, wizened and shriveled as an Egyptian mummy, lived with them. The old man was incontinent and barely lucid much of the time. The senior wives, harried to their limits between the demands of the children and the demented patriarch, fully approved of and hoped for the match, knowing that the newest and youngest wife would be theirs to command.

"I shall never marry you! I honor and follow the example of our great Afghan queen, Soraya Tarzi, as my mother did before me! I will never wear the chador or be the second or third wife of any man! Get out of here, and take Khalid with you!"

Sartor smiled condescendingly, and appeared unruffled by Reshtina's outburst. Khalid coughed nervously. At just over five feet and not much over one hundred pounds, Reshtina's outraged anger had no effect on Sartor whatsoever, and in any case he regarded all women even nominally under his influence as little more than children, whose desires and wishes, like children's, were something to be patronized but ultimately put aside, having no significance compared to his own needs. His was an arrogance to rival his great girth.

"Yes, yes... I know all about your idols; the disgraceful Soraya—Mr. Karmal and his whore, Anahita—your communist friends. Infidels and traitors all! Soraya brought dishonor to our country, and for that she and king Amanulla were made to abdicate, as you well know from your study of Afghan history. It is not for our people to take on the foul habits of the foreign unbelievers. That is most assuredly against the way of our beloved ancestors—the Pashtunwali!" he retorted.

"Dr. Anahita Ratebzad is my friend and teacher, and an inspiration to all Afghan women! I will never consent the three times to marry you, but I ask you now three times to leave! As you follow the Pashtunwali you must respect my wishes in my home!"

"They will not go away until you agree to leave with them," her brother finally spoke.

"Just where have you been this morning, dear love? You were not at home when I called earlier." Sartor spoke softly, but his voice carried more than a hint of menace.

For the past several mornings Reshtina had felt bilious, and had been unable to eat breakfast. She felt a sudden urge to vomit. She rushed to the bathroom and locked the door behind her. The feeling gradually subsided. She splashed cold water on her face, brushed her teeth and washed her thick glasses, all the while trying desperately to think of a way to get rid of the men. After a few moments she heard pounding on the door.

"Are you ill my flower?" Sartor called.

She heard his huge fat hands working the doorknob.

"I'll be out in a minute!" she called.

The bathroom window was high and small, but Reshtina was a compact and agile young woman. She pulled herself up onto the sink vanity cabinet, opened the window and removed the screen. Sartor threw his substantial weight against the door and the jam split easily, but he was a few seconds too late. Reshtina was already running down the sidewalk, her stomach and shoulders smarting from the scrapes she had received in her hurried escape. Her luck held—a taxi idled a block away. She gave the driver directions to David's apartment. She did not know where else to turn.

Khalid, Tariq, and Sartor watched as the taxi accelerated away.

"Where will she go, Tariq?" Khalid asked.

"How should I know?" the youth replied insolently. He too had spent much of the night drinking with his lover, Steven Webster. His head throbbed.

With a movement surprising in its swiftness for such a large man, Sartor grabbed the slim youth by the collar. He lifted him off the pavement so that his feet kicked in midair, and shook him as a terrier would a rodent. A homicidal expression had entirely replaced Sartor's usual unctuous mien.

"Now look here boy—I've had enough of you and your sister's games! You know where she has gone. Now tell me, or it will go hard with you!"

The boy's uncle, Khalid, wrung his hands in anguish, but dared not interfere. Sartor had a reputation for violence when he was crossed, and just as importantly, now that his sister-in-law was dead, Sartor's tribal connections in Paktia would be even more important to Khalid's business interests than before. Still, he had an obligation to his brother, and he could not stand by and knowingly let harm come to his nephew.

"Please, do not hurt the boy, perhaps he does not know after all," Khalid ventured timorously.

"Oh he knows. They plot together the two of them—like little foxes in their den! I have had enough of waiting. I am a busy man, and have no time for you and your sister's childish games, boy!" he said, striking Tariq in the face with the palm of his fleshy hand.

Sartor had only meant to shake the boy up as a warning, but Tariq's nose gushed blood all over the front of his American faux cowboy shirt, a recent and precious gift from Steven Webster. Tariq began to wail.

"She has American friends from teaching Pashtu at the Peace Corps school. Perhaps she will go to them?" Khalid volunteered, hoping to save the boy from further abuse.

Sartor hesitated, scowled, and let go of Tariq.

"Clean yourself up now, boy!" he said taking a kerchief from the depths of his kameez. Tariq accepted it meekly and wiped his face. Tears dissolved little trails through the blood on his cheeks.

"Don't worry, your face is still pretty. Your nose is not broken, but I warn you—if you do not tell me where you sister has gone, I will not be as gentle with you next time!"

"You will not hurt her?" he whimpered.

"Of course not—your father has promised her to me. I mean to make her my wife, and you will be a brother to me!" Sartor answered. His fit of pique had vanished as suddenly as it had appeared.

"The prophet allows each man his four wives if he can support them. It is written! As you know I have but two wives, plenty of room in my home, and plenty of money to provide for my children. However both my wives are too old now for the making of babies, and I have but one son between them, and he sickly at that. Reshtina is young and healthy, and God willing, she will provide me with a healthy son—perhaps a pretty boy like yourself—ha, ha!" Sartor clapped Tariq rather too warmly on the back, causing the boy to stumble forward, but Sartor caught him before he could fall.

"Ah, you are but a young sapling swaying in the breeze, Tariq, but someday soon you shall be grown to a man, and perhaps I can help you with your mahr and other wedding expenses. I am a wealthy man as you well know. I have promised your sister a handsome mahr, and it is no business of mine if she chooses to give much or all of it to your father, whose affairs have suffered greatly since your blessed mother died."

"Has Reshtina told the mullah three times she accepts the marriage? I do not think she will do it."

"Truly she has not yet, but when she comes with me to see your father and the mullah, and understands that we will be King and Queen for the night at her Nikah, and that our Nikah itself will be a splendid ceremony in the best traditional Islam and Pashtun fashion, she will accept my proposal a hundred times over! It is time for both you and your sister to give up your bad habits and your shameful life in Kabul, and take up the Pashtunwali. It is time for you to grow up and quit your childish dalliances with the infidel communists, atheists, and idolaters! They have no shame and are worse even than the Christians—heathens—not even people of the book!"

Tariq did not respond. Although he wanted nothing to do with tribal tradition, and had every intention of educating himself and adopting the modern western ways, he knew better than to argue.

"Come, your father has given the permission, as you surely know, and it is your duty as a son and brother to help see that your sister is well provided for. You must tell us where she has gone. What if your father, poor man, already grieving from the so recent loss of your mother, were to find out about your behavior with your young American boyfriend? What would he say if he knew how you spent the night in the bed of this unbeliever, in the manner of the ancient pagans—without shame!"

Sartor squeezed the boy's upper arm with a certain measured pressure, and his smile once more transmuted to a grimace.

Tariq blanched at this revelation, and the boy began to tremble. He could not imagine how Sartor had learned about Steven Webster. It was this final threat which overcame his loyalty to his sister, to whom he had become much closer since their mother had died and they had taken the apartment in Kabul together. He told Sartor where the Americans lived without any further prompting.

Khalid and Sartor got into Sartor's car and drove off to find David's apartment in Shari Nau, leaving Tariq sobbing and shaken on the curb. He had a sense that he had totally and irrevocably betrayed his sister, and he wanted nothing more at that moment than to submerge himself completely in the embrace of his lover, Steven.

Reshtina was greeted with some surprise by Aletheia at her apartment, located on the third floor above David's residence. She too had taken Farsi lessons from Reshtina her first months in Kabul, and she liked and admired the Afghan woman for her spirit and intelligence, though she knew next to nothing of her personal life.

"What is it Reshtina? You look awful!"

Reshtina was breathing hard from her dash up the stairs. Her glasses were bent askew and blouse torn from her window escape. She was obviously distraught.

"Do you know where David has gone? There is no one home at the apartment!"

"Slow down girl and come on inside. You're going to give yourself a heart attack or something! Here—what you need is a shot of this."

Aletheia, who thought nothing of having a drink any time of the day if it suited her, opened a cupboard door and pulled out a half empty bottle of vodka that had somehow survived the party. She poured a generous shot for Reshtina and one for herself.
Reshtina accepted the drink reluctantly, but took a sip, and then another.

"There you go. Hair of the dog I always say. Now what the hell is eating you so that you need to run after David like this. Hasn't anyone ever told you that is not the way to lasso a guy?"

Like everyone else in the apartment building, Aletheia was well aware of Reshtina's infatuation with David. She felt sorry for the woman and identified with her plight. She had never dated in high school, and knew the misery of watching friends with more charms get the invitations to the dances and proms, and of being one of the girls who watched from the sidelines while her more attractive girlfriends were getting engaged and married. Like Reshtina, she too had imprudently gone 'all the way' with the first guy to take an interest in her, only to learn at an early age the sad lesson that men certainly took the act far less seriously, and that mere copulation did not assure a future attachment.

"Oh I know that now. I wish that was my only problem," Reshtina said, and began to cry softly.

"Oh, you poor girl—what is it? Stay awhile—I'll make us some tea to go with the vodka. You must be very in love with David, but don't you see it's just no good? Can't you see he is just using you? Here—have some tissue. Cry as much as you want—it's just the two of us girls here."

Aletheia, bustled about the room putting water to boil in the old teakettle, and setting out her two best mugs with a bowl of sugar on the packing crate that served as an end table next to the bedraggled sofa, where Reshtina continued to sob quietly.

"You don't understand. I am promised to another—a man I despise with all my heart!"

"Well, that is another thing entirely, of course. But do you really have to marry this other man? Can't you just refuse his offer and continue to support yourself teaching, or is your family more traditional?"

"My mother was modern—what you call progressive or liberal I think, but she is dead many months, and father..." more sobs wracked her small body.

Aletheia sat down next to Reshtina, held her hand, and cooed comfortingly until Reshtina finally regained control of her emotions.

"I must admit that even though I've lived in your country over a year, I still don't quite understand your marriage customs. I thought the bride must agree to the marriage, even if arranged. Don't you have a choice?"

"Yes, that is true in many families—even some traditional families, if the father cares deeply for his daughter's welfare. But my father is very near ruin now. When my mother was alive we had the help of her family, and she kept control of our family finances, but without her father has managed to lose nearly all of our money and livestock. Sartor himself holds the deed to our home, and if I do not marry him I am sure he will throw my father out!"

"Can your father move in with you and your brother, or another relative?"

"He would never agree to that. He will never leave his little village. It is all he has ever known. He is a very simple man and could never adjust to Kabul—and he is old and infirm—but that is not the only reason... There is something else which makes this marriage impossible—something I have never told anyone until now, but everyone will know soon enough—I am pregnant—with David's child!" Reshtina covered her face with her hands and began to cry again.

Aletheia sat back suddenly, shocked at this unexpected revelation, but with this confession everything about Reshtina's behavior around David immediately made more sense. Her first reaction was anger at David for taking advantage of the naive girl, but upon reconsideration she decided the girl's plight would be difficult enough even without the added complication of the pregnancy.

"Will you have the baby?" Aletheia bluntly asked. She divined the time had come for straight talk and concrete plans.

Reshtina looked out through her tear smudged glasses at Aletheia with horror. Her deep brown eyes, already magnified behind the thick lenses, grew larger yet. Her guise of modernity and sophistication served her well in the bustling city of Kabul, and the cosmopolitan, well-educated, but essentially limited circle of her associates there. This however was little more than a veneer over her essentially orthodox Pashtun and Islam view of morality. She was appalled at Althea's insinuation.

"Okay, okay, I get it. I didn't think you would consider it, but it had to be said. Don't worry, I won't bring it up again. Anyway, what we have to do now is figure out some way to get you out of Kabul, and to some place where this man you are supposed to marry will not follow you—at least that is the way I see it."

"But my father—who will look after him, and Tariq is....he is....so delicate..."

"Yes, yes, we all know Tariq is a queer, but that does not mean he is helpless, and he has well-connected friends in Kabul. He will be all right—but Reshtina, I am probably not the best person to help you with your problems. I think we should go see Conrad. He will know how to get you safely away somewhere, and he is not a man to be intimidated by anyone, as far as I can tell."

"No! I would be too ashamed for him to know!"

"Now listen here Reshtina," Aletheia said, adopting a stern tone.

"The time for playing the young innocent is over. You are not a naive little girl anymore as you well know. You have got to put your modesty and your concern for your brother and father aside, and start thinking about what really matters—you and your child! The welfare of the child you bear is more important than your responsibility to your father or your brother—who after all are adults with some control yet over their circumstances—but the baby growing within you is your complete responsibility now and in the future, and its welfare must be your first priority. Do you want this man you are supposed to marry to have absolute control of your son or daughter—to raise her to wear a chador and to be traded off like livestock to whomever your husband wishes—or your son to learn only what the mullah approves? Is that the family you really want?"

"No, but one does not chose one's family. Fate and Allah alone make that choice," she replied dolefully.

"Bullshit! It is true you cannot choose your blood relations, but you damn sure have some choice in who you marry or live with, and you sure as hell had something to do with choosing who you slept with! What would your mother say if she could see you now—behaving as though you have no responsibility for your future? You are talking crap, sister, and you know it!"

Reshtina considered this. She imaged her late mother, tall and regal in bearing where Reshtina was

short and common—the icon of her desires—of woman-
ly perfection. Yet, she reflected, even that nearly perfect
being had made the obvious mistake of marrying her
father.

*What could have possessed a woman of such char-
acter to have married a toady like him?* And then suddenly she knew. Math was not her forte, but it came to her
in a flash that she had been born less than seven months
after her parents marriage, and there had never been
any suggestion that Reshtina was anything but a healthy
full term baby.

As her mother's star declined to something
more akin to the terrestrial plane in her perception,
Reshtina experienced a sensation of near vertigo.
Though the idea of a future with Sartor was abhorrent,
it was at least part of a familiar world. It dawned on her
that her short dalliance in Kabul, first at the university,
and then as a Peace Corps teacher in the rarefied air of
what in Afghanistan was the closest thing to a modern
enlightened society, had allowed her for a few years to
put off any real decision about her future.

Ever since she could remember, Reshtina's
mother had nourished the hope that her only daughter
would somehow escape the medieval village background that she, for all her family connections, intelligence, charm, and native refinement, had become ensnared in. It came to her that the best way she could
honor her mother's memory was to refuse to accept a
similar fate.

As for her father; he was limited by his age and the only way he knew, that of the traditional village life. She could not be angry with him for arranging her marriage to Sartor, but she also realized, as the vertiginous sensation passed, that she no longer cared overmuch what her father wanted, nor was she very concerned with what happened to him or anyone else in the village. She was shocked with herself at these new insights, but there they were, and she could not deny them.

"Well, what will it be Reshtina?" Aletheia said, intuitively aware that at least some of her words had hit home.

"Yes, I am ready to leave this place. You are right. I should try to make my own future—for myself and my baby—as mother herself would have advised me."

She had done with her sobbing now. She polished her glasses pensively on her blouse. She wished to see the world as clearly as possible.

"Okay then, let's get going." Aletheia said. "Maybe we will be lucky enough to find Conrad at home, but if not we can at least leave him a note."

CHAPTER 19

Sartor And Bagnur

The area of Kabul where the Peace Corps apartments were located was familiar to Sartor. He had transacted a few business dealings with Bagnur, the manager, in the past. As soon as Tariq described the location, he realized it was one of Bagnur's family properties. Sartor and Khalid took a round about way, stopping for a midmorning meal at one of Sartor's favorite eateries. Sartor did not like to go long between meals, and the morning's confrontation had left him especially peckish.

After an ample brunch and some small talk with the proprietor of the restaurant the two men continued on to the apartments, arriving well after Reshtina, Aletheia, and the rest of the Peace Corps residents had left the apartments for their separate destinations. Sartor and Khalid found Bagnur in his shop. They exchanged the customary pleasantries in the usual manner of Pashtun acquaintances and business associates. In the process Bagnur recalled the details of his last business deal with Sartor, and how he had found, some months later, that he had been deftly and subtly gulled by the man. It was not so severe a matter as to amount to a mulcting or fraud, but it was nonetheless true that Sartor had taken unfair business advantage of Bagnur, with the result that although Bagnur did not actually lose any money, he did not realize the customary profit that would have normally been expected for the transaction. It was very rare for Bagnur to be duped in such a manner, and as he recalled the incident he became secretly angry and hostile, but he was careful to hide his feelings from the huge man.

"I have come to you today because I understand one of my young American friends, a Mr. David Stork, rents a room from you here. I have some news for him which he will be especially happy to receive," Sartor said.

Sartor's mispronunciation of David's last name immediately revealed to Bagnur that Sartor did not know David well, if at all. In any case Bagnur was very protective of the Americans—his Americans, and did not like the idea that someone else might be doing business with them without his knowledge and approval—especially when that someone had previously taken advantage of him. Perhaps Sartor was out to take similar advantage of his young and rather naive friends as well.

"I believe that mister Stuckrath—he pronounced the name slowly and carefully—is out. If you could write down this information and entrust it to me, I could easily see that he receives it when he returns," Bagnur said ingratiatingly.

"I appreciate your offer, but the information is of a rather a personal nature. Can you tell me perhaps—

was he accompanied by a young Afghan woman?" Sartor continued.

"I spoke with David not long ago. He left this morning with two American friends only—no women accompanied them."

Bagnur found this last question odd as well as intrusive, and decided this visit must be of some consequence to Sartor. Probably Reshtina was a kinswoman. Perhaps, Bagnur thought, he might be able to retaliate somewhat for Sartor's previous ill use of him. He elected not to tell the Sartor that he had also seen Reshtina leave with Aletheia earlier, choosing instead to hold back that information, to see if the man might yet reveal the true purpose of this visit.

"Perhaps you would not mind if I inquired myself? There might yet be someone home in one of the rooms above. It is a matter of some urgency."

Sartor continued in a conversational manner as easily as before, but to Bagnur's secret delight the corpulent man had begun to perspire profusely.

"The stairs unfortunately are rather narrow and steep, and I should be ashamed to let a respected businessman and esteemed guest such as yourself exert himself in such a manner on my property, when I could so easily be of service. I would be honored to enquire for you myself. In the meantime, may I offer you some tea and a more pleasant seat out of the sun inside my shop?"

Bagnur knew Sartor could not object to this offer without committing a serious social gaffe, or impugning his hospitality. It would be gratifying to make the fat man wait while he pretended to investigate, he thought as he ascended the stairway. Taking his time, Bagnur inspected the rusting bolts holding the balcony railing, checked the exterior light fixtures, and made a mental note to scold Samot for the piles of debris still left over from the roof top party.

When he felt he had wasted enough of the man's time Bagnur started back, feeling that he had at least incommoded Sartor some as partial retribution for Sartor's earlier slight against him. But Bagnur, just as in their previous business dealing, had not taken the true measure of Sartor's devious character. Suddenly the huge man appeared, sweating and livid, his massive bulk almost entirely blocking the stairway.

"So this is how you treat a guest! Making a busy man wait at your pleasure while you dawdle!"

For a brief instant Bagnur feared Sartor might actually strike him, but the man merely brushed him aside and strode up to the first apartment, forcing the door with one movement of his massive shoulder, much as he had Reshtina's bathroom door earlier.

"Wait! Stop! You have no right to destroy my property! I will inform the police!"

Bagnur made sure as he shouted out his protests that he was sufficiently distant from the Sartor to run for the stairs if need be. Bagnur was a slight man, and not at all valorous.

"Go ahead, and then see what happens when it is discovered that you have interfered between a husband and his betrothed!"

Sartor had stopped in the doorway. They were at an impasse it seemed. Although it was a serious matter to violate another's property and privacy, Bagnur quickly realized that he might be in even bigger trouble if it were to come out that he knowingly ran a property where Afghan women spent the night with foreign men —especially if one was a woman pledged in marriage to a powerful and wealthy businessman. It seemed he must extract his revenge on Sartor another day.

"You should have told me this news in the beginning! I had no idea she was promised to you—that is another matter, of course. She was visiting earlier with her American friend, a Peace Corps woman who lives in the upper apartment. Reshtina went with her earlier this morning. I know not where," Bagnur quickly replied.

Of course Bagnur was perfectly aware Reshtina had spent the night with David Stuckrath. He made it his business to know as much as possible about the young westerners, and he was on the best terms with most of them, but he thought it best to dissemble under the circumstances, for the protection of both himself and the girl.

"You are sure you do not know?" Sartor asked, menacingly.

There was no doubt in Bagnur's mind that this was meant as a direct threat. He would have to be sure to keep his pistol at hand in the shop for the future.

"I swear to you on the grave of my parents I know nothing of their destination," he replied.

"I expect you to call this number when they return. Do not fail me!" Sartor exclaimed. He extracted a business card embossed with a highly figurative Farsi script, and shoved it at Bagnur.

"And what if the American woman returns without your betrothed?" Bagnur replied.

"In that case we may once again do business together. If the American woman returns without Reshtina, I will make it well worth your while to find out where my fiancé has gone by whatever means you can, for our wedding date draws near. I fear that she has fallen under the influence of her heathen friends, and her father wishes that she return and honor her marriage vows, as do I, of course."

Sartor's anger seemed to have vanished as suddenly as it had appeared. He feigned the demeanor of a concerned and loving fiancé.

Since their first salutations Reshtina's uncle, Khalid, had said nothing. He had remained in Bagnur's shop, helping himself to tea from the ornate samovar while the angry Sartor confronted the shop owner upstairs. Several prospective customers had stopped by to shop while Sartor and Bagnur faced off, and Khalid had informed them politely that the proprietor would return shortly. He was considering whether he too should go upstairs and see what was keeping Sartor so long, when the two returned at last. He noticed that Sartor was perspiring profusely and the shop owner looked anxious.

"It seems your niece is no longer here, though she did come here after foolishly crawling through her window. Bagnur has graciously consented to let us know if she does return," Sartor informed Khalid.

The three men repeated the polite Pashtun farewells, as though no altercation whatsoever had occurred.

That fat son of a pig! I should send a policeman with a bill for my broken door jamb. May your house be destroyed and worms infect your bowels! Bagnur thought, as the two men drove away.

But later he smiled privately, reflecting that he had at least put something over on the man. Although he had sworn on the graves of his parents that he did not know where Reshtina had gone, the fact was they were both still living.

CHAPTER 20

Sorting Things Out

Until I was twenty-five, I had no development at all. From my twenty-fifth year I date my life. Three weeks have scarcely passed, at any time between then and now, that I have not unfolded within myself.—Herman Melville

After the night's adventures at the Tolkif Prison, Conrad slept soundly until after eight o'clock, long past his usual rising time of five-thirty. The fact that he had not been disturbed earlier by either a phone call or a visit from agent Sherman or the Kabul police, meant his role in Brian Peccanter's jail break must not have been discovered, as he had hoped. Later he would be glad for the extra sleep, for the remainder of the day proved to be as eventful as the previous one, Friday the thirteenth, had been.

The first interruption came just as he was sitting down to eat his belated breakfast. It was totally unexpected. Aletheia and Reshtina, both of whom he knew only slightly through his friend David, arrived at his apartment. They refused his left over palau and lamb kebob, but accepted his offer of tea. After the teacups were filled, while Conrad finished his meal, the two women explained the reason for their visit. Aletheia did most of the talking. Reshtina, obviously in distress, stared sullenly at the floor, and confirmed the other girl's story with occasional nods.

"Now listen Reshtina," Aletheia lectured her. "There is no need for you to feel humiliated or embarrassed among your friends. We're going to help you in any way we can. We are not here to judge you—and anyway you should understand that in our culture and in these times there is no longer the stigma that used to exist. Most importantly—even though you may not want to tell him—David must be told, and he must take responsibility for the child as well—certainly financial responsibility at the very least, since you are determined to keep the baby."

Reshtina nodded again, but still remained mute.

"I'm not exactly clear on why you two came here or how I can help, but I am expecting David to drop by today. I guess this is as good a place and time for him to hear this as any," Conrad offered.

He was not very optimistic about the effect this news would have on David. David's friends knew he was doing his best to distance himself emotionally and physically from Reshtina, while trying at the same time not to hurt her too much—a strategy Conrad knew from even his own limited experience that nearly always came out badly in the end. He suspected David would lose his position in the Peace Corps if he did not marry the girl and her condition became known, which it surely would in their small and incestuous society. Conrad knew marriage to Reshtina or any woman was not something David wanted. They were close enough that David had told him one boozy evening of his first serious girlfriend, Clio. The prospect of that potential marriage had been the main motivation for David joining Peace Corps, and fleeing the predictable future he had imagined would result from marriage to his college sweetheart.

Shortly after Conrad heard Reshtina's sad tale there came a second rapping at his door, and as if on cue David entered, followed by Tony and Dennis. All were looking somewhat the worse for wear after the night's adventures, especially Dennis with his stitched and swollen face.

"Well, if it isn't the Three Stooges themselves! It seems I have become suddenly very popular. Have you come to continue last night's festivities?" Conrad greeted them sardonically.

The three were surprised and baffled to find Aletheia and Reshtina there before them, but they did not have long to wait for an explanation. Conrad had decided an immediate and complete airing of the situation was in order.

"David! Reshtina has something to tell you, and though it is a personal matter we will all know soon enough, so I think it best we hear what she has to say to you immediately. Important decisions need to be made —and soon."

Conrad spoke as though he were issuing a command, and his statement was taken by everyone in the same spirit. They all looked at Reshtina expectantly.

Now that David was in the same room with her, all of Reshtina's previous decisiveness and determination vanished. She trembled and felt her heartbeat accelerate. She stared wildly around the room through her thick lenses, her expression bringing to mind some hunted animal brought to ground by a pack of baying hounds. She felt a sudden urge to run, as she had earlier that morning when she had escaped from her fiancé through the bathroom window.

"Oh for Christ's sake! Don't torture the poor girl anymore! Can't you idiots figure it out? She's pregnant!" Aletheia intervened, glaring at David. "... and she has every intention of having this baby—so don't even think of bringing up the alternative. We are not back in the states after all!"

Aletheia put her arm around Reshtina's shoulders, fearing the girl would start weeping again, but surprisingly Reshtina, though mortified and still shaking from the surge of emotion she had experienced when David entered the room, felt not the slightest urge to cry. Instead, under the gaze of these concerned friends, she felt a kind of new empowerment well up from some previously unknown depth, and an expansion of the insights she had experienced previously in Aletheia's apartment. But that was not the end of it. She seemed to herself to be like some formerly mundane and drab pupal creature that was apparently destined to burst forth from its larval state into something quite different entirely. She had made a profound new discovery.

Although she had been at least somewhat aware that David might not feel for her the passion and warm protective emotions a man should for a lover or wife, she had imagined her own ardor would eventually win him over. Now it came to her that she had no such feelings for David either. Somehow her earlier infatuation had simply evaporated! This was a completely unexpected and miraculous revelation.

Later she could never pinpoint just exactly when the attachment had ended. It might have been the night before, as she had gently moved David's heavy arm from off her chest, when he had fallen directly to sleep without so much as a word immediately after their drunken coupling. Or it could have been the next morning after breakfast, when David had left abruptly after their hurried meal together, without even thinking to call her a cab. Or perhaps later that day in Aletheia's apartment, when Aletheia had commanded her to think first of herself and the baby, and to forget all about David's feelings or welfare.

"I have to ask you though, Aletheia, now that we are all here together like some big happy family, and the cat is out of the bag... What the hell is it you think I can do to help out here? This seems to me to be David's problem and responsibility," Conrad exclaimed, aiming an accusing gaze at the culprit.

Now it was David Stuckrath's turn to feel the eyes of all upon him, and like Reshtina, he felt cornered and exposed. His discomfort and embarrassment were extreme, but before he could respond, Reshtina spoke up. Her normally muted voice was shocking to her friends in its uncharacteristic volume and shrillness.

"I do not care at all what David or any of you may think. I know he is the father, but he does not want me for his wife—nor would I marry him even if that was his wish, because I know he does not love me—and I shall never marry any man against my will!"

She spoke with such force and determination that the others were entirely taken aback. No one responded for several seconds.

"Now that is what I call a pregnant pause!" Conrad quipped at last.

"Well, then, that part at least is settled—we understand Reshtina will not be marrying David. But of course there is the not-so-little problem of the stout Sartor, your hopeful hubby. At the very least it seems Reshtina should make herself scarce around Kabul—and where will she then have this baby?"

"She can come to Jalalabad with me. I'm leaving next week to return to work at the clinic. She can have her baby there," Aletheia volunteered.

"Thank you Aletheia. You are a true friend," Reshtina said.

She took the American woman's hand in her own and squeezed it quickly, then removed her heavy black-framed glasses to wipe the welling tears from her eyes. She was moved by the woman's offer, but it would not solve her biggest problem.

"Sartor will find me in Jalalabad just as he would in Kabul. He has many relatives and his reach is long. I must leave Afghanistan. I can only safely rely on the family of my mother in Iran, whom Sartor will not be able to bully so easily."

"Then how to get you safely there is the challenge," Conrad responded.

"Seems easy enough," Tony chimed in. "She could take the bus or fly. We can take up a collection to get her a ticket."

The others all made noises of agreement.

"You are all so kind," Reshtina said, tearing up yet again. "I have some money in my savings—enough I think to buy the tickets and a little more for when I get there. The money is not so much a problem, but where will I stay until I leave? Sartor will have my apartment watched, and all my things are there, including my passport. I can't afford to buy all new clothes in Iran, nor do I want to risk asking Tariq to bring them to me. I don't think Sartor will give up very easily."

"As for a place to stay for a few days—no problem—you can stay here," Conrad answered. "That is, if you are not concerned about ruining your reputation."

They all laughed at this. Their laughter dissipated the remaining tension and anxiety which had permeated the room since David had entered, though their levity did not quite disguise the concern they continued to have for Reshtina's situation, or their disapproval of David's role in the affair.

Through all of this Dennis uttered not a word. While the rest carried on with the discussion, he left the room and went down the hall to the bathroom. He stood for several minutes in front of the mirror over the sink, and came finally to his decision.

"I have got a better idea," Dennis announced abruptly, upon his return.

"You all know I am scheduled to fly out of here —to bid this pleasant city adieu, very soon. If Reshtina can get packed and ready, and a ticket and visa can be found on such short notice, I would be glad to escort her back to the States," he stated, matter-of-factly.

This offer was so unexpected that the little group was shocked into silence, much as they had been after Reshtina's earlier declaration. Dennis took advantage of the interlude to walk over to Reshtina, still sitting with the others among the soft and colorful cushions scattered about the luxuriant carpets. He knelt directly in front of her and took her hand in his.

"And Reshtina—when we arrive—and only if you agree—we can be married, and you can remain in the United States as my wife for as long as you want, to raise your baby."

Reshtina's eyes, already preternaturally exaggerated behind her thick lenses, enlarged remarkably, giving her face a cartoonish appearance. She opened her mouth to speak.

"No! Please don't answer me yet—until you have thought it over—I mean about the marriage," Dennis said. He let go her hand and delicately applied his fingers to her lips in a gesture that was at once tender but insistent.

Conrad was the first to overcome his astonishment.

"Are you absolutely sure about this, Dennis? I am not saying your motivations aren't noble, but anyone can see by the condition of your face that your judgment isn't always the soundest."

There were a few nervous giggles.

"You would have to take total responsibility for her. This is no light matter. Reshtina has no experience or connections there, and will be totally reliant on you —whether or not you get married—and of course there is the added expense and responsibility of the baby," Conrad continued.

"Of course I will help with the financial part," David said, feeling his moral stock plummet to yet a new low.

"At the very least," Conrad remarked sternly.

"Well, Reshtina? Will you come with me, at least?" Dennis asked, gently.

His attention and gaze had never strayed from her face. He had made no acknowledgment of the comments by either Conrad or David. Dennis had so focused his attention on Reshtina, that for him, it was as if they were the only two in the room.

Reshtina was initially as bewildered as the others were by this sudden proposition. She was on friendly terms with Dennis both from the language classes he had taken from her, and because of his association with

David and the other Americans, but she was completely confounded by his offer. He had never to her knowledge shown any special interest in her in the classroom setting, and never spoken more than the usual pleasantries to her in the course of the year she had functioned as one of his teachers, and more recently, as his roommate's lover. He was shy she knew, and perhaps it was possible that he had cared for her all along without her knowledge. She now realized she had been so obsessively focused on David, that she could have easily missed the subtle signals of his attraction to her.

The more she pondered it though, the more appealing the offer seemed—at least the first part of his suggestion. Like most educated Afghans, she had long fantasized about visiting America or Europe, and like many her ideas of the western countries were a fantastic concoction based upon popular Hollywood movies and American pop songs, mixed with the impressions of incredible wealth and freedom that she associated with the foreign travelers and expatriates. Her contact with the generally much less well off Peace Corps volunteers, their more modest life style, and more realistic descriptions of their homelands, had done little to dull the luster of the fabled promised land America represented to her. Her view of the West, though perhaps somewhat more nuanced than most Afghans, still contained substantial elements of fantasy.

Reshtina could not believe her good fortune. Only hours ago her life had seemed in ruins, and her future a choice between a loathsome marriage, or an obscure role as a fallen woman, wholly dependent on the good will of distant relatives. Although, like the rest of the little group in Conrad's apartment, she was not sure of Dennis' motives, she did not hesitate to accept at least the first part of his offer.

"Though I don't understand your reasons, I know you are a good man. I can be ready to go whenever you wish. I will go with the clothes on my back if I must, but my passport is at my apartment," she answered, returning Dennis' gaze.

"I promise you will not regret it," Dennis replied solemnly.

"Well, I'm glad that is settled!" Tony said, shaking his head in disbelief.

"Okay then, it looks like our biggest problem is getting into Reshtina's place to get her things. But having recently broken a man out of jail, I don't suppose that will present us with much of a challenge. The sooner the better, and David of course will help me," Conrad proclaimed.

"I've got a few afgahnis stashed away. I'll go down to the money bazaar and get as many dollars for them as I can. I don't have a lot, but it should come close to buying your ticket," David said, looking guiltily at Reshtina.

Reshtina, who was now feeling positively elated, was also in a generous state of mind. She stretched her compact torso across the carpet, placed her hands on either side of David's face, and kissed him gently and fondly on the mouth, lingering slightly longer than was comfortable for David, given the circumstances. David understood it was a kiss of absolution, as much as anything. He felt a flush of intense emotion—a combination of thankfulness and relief, and an appreciation of her generous nature and personal courage that was if not love, something closely akin to it.

"Hey man—that's my fiancé!" Dennis said.

They all laughed.

"Well, I think this calls for a toast, at the very least. We must salute the lovely couple with something besides this stale tea! I'm sure I can come up with something a bit stronger," Conrad declaimed. He rose and went to the cupboard where he kept his well stocked bar.

"There is one very important detail we must attend to quickly. Reshtina needs a visa to fly to the States. I do have some connections along that line. I will do my best, but in the worst case you may have to delay that flight a few days."

David was aware that Conrad was one of the lucky few expatriates who were welcome at Louis and Nancy Dupree's notorious 'five o'clock follies,' a frequent gathering for a wide variety of influential Afghans and westerners hosted by the couple, famous for their unparalleled knowledge of Afghan history, archeology, and culture. His reasonable assumption that Conrad would use one of his contacts there to secure the essential papers was wrong in this case. Conrad had already decided Paul Sherman would be his best connection for such a favor, and he intended to use his bargaining power with the agent to do Reshtina this favor. The problem still remained of how best to gather Reshtina's essential belongings—especially her passport.

While his friends spent the afternoon socializing and reducing his liquor supplies, Conrad reconnoitered Reshtina's apartment building and the immediate neighborhood. He determined Sartor had hired two guards, neither visibly armed, who were watching the front and back entrances of the building. Conrad knew that simple strategies often worked the best, there being less opportunity for miscalculation or unexpected contingencies. Accordingly his plan was simplicity itself.

Just after dark Conrad engaged the taxi driver he knew to be both trustworthy and discreet from several previous outings (including their latest escapade—the freeing of Brian from the Tolkif jail). He decided to take only David and Reshtina. Besides the fact that David was already involved with Reshtina, he considered David to be the best choice of the three roommates for what he had planned. Dennis seemed to attract trouble, Conrad reflected, and was too liable to act first and think later. Tony, though he had proven himself at the prison, did not seem to have the required bravado for such an errand. The only other potential accomplice, David and Dennis' roommate John Mesmer, was still too weakened from his recent bout with dysentery.

Conrad donned the clothing and headgear of a typical Pashtun tribesman. Since his Pashtu was fluent, and the lighting would be dim, he was confident he would have no trouble deceiving Sartor's guards. They left the taxi idling a block away from Reshtina's apartment building, with instructions for the driver to await their return. The driver, who had been assured of an especially large fare, could be relied on. The hardest part, Conrad knew, would be drawing the sentries away from the building and diverting their attention long enough for Reshtina to get inside, gather her belongings, and make it safely back to the taxi.

Shortly before they came into the guard's field of vision and according to plan, the two men began to run, Conrad keeping just ahead of David and yelling loudly in Pashtu that he was being attacked. Conrad had concocted a ruse whereby David played the role of an American tourist who was convinced he had been cheated in the nearby bazaar by the Pashtun. As they had hoped, both guards came out to investigate the disturbance. The man guarding the front door came out to the sidewalk first, followed a few seconds later by the second guard, who came running from the rear of the building.

After some initial confusion, with Conrad pretending to understand very little English and David playing the part of an unsophisticated tourist, Conrad convinced the men that it had been a case of mistaken identity, due no doubt to the darkness and miscommunication. While the four men sorted things out, Reshtina was able to get into the building unnoticed.

Conrad did his best to keep the men occupied, producing cigarettes and offering his profound thanks to the guards for their help, and drawing them into a long conversation about the general silliness and ignorance of the westerners. Meanwhile David, pretending to be satisfied with the outcome of the dispute, walked away from the group and back to the waiting taxi cab. For several minutes the guards genially smoked their cigarettes and laughed with Conrad, but all too soon their eyes began to wander back to the apartment building.

Unlike most hired security, they were unusually devoted, Conrad noted with annoyance. As he was offering the remaining pack of Camels to the men in a last ditch effort to delay them further, Reshtina, a suitcase in hand, emerged from the building. Both guards caught the movement and started towards her, yelling as they ran. Conrad was able to trip and shove the first guard to the ground, but the second guard managed to get to Reshtina and grab hold of her just ahead of him. It was unfortunate, but Conrad had no choice. Three quick blows and that guard was rolling on the ground in pain, blood streaming from his face. They made it to the taxi while the first guard went to the aid of his partner.

"They will call Sartor right away," Reshtina said as the taxi pulled away.

"Too late now—you have your things. All you need is an Ariana ticket and a visa," David said.

"I hope you remembered your passport," Conrad reminded her.

Reshtina smiled widely and held up the precious document.

"We had better get some rest now. It's been an eventful day," Conrad suggested. He had instructed the driver to take them back to his apartment.

"I won't argue with that," David said. "I think I could fall asleep right here in this taxi!"

Later that night, after further diminishing Conrad's liquor stash, David, Dennis, and Tony returned to their apartments. Reshtina and Aletheia spent the night in Conrad's bedroom, while he slept in the office, which served as his backup sleeping room. Conrad insisted the women stay under his protection—at least until Reshtina was on her plane out of Kabul. Conrad had never met Sartor, but knew of him through several of his business connections. He was aware that the man had a reputation as a well-connected and aggressive business man, prone to violent outbursts.

As she drifted off to sleep Reshtina wondered if she would ever see her country or family again, and silent tears came. Her American friend Aletheia, already snoring quietly next to her on Conrad's bed, was of course correct. Her first concern now must be for the new life within her, and of her own and the baby's welfare. Still, she could not help worrying about her brother, Tariq, and even feeling some remorse for defying her father, though he had betrayed her and her mother's wishes. She had left a brief note for Tariq in the apartment, but she did not dare tell him of her plans or where she stayed, only that she was safe and he should not worry.

She pondered the mystery of Dennis and his strange and wonderful offer. The more she thought about it, the more attractive he became to her, while her previous infatuation with David declined to virtual insignificance. Finally, the fears and anxieties of the day vanished, and she slept at last.

CHAPTER 21

Paul And Conrad

Paul Sherman was surprised to get the call from Conrad Sunday morning. He had been hopeful that the young informant would eventually accept the Agency's offer, but Paul had not expected to hear from him so soon, especially since the prospective recruit had not offered any help with the search for seaman Peccanter, and they had not been in touch since their earlier conversation.

They met downstairs in the bar of the Hotel Intercontinental. The room was cool and conditioned. Quiet western instrumental pop music played over the barroom speakers. The noon gun had yet to sound, but they were not the only ones present even at that early hour. Several other men sat at the barstools and tables, having their mid-morning drinks, and reading the newspapers flown in daily from various cities around the globe for the patrons of the hotel. At least one of the men Paul knew to be in the employment of the same agency he worked for, and another worked for a similar European intelligence gathering organization.

After exchanging greetings with Conrad, Paul suggested they move outside to the deck dining area for more privacy.

"I have come here to accept your offer. I also have a special request," Conrad said without preamble, after they had both ordered drinks.

Conrad was dressed neatly and freshly shaven. His manner was crisp—even terse, but he had dropped his former belligerent attitude, Paul was relieved to note.

"I hope your conditions are not too severe. I am given some latitude to negotiate, but there are certain limits to what I can offer in the way of salary, benefits and so forth." Paul continued to conceal the fact that he had nearly carte blanche in the matter.

"Salary is not the issue. Your—the Agency's offer, is perfectly acceptable in that respect, but if I was not interested, nothing you could offer would entice me."

"Yes, you made that pretty clear the last time we met. So what is your 'special request,' then?"

"Well, it is more a personal favor from you, I should think. You see, I need to get a visa for a friend, and it's somewhat of an emergency. I need it by Wednesday, the eighteenth, if at all possible."

"I assume you mean a United States visa."

"Yes, for an Afghan woman."

The waiter, dressed in a starched white uniform, delivered their drinks. Paul had been briefed to some extent on Conrad's domestic arrangements. He wondered why he would want to send his Afghan lover to the United States.

"It can be done I think. Of course I will need the woman's passport, and I must have your assurance she is not wanted for any crime here."

"Hardly. She is more the victim. The woman is pregnant by an American—no, not me—one of my Peace Corps acquaintances. He has offered to take her back to the States. Unfortunately, I was only informed of all this yesterday. I don't know how well you understand Afghan laws on marriage, but suffice it to say she cannot marry him here unless he converts to Islam, and with his flight leaving so soon, there is hardly time for that, even if he was willing to go through with the ritual."

Conrad produced Reshtina's passport and handed it to Paul. Paul looked over the document while Conrad sipped his drink.

"Which one is he—the one who got her pregnant?"

"The same guy you kicked in the face Friday night, when you picked up Brian and Karen. His name is Dennis Butler."

Conrad had decided there was no reason to tell Paul that it was in fact David who was the father. He did not want to make things any more complicated than they already were.

"I'll see to the visa, and I will get you the paperwork from the Agency that you will need to fill out and return to me for your new position. Consider the visa my amends to the young man for damaging his face. As far as I'm concerned you can start drawing your pay from today's date. If you need any cash, I should be able to get you an advance on that pay tomorrow afternoon or Tuesday morning at the latest, along with the woman's visa."

"The advance won't be necessary, but thanks. I will do my best to get the information you want, but you have not given me directions for getting that intelligence to you or anyone else. Not the same contact I have been using, I am guessing. I have reason to believe he is not reliable—if not actually compromised—and if I know that, I'm betting you do too."

"You are correct; we do have a problem there. Your new contact will be one of our most trusted liaisons, Mr. Green—whom I believe you are acquainted with—and you will receive instructions from him as to where and how you are to deliver your intelligence. Some things will obviously change. You will be given new tasks and additional responsibilities, though I doubt you will find them too onerous. Communications from Ambassador Neumann's staff and other reliable sources have informed us that a coup attempt may be expected in the next few months, or even weeks, so things may be pretty busy in the immediate future."

"I would bet a coup attempt happens sooner than that," Conrad said.

"Yes, I'm guessing you must have valid reasons to think so. Whenever and however it occurs seems to matter little to the current administration, as long as the basic relationship we have to whatever government ends up holding the reins of power here does not change. As always our main concern is that Afghanistan is not pulled any closer into the Soviet Union's orbit, as I am sure you are aware. The Chinese communists do not really seem to worry my superiors much, though any information you might impart there would be welcome, of course."

"You're absolutely right about the Chinese. The Eternal Flame Maoists are a tiny minority among the communist parties on campus. The real issue in the long run will be the Organization Of Muslim Youth and their followers. I won't be at all surprised if they someday become a much bigger problem for both the Afghans and us than the communists."

"I'm not sure I understand what you are getting at?"

"Professor Mojadedi at Kabul University is an Islam fanatic who is completely against the modernization of Afghanistan. He has a large and growing following of young Muslims, likewise fanatics, and he has convinced many of them that all things modern and western are evil. Some of his followers have recently been throwing acid on women who refuse to cover their faces in public, intimidating and terrorizing fellow students whom they accuse of not being sufficiently orthodox, and beating up those who have the courage to disagree with them publicly. These people want to turn back the clock to the middle ages, and do away with all of the freedoms women have gained under king Zahir and his predecessors' reigns."

"That puts both you and I in a somewhat awkward position, Mr. Slocum," Paul said.

"How is that?"

"The current administration believes we must encourage and develop relationships with the Islamic groups in order to bolster our position against the communists. The most influential advisors in our department seem to think they are our best chance to resist further Russian expansion into Central Asia."

"But that is crazy! If the Islamists take power they will set the country back five hundred years. In my opinion our best policy should be encouraging and backing up the more progressive elements in this country—regardless of their political views."

"Ah, but as you know, neither you or I make policy. Do I understand you correctly—we cannot count on your cooperation with respect to this particular strategy?"

"That is not what I said. I only mean it seems a stupid strategy to me. I have no objection to spying on the communists, religious fanatics—or any other group for that matter—but it does not mean I have to like the radical Moslems or their goals for this country."

"Goals for Afghanistan? Have you forgotten you will be working for the interests of your own country, not this one?"

Paul had been warned before leaving for Kabul that Conrad might have in some ways 'gone native.' But

Paul and his supporters had argued that even if that was the case, he could still be very useful. At one conference an Agency officer brought up the historical example of Sir Richard Burton from the previous century. Though not entirely controllable, and not always sympathetic to the prevailing British interests, he had supplied much valuable information to the British Empire in spite of his essentially independent nature, and even outright hostility to some of the empire's practices.

"Has it never occurred to anyone in government that our interests and the interests of the common people of this country might be complementary—that even for a country like ours—obsessed as we are with commerce, profit, and military domination, it would be to everyone's advantage to see better education, less superstition, and the emancipation of women here—if for no other reason than it would create more consumers for our products! Who gives a shit whether they call themselves socialists or capitalists, as long as the general standard of living and literacy rates improve. Hasn't Viet Nam taught us anything? Didn't we learn anything from the British Empire's experiences during the first and second Afghan wars, or their experiences in India?"

"I think we decided previously that we must agree to disagree about Viet Nam. I understand your reticence, and I appreciate your candor, but I too have not always seen entirely eye to eye with our government on some of its policies. At times I have had to take part in certain activities which have disturbed my conscience, but the very few times I have had serious objections to an assignment, the Agency has always found some way to accommodate me. I think I can assure you of the same thing. Your assignments with regard to the Islamists will be limited to information gathering for the time being, and if that should change to some more active form of support at a future date, you will be offered less disagreeable duties."

"Are you hinting we might actually help arm those fanatics? That would be madness!"

"I am not suggesting anything except that you will not be asked to do anything that you absolutely object to on moral or ethical grounds. Now, have we perhaps set the boundaries of this relationship to your satisfaction?"

"Well, for now at least I think I can live with the arrangement, but as I feared, it is beginning to sound more and more like that Faustian bargain."

"That strikes me as an overstatement at the very least. Doesn't all employment demand some sacrifice of ego and entail certain compromises? Now about the other matter—seaman Peccanter. Have you been able to find any information at all concerning his whereabouts?"

Paul found the direction of the discussion uncomfortable. He was well aware of his government's plans to arm the Islamists, and to provide military advisors in order to help trip up the communists as much as possible. In fact his main purpose in Kabul was to set up just such a connection with one particular Pashtun leader. The plan was no different in character from similar operations he was aware of in Central and South America, several of which he had played some small role in.

Paul had been in his twenties during the outbreak of McCarthyism, but he had never bought into the general hysteria, and had disliked the senator and his methods. He had even felt a certain private pleasure when the odious man was laid low at last. Paul's political views were far more nuanced than many of his colleagues, but stopped short vocal criticism of his country's actions, even in private. For the most part he preferred to believe that those above him who made policy decisions were privy to knowledge he did not have, were more aware of the 'big picture,' and thus more qualified than himself to make such decisions. Ironically though, the higher Paul moved up the chain of command, the more he had come to question those assumptions.

"Look Paul—I assume now that we are officially working together we can be on a first name basis—unless you prefer we use numbers or some other cloak and dagger sort of code system. You put me in an awkward position here. These are friends of mine, and as I told you in our last conversation, I don't give a damn about the war in Southeast Asia, which is of course officially over, even though we continue to bomb the fucking hell out of everything in the region. I also do not give a damn about your Captain Ramsy. I mean no disrespect to you, and I will not interfere in any way with your efforts of course, but don't expect my help with that."

Actually, Conrad had every intention of doing what he could to help Brian retain his freedom. He paused and downed the rest of his drink before continuing.

"Regardless, I think you are getting a pretty good deal for your money all things considered. I will get you the information you need on the OMY, PDPA, Eternal Flame, and more, just don't expect me to help you out with your manhunt. And one more thing; I will not have anything to do with the drug interdiction bullshit here. Let's just say that is not my area of expertise, and I don't want any association with those bottom feeders."

Paradoxically, Paul had earlier decided that he would ultimately need to be more honest with Conrad, in order to have any chance of gaining his full trust and cooperation in this or any other matter. That was the odd thing about his line of work. Much of the time it was necessary to deliberately mislead, fabricate, misinform, or lie outright, but on other occasions complete honesty was more effective.

Up until now Conrad Slocum had been what in the service was known as a 'CAS,' a 'Controlled American Source'—essentially an information subcontractor. Now he would have status and some authority as a full-fledged if junior agent. As Paul's protege, Conrad's actions would reflect on them both, and he wanted the partnership to get off to a good start. Paul felt the time had come to be more forthright with Conrad regarding his real feelings on the Brian Peccanter manhunt. He also realized their relationship would improve if he could assure Conrad that the Agency—to some degree at least—had his back.

"What if I told you I have come to believe seaman Peccanter may actually be innocent of at least some of the charges he has been accused of? And since you bring it up, and for what it is worth, you probably already suspect we know something about your particular tastes in local drugs. I am not here to moralize or lecture you about that, let alone forbid it. In fact, I will be absolutely frank with you on this. Concerning the drug issue in particular—short of you actually being involved in an international smuggling operation, you will always be immune to any kind of harassment or charges for personal use—at least as long as you are able to supply the kind of information we need, and do nothing to publicly embarrass the Agency. I can guarantee as long as you are reasonably discreet you will not be bothered by Burke or any of his bunch, but I suggest you refrain from further antagonizing him and his crew, as I can only do so much to restrain that group."

Conrad did not respond to this immediately. He realized Paul must know everything about his recent altercation with Burke and the agent's subsequent threats. Conrad knew most of the American drug agents in Kabul were users and dealers themselves, and largely a debauched set of opportunists and hucksters. He was not the least bit intimidated by Paul's implied warning. He knew he was too valuable already to be the target of a drug investigation, and in any case that set of bungling blackguards would never find him if he should choose to disappear. His casual dealing was a part of the basic social fabric of his age group that Paul, from an earlier generation, simply did not understand. He really could take or leave drugs and had no problems with addiction himself.

"Fuck Burke and the rest of his stooges. I just wanted you and the Agency to know I will not be a part of any anti-drug hippie-bashing obsessive bullshit, just as I don't want any part of arming fanatical fundamentalists. I still have some scruples. As for Brian—I am wondering what, or who, changed your mind?"

"I have to admit Miss Truman has been very persuasive in arguing on her boyfriend's behalf, but I reached my conclusions mostly on my own. I'm willing to admit some of it is intuition, but I have been at this work long enough to learn to trust my instincts."

Paul would not reveal his personal doubts about Cecil's character. That was something he could discuss with no one.

Conrad could not help wondering just how persuasive Karen had been. She was a very pretty girl, and Conrad had to admit that he too was not immune to her charms. He could not rule out the possibility that she might have struck up her own sort of bargain with Paul, nor did he know enough about her to hazard a guess as to what lengths she might go to protect her boyfriend. He did not think Paul, or many men for that matter, would be capable of resisting her attractions if it came to that.

Conrad could indeed deliver on his promise to provide inside information on the actions of the local communist parties as well as the Islamists. Two of his best contacts were Reshtina and her brother, Tariq, both members of the Parcham faction of the PDPA. Reshtina was dedicated to Dr. Anahita Ratebzad, one of the founding members of the PDPA along with her lover Barbrak Karmal. Karmal himself was considered to be one the three most influential communist party leaders, along with Amin and Taraki. Through his friendship with the siblings and several other Afghan acquaintances, Conrad had developed the ability to move freely in their social circles, and had gained a very accurate picture of the most important relationships and connections between many of the PDPA party leaders and strategists.

He was in fact attracted to many of them personally, as well as to their idealistic goals for improving the lot of the people of Afghanistan. He found their optimism, enthusiasm, and energy refreshing and stimulating. In particular he liked the communist party's emphasis on education and the liberation of women from the tyranny of Islamic feudalism, where women were mere chattel. He also approved of the party's disdain for the Durrani monarchy, whose members had done little but enrich themselves and the tribe for generations, while the country as a whole remained one of the most impoverished in the world.

Of course Conrad's family background had something to do with his sympathies, as Paul and others in the Agency obviously knew, but that did not override Conrad's potential value as an informant. Regardless of what the Agency understood of his political sympathies, they needed Conrad's skills and social connections. Even if Conrad did sympathize with the PDPA's efforts in Afghanistan, the Agency could not afford to chastise him as long as he continued to supply the information they needed, and as long as he refrained from actually confronting or interfering with other operatives, Paul reasoned.

In addition, Conrad's social connections with certain members of the Islamist sympathizers were just as useful to the Agency as was his familiarity with the communists. He knew many of the former through his carpet exporting business. Those business interests gave him access to the homes of several Pashtun traders who were deeply involved with supporting the Organization of Muslim Youth, and he had a passing acquaintance with professor Mojadedi himself, having once sold an especially nice Shindand rug to one of his relatives. Conrad, as far as any of them knew, was just an American trader who provided a convenient link to certain western markets. It was surprising how many of the wealthy and conservative Koran thumpers had no problem dealing with him and other infidels where profits and fine woven goods were concerned.

Though he sympathized with much of the PDPA's agenda, Conrad was no communist himself, or at least not in the Russian or Chinese sense. He liked many of the ideas of Marx, Trotsky, and Lenin, but recoiled from any sort of tyranny by any name. Although both his mother and grandmother had at one time been registered communists (he had barely known his father, who had died while he was young), Conrad had never formally joined any political party. Thomas Paine was Conrad's prime political muse when he thought much about the subject, but mostly he was motivated by self-ish interests and an essentially pagan sense of ethics. He needed to work to live, but his temperament, unusual childhood, and unorthodox education ill-suited him for most occupations. Intelligence work seemed to fit him best of all the work he had tried his hand at to date. In many ways, though they were some fifteen years apart in age, Conrad and Paul were cut from the same cloth.

"I will get that visa for you, as I promised. Obviously it would be best if your friends did not know of our connection, or how you managed to procure the papers. Of course I would appreciate your help locating the American if you have any suggestions or hear anything at all. I'll tell you the same thing I told Karen—Miss Truman—that if I do find Mr. Peccanter I will do everything in my power to see he gets a fair hearing. I will take personal responsibility for his safety if I can locate him before Captain Ramsy does."

"Yes, of course. My Peace Corps friends are completely unaware that I'm a two-bit spook. As far as I know only a handful of agents here even know my identity, and I have to hope they are at least competent enough to keep that secret."

This was not entirely true. He was sure Shamsher at least had his suspicions.

"I can't stay in Afghanistan beyond next week. The captain will arrive tomorrow, and if we have not located Peccanter by the end of the week he will be on his own, as I need to get back to Washington."

"So the captain does not think you can find him by yourself?" Conrad asked.

"I'm not sure if it is that, or that Ramsy wants to take custody of Peccanter himself, if he is found. Like I said before, and just between the two of us and Miss Truman; I now have some doubts about this whole affair, but regardless of my feelings, Mr. Peccanter is not helping his case any by running."

"That depends on whether you think staying alive helps his case or not."

"What are you suggesting?"

"You know damn well what I'm saying. Brian told me himself he was afraid his captain would kill him if he got the opportunity, and that even if he did survive long enough to get to the court martial, it was all rigged anyway. If Brian's story is true, why would the captain stop at murder if he thought he could get away with it? He could just say Brian tried to escape."

"All the more reason for you and your friends to help me locate him first, if that is what you really believe."

"That still seems riskier to me than just letting him be on his way, as far as I can see," Conrad countered.

"That might be true in the short term, but sooner or later either the captain, some other officer, or Interpol will catch up with him."

Paul could see Conrad would not be convinced, and although his new recruit had made it clear he would not help with the hunt for the AWOL seaman, otherwise they parted on better terms and with a closer understanding than after their previous meeting. Paul felt they had established a good initial rapport, in spite of Conrad's refusal to help with the seaman's case and his antipathy towards the Islamists. He was reasonably sure he had made the right decision in enlisting the young new agent, and that Conrad's contributions would be significant. Paul's task of gathering crucial intelligence in this country, which had become his main responsibility since his recent promotion, was not an easy one, and he could not afford to set too many conditions on the sources of that information.

CHAPTER 22

Paul And Cecil

On the morning of Monday, July 16, after an overnight stay in New Delhi, Cecil Ramsy arrived at the Kabul airport. He was grumpy and out of sorts from the interruption to his normal routine and lack of sleep the last two days. His head ached, his clothes were rumpled and sweaty, and he was stiff from too much sitting. He cleared customs without any problems, retrieved his only piece of luggage, and found Paul in the waiting area.

"How was your flight?"

"Miserable as usual. Any more news yet on Peccanter?" he replied. Cecil was in no mood for small talk.

"No, but I did find out he had the help of a local Afghan breaking out of jail, and I'm assuming he is still traveling with him, as I have not been able to track down either of them. He has most likely left Kabul and probably the country, but so far I have no leads as to which direction they may be headed. I don't have much hope that we will find him in Afghanistan. Interpol may have more luck."

"Fuck Interpol—we can do better than that bunch on our own."

Paul showed Cecil out to a waiting taxi.

"You look like hell," Paul observed as they took their seats in the cab.

"Just get me a drink, a decent meal, and a shower, and I'll be good as new," Cecil replied.

On the way to the hotel Paul explained in more detail the capture and subsequent escape of seaman Peccanter, and his efforts since then to find him. When they arrived at Paul's room at the Hotel Intercontinental Cecil ordered a drink from room service, downed it quickly, and headed immediately for the shower.

In the bedroom, where Karen and he had enjoyed the previous night together (and slept very little), and where Cecil, ironically, would sleep tonight, he found himself drawn to his friend's half open suitcase. Quickly he sorted through the contents, while listening attentively to be sure the shower still ran. There were two light cotton golf shirts of the style his friend was so fond of, several changes of socks and underwear, two pairs of slacks, and a V-necked sweater. He felt a hard lump in the folds of the sweater, which proved to be a . 38 short barreled revolver—the kind called a 'Saturday night special' stateside.

Definitely not Navy standard issue, Paul thought as he carefully replaced the items, making sure the suitcase appeared undisturbed.

As he waited in the next room for his friend to finish his bathroom routine, Paul wondered if Cecil Ramsy's problems with drinking and evident dissipation might stem ultimately from his unhappy youth. Cecil's parents had separated when he was in grade school. Thereafter Cecil had idolized his seldom seen military father, who had been his main inspiration for joining the Navy. Cecil had been devastated when his mother eventually married again, having for years fantasized that his parents would eventually reunite. The stepfather brought his own two children into the family, and suddenly Cecil, who had been an only child, was forced to share his bedroom with an older boy, and could no longer command the uninterrupted attention of his mother. His older stepbrother was tall and strong for his age, and enjoyed taunting and teasing Cecil in private.

Because of these traumatic domestic changes Cecil began spending much of his time at Paul's house, often spending the night, and sometimes even whole weekends. Paul's parents were understanding and somewhat aware of the boy's unhappy home life. During his high school years Cecil essentially became another member of Paul's family—a family he preferred to his own.

Paul recalled a camping trip they had made together in their early teens. They enjoyed hunting, fishing, and cooking their catch afterwards on the open campfire. That particular day the two had separated to try and flush out quail they knew nested in the area. Paul had no luck, but he had heard the sharp snap of

Cecil's twenty gauge shotgun, and circled back to see what his friend had bagged for their dinner.

Paul had stopped short in a wooded area at the edge of a meadow, where he could see his friend behaving strangely. He had come up quietly, and Cecil had not been aware of his presence. Cecil had wounded one of the birds. He could see it flapping wildly on the ground. Dumbfounded, Paul had watched as Cecil prodded the creature with a short stick. Instead of finishing off the bird quickly, he was tormenting the animal cruelly. Paul could hear Cecil talking to the bird as he tortured it, poking and striking it with the stick and laughing at the quail's pitiful efforts to escape.

"That'll show you who's boss—yeah, that's right —just try it again and see what you get. Oh, now you see how it feels, don't you!"

He realized that Cecil was pretending the bird was his stepbrother, and he was acting out his fantasy of revenge at the poor animal's expense. Though Paul had no qualms about killing animals for food, he took pride in a quick clean kill and hated to see an animal suffer. Still, he knew Cecil would be embarrassed if he was caught doing something so low, so Paul had backed off a ways, then announced his presence with plenty of noise so that Cecil had time to finish off the bird before he arrived on the scene. He had never told Cecil of witnessing this incident, and had not thought of it again until now.

We are sometimes most blind to the true character of those we are closest to, Paul thought. Even as this realization struck him, Paul remembered a second incident, from a decade later, while they were university undergraduates.

A freshman coed had accused a group of fraternity men, including Cecil, of blindfolding and stripping her in a hazing incident related to the annual rush season. The matter had been hushed up quickly. The girl had been pacified by being accepted into her sorority of choice, and it was rumored the fraternity members had paid her a large sum of money to keep quiet. Disturbingly, there had been a persistent rumor that one of the men had fondled her breasts and rubbed his penis on her pubic area. One of Paul's college acquaintances had dated a friend of the victim. He had told Paul that the victim was absolutely sure the man who had molested her was Cecil Ramsy.

Paul now understood that he had repressed the memories of both these incidents. He was only drawn away from these disturbing recollections when Cecil at last emerged, freshly showered and shaven from the bathroom.

They had lunch at the hotel restaurant. Paul watched as Cecil downed his second drink, also a double, before ordering desert.

"A little early in the day for so much booze isn't it?" Paul commented.

"You always were a bit of a bluenose, but I do seem to recall a time when even you would not hesitate to have a little nip with breakfast."

"That was a long time ago."

"Okay, so I admit I might drink a little more than I should some days, but everyone needs at least one vice —right old boy?"

I wonder if just one vice is enough, Paul mused, and then it came to him in a flash—the intuition that the story Brian had told Karen was the truth—all of it. This insight was so spontaneous and overwhelming, he understood why cartoonists resorted to the light bulb illustration cliche when a character experienced a sudden revelation.

That sensation vanished quickly though, and left him with a profound feeling of desolation and loss. Cecil Ramsy was his oldest and closest friend, the brother he had never had, and the only person besides his parents he would have trusted with his life. Later, he was never sure exactly what had opened his eyes. Something in his friend's tone of voice, the obvious alcoholism, the gun in the suitcase, his recollection of the two earlier unsavory incidents, or something else entirely; but at that moment, while his fork with its impaled egg hovered midway between his mouth and the plate, Paul was absolutely certain that his old friend was entirely capable of the acts Karen had described. Somehow he must have been subliminally aware all along of Cecil's depravity. How else explain that he now accepted so readily the idea that his old comrade was capable of such evil?

Ultimately Paul was just as adept at dissembling as his friend, if anything even more so. It was an essential part of his job. Beyond that, Paul had observed over the years that what society called 'maturity' was only the knowledge, skillfully applied, of when and how much to conceal of one's feelings, motivations, and actions. So he began the by now instinctive process of disguising his true sentiments, while continuing to pretend the old comfortable relationship with Cecil still existed. It distressed him to dissimulate this way, for he knew it marked the end of a lifelong friendship that had meant much to him in an existence which allowed so little in the way of real candor, let alone intimacy.

"I guess I am getting a little conventional in my old age," he joked, "but I was thinking we might have our work cut out finding our man before he gets too far away."

It was important that Cecil think nothing had changed in their relationship, if Paul was to protect seaman Peccanter now that he believed the young man was innocent, and that his old friend must be the true villain.

"You worry too much, as usual. How far away can he be? He won't take the risk of flying, and the main roads have too many checkpoints. He'll need a place to hide out for a while, and my bet is he will stay with relatives or friends of the Afghan who helped him escape. My guess is he is still in Afghanistan, probably even here in Kabul somewhere. With a little research and a few well placed dollars we shouldn't have much of a problem finding him, unless as you say, he has really flown the coop. In the meantime, let's relax a little and enjoy ourselves, how about it?"

"Whatever you say, Cecil. This whole affair is really only your concern. I'm just here to help you out any way I can," Paul said, feigning indifference. "If it is all the same to you I guess I will have that drink after all."

Paul motioned to the waiter and ordered an Irish Coffee.

"You call that a drink! Well, at least it is a step in the right direction. Now tell me; you must have some sort of a plan for finding Peccanter?"

How can I keep Cecil occupied while making sure I find the man first, and he does not discover my collusion with Karen? Paul thought, turning the matter over with one part of his mind, while he focused another part of his attention on keeping up the pretense that he was still working to help the captain.

"Well, it's not much of a plan, I admit. I could get nothing out of the owner of the hotel where he was staying. I honestly don't think he knows anything. We could go back to the jail and ask some more questions— maybe interview a few more officers, but getting answers in this country means coming up with the right payola."

"That's no different from anywhere else. Anyway money is not a problem," Cecil said, patting his wallet. "What about your intelligence connections here?"

"I doubt we will get much from them either. There are dozens of operatives from several agencies in Kabul at the moment, but most of them are just your standard issue drug investigators and informants, and the rest are all busy with tracking the Russians and the local communist parties here. Rumor has it a coup d'etat is imminent. (Paul knew this to be much more than a rumor, but had no reason to reveal this to Cecil.) The Russians are backing the return of a previous high ranking official in the Afghan government who is more sympathetic to them than the current king. The king, Zahir, is out of the country now with health issues. Some say the coup could happen at any time," Paul explained.

"What about the girl—Peccanter's girlfriend? Did you question her? Maybe I should talk to her."

"No point in that. It would just be a waste of your time. I've already interviewed her and she doesn't know anything. I had her in my custody the whole time her boyfriend was locked up, so there was no way for her to contact him or anyone else. My own feeling is that Peccanter himself had no plan or particular destination in mind, and probably relied on the Afghan who helped break him out to choose the best escape route. The only thing she could tell me is that they had hoped to eventually make their way to Europe."

Paul was determined to keep Captain Ramsy from having any contact with Karen.

"So it sounds like we are on our own then. Just as well," Cecil said, finishing his drink.

"I've got one appointment that I must keep this morning. After that I am all yours for the rest of the day. We can head over to the prison, or anywhere else you want to go," Paul said.

Paul instructed the waiter to put the meal on his room account, and both men left the restaurant. Cecil took the elevator back to the hotel room while Paul took a cab down to the city.

While Paul attended to his errands, Captain Ramsy decided to do some investigating of his own. He was not happy with his friend's seeming lack of enthusiasm and inventiveness in pursuing the AWOL seaman. He suspected Paul simply had too many responsibilities and duties here to turn over every stone or follow every lead that might lead them to Peccanter.

There was something else too. Although Cecil was an alcoholic who normally imbibed steadily from breakfast on, and generally drank himself to insensibility each night, it did not prevent him from perceiving that their friendship had cooled somewhat. He detected an impatience and lack of sympathy in Paul's manner. This too he attributed to Paul's new responsibilities and worries. He was aware of Paul's recent promotion within the Agency. Cecil regretted somewhat that he had asked Paul to help in the manhunt. He was beginning to think he had asked too much of his old companion. He reasoned that Paul was probably simply too distracted with his other duties to be as helpful as he had hoped, and he would have to take on the responsibility for locating his quarry himself.

CHAPTER 23

An Unlikely Hero

In the early hours of July 17, 1973, General Daoud's rebel troops converged on the king's palace. The operation had been planned months in advance. King Zahir was in Italy recovering from an eye injury incurred in a volleyball game. Volleyball was currently all the rage with Kabul's elite. General Daoud, who had been Zahir's Prime Minister ten years earlier, had secured the loyalty of the important military leaders as well as the blessings of the local communists.

Shamsher and Brian Peccanter, both armed with rifles provided to them by the rebels, rode in the old Chevrolet 'Two-Ten' with four other rebel troops. General Daoud's men had (temporarily, they assured them) commandeered the venerable old vehicle. Their particular leader, an officer of uncertain rank, directed from the front seat while a subordinate soldier drove. The six men were wedged in tight, their rifle stocks resting on the floorboards between their feet, swaying in unison as the loosely sprung coupe negotiated each turn. The city was enveloped in a shadowless darkness, but the waning gibbous moon allowed them to see just well enough to drive with headlights off. The streets had been relinquished hours earlier to the stray dogs that roamed in search of any residual scraps of nourishment.

Several blocks before the palace they parked the car and assembled with the other groups of revolutionaries. Together the rebels advanced as silently as they could towards the gated enclosure. The two sentries at the entrance were swiftly dispatched by their group, but the disturbance had alerted the inside guards. They had expected little or no resistance. Most of the Afghan armed forces had by earlier arrangement agreed to back General Daoud Khan, who had years ago been head of the Kabul divisions, and for a decade from 1953 Prime Minister, but some of the king's elite personal unit either hadn't got the message, or had decided to resist.

The soldiers quickly took positions inside the walled compound according to their plan, but their deployment had been detected. There were loud calls in the dark and the courtyard was lit up by blinding flood lights. Guards still loyal to the king fired down on the men in the square. Brian and Shamsher found themselves pinned down along with their patrol behind a large concrete fountain and pool. From their vantage point on the building's roof the guards rained down furious bursts of fire. Each time one of the rebel soldiers raised a head above the rim of the fountain pool shots rang out, some landing uncomfortably close—the bullets sizzling into the shallow water or sending up puffs of dust and pieces of concrete shrapnel from the courtyard behind them. It was a precarious position. The expected reinforcements had yet to arrive.

"I've got an idea," Brian told Shamsher.

"You see those trees," he said, pointing to a grove about twenty yards from the fountain.

"I'll create a diversion by heading for them, laying down fire as I go. The rest of you should be able to make it inside while they're busy with me."

"That is too dangerous. You maybe cannot make it. This is not a fight for you, Brian," Shamsher said. "It is a good idea, but I must be the one to go."

Several more shots kicked up dust directly behind them in the courtyard.

"Listen, I've done just this sort of drill in basic training. It's no big deal—it's not very far, and I'm a good sprinter, but if it makes you feel any better you can cover me while the soldiers make for the palace door, okay?"

With Shamsher translating the men discussed the idea. Finally the leader nodded and spoke.

"What the fuck did he say?" Brian asked Shamsher.

"He said, 'go with Allah,'" Shamsher replied.

"It sure took him long enough to say three words."

"He also said, 'the infidel is a crazy man,'" Shamsher deadpanned.

"What the hell—at least this is a cause to believe in. You all seem to know exactly what you are fighting for, and have a leader who promises change. I never could figure out what or who the hell I was fighting for in Viet Nam. Are you ready, Shamsher? Let's do it!"

With that Brian ran, weaving and firing as he went, while Shamsher fired as fast as he could at the soldiers on the roof with his antiquated Martini-Henry bolt action rifle, a weapon that had first seen use a century earlier during the second Anglo-Afghan war. The other rebels were able to make it unharmed through the palace door during the distraction, as Brian had hoped. The sounds of muffled firing came from inside the building. At the same time the reinforcements arrived, driving fast in pickups and Jeeps into the courtyard of the mansion. Dozens of armed soldiers quickly dispersed into the building and the surrounding grounds.

"Are you unharmed?" Shamsher called out, when the firing from the roof had stopped.

"I took one in the leg, but I think I will live," Brian yelled back, from his hiding place in the trees.

"I think I maybe shot one man on the roof, and the others have gone. Our soldiers will silence those left inside you can be sure," Shamsher said. "Now may we enter the palace in safety!"

With no resistance, the two men made for the mansion door, Brian gamely dragging his right leg and leaving a trail of bright red as he went. Inside, in a large reception room, a group of the rebels had gathered. Some of the men held guns on captive soldiers—the members of the king's private guard who had deemed it wiser to surrender than to fight, or who had been wounded in the fray. It appeared the action was over, with casualties light. A rebel soldier who acted as medic expertly cleaned and dressed Brian's wound. Shamsher translated as the medic spoke.

"He learned medicine from the Germans. He wants to become a doctor," Shamsher said. "He says this is good practice for him, and you will be fine."

"I'm more than happy to oblige him," Brian said, with false bravado. His leg was really beginning to hurt.

"He says also you are lucky this bullet went through your leg without hitting an artery or bone. You must mostly worry about the infection and to keep the wound clean."

As Brian's wound was dressed there were cheers and shouts from outside the palace.

"What's going on?" Brian asked.

"Daoud Khan has arrived and the revolution will be a success," Shamsher replied. "The king Zahir was not in the palace. The rat had already gone off to one of his nests in Italy, where he spends most of his time and the people's money, living a life of ease while his subjects in Afghanistan live like dogs—but no more!"

They went outside, Brian leaning on Shamsher and limping along as best he could. The sun barely peaked out from behind a mountain ridge, casting its rosy glow on the compound. There was light enough now that the long shadows of the men were discernible. In the courtyard a crowd of Daoud's soldiers and civilians massed around an old Russian T-34 tank from which General Daoud spoke to the assembled.

"What the hell is he saying?" asked Brian.

"He is thanking to all the soldiers who helped taking the palace. He says here was the only fighting in Kabul. The military leaders have all sworn to be loyal forever to Daoud Khan. Only these palace guards fought for King Zahir, but they will be set free if only they swear also the loyalty to Daoud and the new republic."

There was a pause in the new leader's speech, and a rebel officer said something to the General. He gestured and pointed in the direction of Brian and Shamsher, standing on the stairs of the palace entrance at the fringe of the crowd.

"What the hell?" said Brian, seeing all the faces turn toward himself and Shamsher.

"You are a hero to the revolution! If not for your actions our men could not have made it into the palace without many injuries or deaths. The general asks to meet you," Shamsher said, smiling widely and slapping Brian's back as the crowd surged in his direction.

To an accompaniment of cheers and raised weapons Brian found himself propelled by many hands toward the general, who descended from the tank to meet him. In spite of the pain in his leg he smiled as he shook the hand of the new leader of Afghanistan. At his side, Shamsher interpreted. General Daoud spoke loudly so that all his supporters could hear.

"We are forever in your debt. For our great cause you have been wounded. You have risked your life for my soldiers and the revolution!"

The general embraced him warmly and shook his hand a second time. The gathered soldiers and citizens cheered.

Suddenly, Afghanistan's new ruler surprised Brian by addressing him in perfectly fluent English.

"They tell me you are an American. Is this so?"

"I am a United States citizen."

"Why do you find yourself in our country, and fighting along side my soldiers?"

"That is a very long story, sir, and I know you must be a very busy man."

"You are most considerate, but just the same, is there any way I can be of service to you? It seems my soldiers and myself are now in your debt, and we surely have the time to listen to how you have come to be here in this place, and to offer you any assistance we can."

As briefly as he could Brian told the general something about his escape from the Tolkif jail and the agent sent to capture him. He described the circumstances of the death of the police officer, and asked for protection for himself and Shamsher.

"Considering your service to our cause, I think I can arrange it so that neither of you will be held accountable for the unfortunate death of the policeman. I am not sure how to deal with this American agent. We must be careful to stay on good relations with your country. There are other pressing matters to attend to, you must understand. However, I can assure you that for the time being, if asked, my government has no knowledge of where you may be, and if in the next several days you decide to leave the borders of Afghanistan, you will have our help and escort if need be with any route you choose."

At the end of this exchange the general again seized Brian's hand in his, and raising them shouted to the crowd. Again the soldiers cheered loudly.

The general shook both Brian and Shamsher's hands yet again, and with another shout to the soldiers, ascended the tank. The antiquated but still formidable machine turned and clanked out of the courtyard and onto the street, with the rebels and rest of the growing crowd following and chanting Daoud's name as they went. One of the soldiers from their patrol found them in the crowd. He took them to the Chevy, still parked conveniently where they had left it, and gave Shamsher back the keys, before saying his goodbyes and running off after the others. No one else from their original patrol joined them, they too having apparently left with the rest of the mob following the new ruler of Afghanistan.

"Now my uncle's car is no longer needed by the revolution, but perhaps we may have need of it for a while longer" Shamsher said, starting the engine.

"Where are we off to then?" asked Brian.

"After a revolution such as this we must have something to eat!" Shamsher replied. "The general will speak to the people of Kabul later this afternoon, but now the men are hungry."

"I just realized I'm half starved myself. At least in Nam we usually got a meal before a battle."

"It is said a soldier fights on his stomach. If that is so then I have no more stomach for the fighting!" joked Shamsher.

The streets of Kabul were busier than ever. The word was out that fighting was over and the populace could go about their business as usual. It was some time before the Brian and Shamsher arrived by a circuitous route to a restaurant in the somewhat misnomered Chicken Street bazaar. Besides chickens, the bazaar offered all manner of groceries, medicines and handicrafts, as well as fine Herat glass, alabaster, lapis lazuli, carpets, pottery, clothing and footwear—and much, much more.

They sat at a sidewalk table in the shade of an awning in front of a small restaurant. The sun beat down on the crowded street before them, while in relative comfort under the shade of the canopy they drank their tea and waited for their food to arrive. To the usual multitudes of merchants and shoppers, women hidden under their tent-like chadors, begging children, hirsute young tourists, overloaded pack animals, stray dogs, and the motley market mix (what David called the 'bizarre bazaar'), were now added the strutting groups of soldiers—only yesterday employed by the now despised and deposed king—today sworn to the service of Afghanistan's latest sovereign, General Sardar Mohammed Daoud Khan.

The atmosphere was one of celebration, though some few had reason to worry whether their employment by or close relationship to the former regime might bode ill—but this was of no concern to the majority of Kabul residents.

The gossip was all of the day's fantastic events, and of the marvelous efficiency and lack of bloodshed with which the coup had been accomplished. The only known rebel casualties had occurred during the fighting at the palace where Brian had been wounded, and when one of the old Russian tanks had suddenly locked up a track and plunged into the Kabul River, killing one of its unfortunate operators.

Their food arrived at last. The two ate rapidly, famished from the morning's exertions.

"How is your leg been feeling now?" asked Shamsher.

"It's starting to throb. I could really use few hits of opium and a couple of glasses of wine. That would be just the thing for this old war hero now."

Shamsher laughed, then quickly grew serious.

"I am thinking even with Daoud Khan as our new leader you will not be safe in Kabul. Maybe he will do as he has told us with the matter of the Tolkif jail, but I do not think he will care to interfere with the American who still hunts you. It is clear he was meaning that you should be leaving soon, though he was careful with his words while in the hearing of the soldiers. He wishes most of all to remain on the good terms with your government. We must get you away from this place soon, where you will not be safe, even with these new changes."

"Yes, that is the impression I got from the general too, but I would like to see Karen again before I leave. Anyway I'm not going to be too spry until my leg heals."

As the spoke, a somewhat disheveled, perspiring man approached their table from behind. His short barreled pistol was at Brian Peccanter's back before either Brian or Shamsher could react.

CHAPTER 24

July 17

David awoke abruptly at five back in his own apartment bedroom. He was instantly aware that something was not right. By habit a later riser, one of the first adaptations he had made to life in Kabul was changing his routine to get up at six o'clock or earlier, as most Afghans, including his domestic and the bazaar shopkeepers below his apartment, were noisily awake and active well before the sun cast its first rays upon the ancient city. But this morning, long after the bazaar should have been boisterous with the combined clamor of voices, radios, and traffic the street was eerily quiet. He dressed quickly and went downstairs. He found Bagnur in his shop, ear pressed against his radio.

"There was fighting last night in the city. General Daoud Khan has returned and King Zahir is no more!" Bagnur told him excitedly, without even bothering with the usual preamble of a formal greeting.

"Where are all the shopkeepers and customers this morning?" David asked.

"Everyone is afraid to go outside until they are sure the shooting is over. There are soldiers and tanks on the streets of Kabul!"

"No other details? Can you tell if it is really safe to go out?"

"I know only what I have heard on the radio, just now."

Afghanistan had several popular radio stations, and only a single television station, whose reception was limited to the city of Kabul. In a country that was still mostly illiterate, and where only a few could afford televisions, the radio was virtually the only source of news beyond the gossip of the bazaars for many citizens.

"General Daoud tells the people of Afghanistan to go about their business, and warns supporters of the king to throw down their weapons and give their allegiance to the new republic," Bagnur continued, his ear still glued to small Japanese radio.

"What do you think will happen?"

"I think nothing will change too much. Life here is always the same no matter who is in power. A few people will die, but the poor will remain poor and those who can will live by their wits as before," Bagnur explained.

"Everyone knows the Russians have supported and advised General Daoud all along. When your country refused to sell Afghanistan weapons it was only natural that our leaders turned to the Soviet Union, and now we see Russians everywhere in Kabul. Our university is full of communist students, and they infest our parliament. We have seen their newspapers and posters and heard their propaganda. Afghanistan will pay a great price for it's dealings with these Soviets."

"I had no idea you were such a political authority," David observed, after listening to Bagnur's uncharacteristic monologue.

"I am only a shopkeeper, but I have eyes to see and ears to hear with. I am not free to say what I wish always. A business man finds his customers where he may, but I will tell you I have no love for these Russians, or their followers."

When David got back upstairs Dennis, John, and Tony were all awake, waiting for water to boil for tea. David gave them the news of the coup.

"It figures—now that I've decided to leave it finally gets interesting around here," Dennis said.

"I hope it doesn't get too hot. We have already got enough problems with Brian and that dead cop at Tolkif jail. I'm going to give Conrad a call and see if he wants to head downtown and find out more about what's going on—you guys up for a walk?"

"Sure, why not—if you think it's safe. How about lunch somewhere on Chicken Street?" Dennis suggested.

"I'll come too," Tony added, still toweling his hair and shivering from his cold morning shower.

Only John demurred, preferring to wait at the apartment, and listen to the radio for more news of the coup's aftermath.

David went downstairs again and used Bagnur's phone to call Conrad.

"It must be an emergency for you to call at this hour. I didn't think you ever got up before seven," Conrad answered, crossly.

He listened as David told him of the coup.

"Well, I guess that does qualify as some sort of an emergency. I wonder what it means for Brian and Shamsher. Hopefully they are already well beyond the border. I'll meet you at your apartment in forty-five minutes, okay?"

Conrad hung up the phone and turned to the woman in his bed. Because of her early morning visit, Conrad was already well aware of the coup, and in any case he had known for months from his own contacts in Kabul that the possibility of a coup was more than just a rumor. He had not seen fit to reveal this to David, nor had he wasted much time with his bedmate on discussion of the event. He spoke to her in Farsi, and she began dressing. At the door Ameena paused. He pressed a five hundred afghani note into her hand. The woman smiled at him and pulled a dark veil over her face before stepping out into the early morning dimness.

Ten dollars was really too generous—I must be getting soft-hearted in my old age, he thought as he dressed. *Still, she does have her charms, and two children to feed besides.* He had to admit, if only to himself, that life had improved in the several months since he had met the woman.

It had started one night when he had been especially vulnerable, drinking and smoking hashish laced Turkish tobacco with Bagnur. Bagnur was Conrad's frequent business associate, though his young American friends were unaware of his close relationship with their landlord. Conrad had grown to admire the man, not only for his market acumen and honesty, but also for his generally accurate and insightful assessments of the character of many of their mutual acquaintances. Bagnur's friendship was useful in other ways too. It seemed one could arrange introductions to virtually anyone in Kabul through him, so extensive were his social connections.

"My young friend," Bagnur had asked that evening, "why is it that you are not married?"

He was not too surprised at this common Afghan query, and it was a mark of Bagnur's sensitivity that he had waited so long to bring up the question. Conrad realized how unusual it must appear for a man with his wealth—at least in this country he was considered well-off—to be unmarried.

"I was married once, but it did not work out," he lied.

"I see, and now you no longer wish to be with a woman?" Bagnur had pressed.

"No, I like women just fine," he answered quickly, not wanting Bagnur to think he preferred boys or men, as was fairly common here, but hidden and spoken of only with extreme discretion.

"It's just that I have not been able to meet any-one...suitable, and the prostitutes have not been to my taste."

Bagnur slowly drew on his cigarette and responded.

"Perhaps you would prefer a women you would not have to share with other men, yet who might not desire marriage?"

"Perhaps," Conrad had replied, and their conversation had turned to other matters.

A few days later Bagnur asked if he might bring a friend over to meet him. He showed up escorting a darkly veiled woman, and after an introduction informed him that he needed to run an errand and would be back in two hours to pick up the woman. In English he told Conrad that if the woman pleased him he should give her two hundred fifty afgahnis, about five dollars, and if she did not please, Bagnur himself would pay her. Before Conrad could protest the merchant was out the door. When he returned to his living room the woman had shed her burkha and stood facing him, a shy smile on her lovely dark face.

Ameena proved to be the perfect cure for his malaise. Widowed and a distant relative to Bagnur, she barely supported her family doing the laundry and cleaning chores for several marginally better off families. The money which Conrad gave her would go to help raise and educate her two boys. He usually saw her once a week, and always at his apartment. Only a few years earlier, and even now outside of a few Afghan cities, she would have been put to death or at least publicly condemned and ostracized for their liaison, but in this more modern section of Kabul her comings and goings, though the object of gossip in the neighborhood, were at least tolerated; but for the sake of appearances Ameena always arrived and left his apartment with a basket of Conrad's laundry.

After a quick shower Conrad dressed and started for the door. The phone rang again. This time it was Cindi Webster.

"Did you hear about the coup last night?"

"David just called with the news. We're all going down to Chahrahi Taurabaz to have lunch and get the latest gossip. Why don't you join us?"

"I've already been invited. We're all meeting at David's apartment first. Hey—have you heard from Karen? She was supposed to stay at my place last night, but she didn't show up" Cindi continued.

"I haven't the slightest idea. Maybe David knows something," he answered, but Conrad had a pretty good idea of where Karen had spent the night.

After Cindi and Conrad arrived at the apartments, the friends set off. By now the 'toilet paper bazaar' in the street below was back to normal, or even busier, the street clogged with shoppers and pedestrians. There was of course a new topic of conversation with the news of the coup, but otherwise life went on much as usual. As they walked towards the city center they saw the first indication that things were not, in fact, exactly the way they had been.

At the first major intersection on the border of Shar-I-Nau a tank bulked. Beside it, in the middle of the intersection, stood a group of armed soldiers. A crowd had assembled on the sidewalks and spilled out into the street. The mood was festive. The soldiers smiled and waved, as though they were celebrities acknowledging their fans. While they stood observing the scene with the rest of the crowd Cindi spied a dirty young girl hawking flowers. She called the urchin over and bought a small bunch of the colorful blooms.

"What the hell?" exclaimed Dennis.

Caught up in the jubilant mood of the onlookers, Cindi, holding her flowers ahead of her as a peace offering, was advancing to the soldiers. The troops, initially distrustful, relaxed and smiled widely as they allowed Cindi to place the flowers in the barrels of their weapons. The crowd roared their appreciation with cries of "Daoud Khan!"

"That was an incredibly stupid thing to do," Conrad said, after she returned and they had resumed their walk to the bazaar.

"These people are happy to get rid of that greedy King Zahir. It's a celebration—a party for the Afghans! Only the king and his supporters are in any danger. My Dad says the royal family has been bleeding the country dry for years and the people are fed up."

"You must be incredibly naive if you don't realize the Russians are behind all this, and the coup has nothing to do with the average dirt-poor Afghan. Did your father not tell you that General Daoud was the man who originally helped pave the way for Soviet military assistance back in the fifties, and that the head of both the air force and the tank corps are Russian puppets? Maybe it is true that Daoud means well, but the fact is the Russians will expect something in return for their help in getting rid of Zahir."

"Why so bitter Conrad?" asked David, surprised at the severity of his outburst.

The little group stood on the sidewalk and listened to Conrad's uncharacteristic diatribe while the stream of pedestrians broke and parted around them.

"What none of you can realize, since you have not been here as long as I have, is that this may be the end of the relatively good times in Afghanistan—for both the citizens and expats like us. The social progress of the sixties may have been set back in the States with King's assassination in sixty-eight and the Kent State massacre in sixty-nine, but here things were still improving. There has been more freedom and educational opportunities—at least in Kabul—since King Zahir created the constitutional monarchy back in sixty-four and five, than at any other time this century. Lots of women go out in public without the burqa; most folks have enough to eat; you are free to come and go as you please, and the police pretty much look the other way when it comes to drugs. Foreigners from institutions like Peace Corps and the World Health Organization get to run around the country doing their humanitarian thing—but I'm afraid all is about to change, and not for the better. If the Russians try to take too much power the conservative Islam groups will rise up, and I wouldn't want to be stuck between those two groups when the proverbial camel dung hits the fan."

"Do you think this coup will really make that much of a difference?" Dennis asked.

"I wish I were more optimistic. I came here back in sixty-nine traveling through Southern Europe and the Middle East as some of you know. I was fresh out of college, and had no idea what the hell I wanted to do next. I liked Italy and Greece but it was just too expensive to stay there on my limited budget. I was only sure of the few things I did not want to do: I wanted no part of that stupid Viet Nam mess, nor did I want to take some boring desk job or dead end assembly line work in a factory, or go back to the academic grind. In fact, the only thing I had discovered I really enjoyed was traveling, and the whole process of learning about and observing other societies and cultures first hand. Maybe it had something to do with all those National Geographic magazines I read from cover to cover when I was growing up."

"So you still haven't explained why you don't believe Afghanistan will continue to get better," David reminded him.

"I'm getting to that. Anyway, when I got to Kabul after nearly a year of being on the road, it seemed like the perfect spot. A fascinating history; a cosmopolitan city of Moslems, Hindus, Christians, and Buddhists living pretty much peacefully side by side; and just as importantly, it was and is amazingly cheap to live here, as you all know. What I did not realize until recently is how lucky I was to have been here during this particular time. It may be true that Zahir and the royal family have not improved the plight of the millions of Afghans living outside of Kabul and the major cities much, but his regime has certainly been great for the city dwellers, and for expatriates and general misfits like myself. Unfortunately I think this coup will bring an end to peace here. This General Daoud has opened a Pandora's Box. I don't think he will be able to keep the Islamic reactionary forces and the Russians from tearing each other to bits—and the citizens will be the real victims."

At this Conrad resumed walking, and the others hurried to keep up with his long stride.

"Sounds like you would do okay in Mexico or Central America," David suggested.

"Maybe so—or even parts of Indonesia or Thailand, but I've been here so long it really seems like a second home to me," he responded a little wistfully.

"It's like that for a lot of people. If they manage to make it a whole year, they have a hard time leaving," David said.

"Well, not this guy," Dennis interjected. "I'm leaving Thursday morning with Reshtina, and I don't care if I ever come back!"

"I hate to disappoint you Dennis, but you and Reshtina are probably not going anywhere right away. The airport is closed, and nobody seems to know when it will open again," Conrad remarked.

"Shit! Well, I hope it isn't closed too long."

"In the meantime there is the problem of Sartor. The longer Reshtina is here the more likely it is that Sartor will find her. He is very well connected, and has a reputation for brutality. I'm not sure how much longer she will be safe at my place, or anywhere else in Kabul," Conrad added.

At the Chicken Street bazaar they were lucky to find a window table inside one of the restaurants in spite of the bustle and crowds. Cindi and Conrad placed orders for all, being the most fluent. While they waited for the food they drank tea and watched the crowds of shoppers through the small dirty window panes of the chaikhana.

"There sure are a lot of soldiers on the street," Tony observed.

"Yeah, I wonder where they got the uniforms. They look like the rejects from Che Guevara's troops after they spent six months in the jungle," Dennis joked.

"Look at that guy! I swear he is wearing pajama bottoms with his Russian uniform jacket," David said.

"Your clothes hardly matter when you carry an AK-47," Conrad noted.

"Wait a minute—over there at that table! Isn't that Shamsher—and Brian?" Cindi exclaimed, pointing at a group of tables under the awning of an adjacent restaurant.

"Jesus, you're right—what the fuck!" Conrad said, standing up suddenly.

As Conrad and his friends started towards the door, a stranger dressed in western clothing rapidly approached the table where Shamsher and Brian were seated, momentarily blocking their view of the two men.

CHAPTER 25

Brian And Cecil

By the time Captain Cecil Ramsy had showered and dressed on the morning of the coup d'état Paul Sherman had already been up for three hours. Earlier, after hearing the news of the coup from agent Green, Paul had placed calls to several of his other contacts and had been briefed in more detail on the latest developments.

"Good morning Cecil—how did you sleep?" Paul said as Cecil emerged freshly shaven and florid-faced from the bathroom.

"Like a rock. What's the plan today?"

"The news is that there was a coup last night, and we will be dealing with a new regime here. It seems General Daoud, who was at one time prime minister under the present king, decided to take advantage of the fact that the king was out of the country. My sources tell me that with the help of the Russians and the loyalty of most of the military, he managed to pull it all off in one night and has already consolidated his position."

"So what does it mean for us?" Cecil asked, toweling his wet hair.

"I don't believe it will affect Americans here much, if that's what you mean. General Daoud has always tried to maintain ties with both the West and the Soviets, and he's a well-educated progressive like the previous king, to whom he is related. As far as I know the only resistance was the king's palace guard, and it was not too violent an affair as such things go. I'm not sure how this will affect us as far as finding Mr. Peccanter. I don't yet know if there are travel restrictions, and I have no idea if this new government will be in any position to help us locate him. They probably have their hands full at the moment. Anyway, I still think he has left the country—he's probably hundreds of miles away by now."

Regardless of Paul's opinion that their quarry was no longer in Kabul, Cecil was not so certain, and was determined to search the city. He had not traveled this far and put up with so much discomfort to simply leave without checking things out for himself. He could sense a certain lack of enthusiasm in his old friend's attitude towards the manhunt. Paul had other more important duties here. He had made up his mind the day before that his friend was simply too busy to focus the time and energy needed on the hunt.

After Cecil had morning coffee and his usual eye opener they caught a taxi to the US embassy, in hopes of finding more leads on Peccanter's whereabouts, as well as updates on the new Afghan government. There was little reliable news. Some whisperings that Iran might support the old regime, but no indication of a counter coup, or even a statement from King Zahir, safely ensconced in his villa in Italy. A curious rumor about a US citizen joining in the attack at the king's palace seemed incongruous. After a stop at the USAID compound bar, where Cecil had his obligatory mid-morning double vodka and tonic, the two friends continued on to the Chicken Street bazaar.

"This is as good a place as any to grab an early lunch if you're hungry," Paul said as they entered the lively public market.

"If we can find a spot. It looks pretty busy," Cecil observed.

They finally did manage to find a table on the sidewalk outside of a restaurant that catered to foreign tourists and expatriates. The waiter knew just enough English to help them order beef kabobs, rice, and tea.

They watched the milling crowd, and Cecil smoked while they waited for their meal. Looking down the busy sidewalk, Captain Ramsy eyed a knot of ragged looking uniformed men idling in front of another tea house. His eye was drawn to two men in western dress, sitting at a table to one side of the soldiers. Something seemed familiar about one of the two men.

A garrulous, long-bearded Afghan at the neighboring table gestured expansively, accidentally whacking the side of Paul's head as he did so. Paul turned to him and the mortified man began apologizing in a torrent of deferential Pashtu. Paul's grasp of the Pashtun language was limited, but he was able to reassure the man with his better command of Farsi. When Paul finally turned back, Cecil was already walking purposefully away. He saw a flurry of motion, heard angry words and saw the group of Afghan soldiers move back. As they backed away, Brian Peccanter stepped into the street. Cecil followed closely behind, with his gun at Brian's back.

"Nice and easy and no funny stuff—or else! I'm only looking for the smallest excuse to pull this trigger," the captain told Brian as he nudged him along.

"Help us!" Shamsher shouted in Pashtu to the group of soldiers standing nearby. "He is kidnapping the young American who was with us at the palace, and was wounded helping our revolutionary forces!"

"Yes, it is true—that is the man! General Daoud himself praised the foreigner!" cried one of the soldiers, recognizing the American from earlier that morning.

Seaman Peccanter had no intention of waiting for Shamsher's or anyone else's help. As the soldiers surged forward and Paul watched helplessly, Brian, hoping to catch the captain off guard, twisted slightly and hammered Ramsy's's wrist with the side of his hand. The gun went off. The shot pierced Brian's back and traveled in a downward spiral through several vital organs before finally exiting at his groin. He toppled to his hands and knees, then slowly collapsed face forward to the pavement. With a roar the crowd fell upon Captain Ramsy, wresting the gun from his hand and throwing him to the ground.

The friends watched helplessly as Karen ran to her boyfriend. She held Brian, sobbing as she felt his life ebb away in her arms, oblivious to the actions of the swirling crowd surrounding them, who beat and kicked Cecil Ramsy as he struggled vainly to dodge their blows.

As his consciousness faded, Brian, lying in the hot dusty street, smiled slightly. He felt no pain. His entire universe contracted to Karen's angelic face, with her halo of copper hair hovering above him. It was the last thing he saw before it all faded into everlasting blackness.

Paul stood by impotently. The fates of both men were out of his hands now. *All was for nothing,* he thought bitterly. *All my best efforts and intentions—too little and too late.*

As if to confirm his worst fears, Karen looked up at that instant. Paul was unable to avoid her accusing gaze. Even through her tears of grief the look of hostility was unmistakable. He knew she blamed him at least partly for her lover's death, if only because he had been the reason Brian's killer had come to Kabul.

"I'm so sorry Karen. I couldn't stop him," was all he could say.

Continuing to hold the lifeless body of her boyfriend, Karen bowed her head and surrendered to her emotions, sobbing quietly as the tears flowed down her cheeks.

Meanwhile another soldier, whose uniform and bearing identified him as an officer, waded into the mob. Shouting orders and brandishing a large pistol, he managed to disperse the angry crowd before they could beat the American captain to death. The officer, a big scowling man with a commanding presence, countenancing no interference from the still agitated but now somewhat more restrained onlookers, forced the bruised and battered Captain Ramsy at gun point into a nearby military vehicle.

"We must keep this murdering infidel alive for a while longer yet, and submit his fate to the judgement of Daoud Khan himself! Stand back!" the officer insisted.

The army vehicle drove slowly away, horn blaring as it carved a path through the unruly throng.

"I need to speak with you—all of you, about this," Paul said, stepping closer to Shamsher and Conrad, and turning away from Karen and Brian, who had been left to themselves in the street with Tony and Dennis while the crowd's attentions focused on Captain Ramsy and his Afghan captor.

Conrad and Paul both needed to conceal their relationship. They continued to take the greatest care to avoid any hint of familiarity with the others present.

"What can you do or say? This is no longer any of your affair. You got what you wanted in any case. Why don't you just crawl back into whatever filthy hole you came out of," Conrad replied, hoping he was not over-playing his part.

In fact Conrad was still ambivalent about Paul Sherman. Although Paul had told him in their earlier conversation that he was beginning to believe in Brian's innocence, Conrad could not be sure that he had not been manipulated by the more experienced agent.

"Please—I know what you think of me, and perhaps you are even correct in believing that I bear some responsibility for this, but I never intended for things to turn out this way. It was my intention to help Mr. Peccanter get a fair trial."

"These people who beat Mr. Brian's killer might wish to show you some of the same, if I only say the words to them," Shamsher said. There was steely menace in his eyes and his hand moved towards the knife he always carried.

"Look," Paul said, speaking quickly, as he carefully observed Shamsher's body language.

"Captain Ramsy's fate—the man who shot your friend—is obviously not going to be pleasant, and is certainly beyond our control, but Mr. Peccanter's reputation and the truth of what he witnessed is another matter. I can help you with this, and I want to."

"Listen," he continued. "I know Mr.Peccanter's story, and I have come to believe it. It's true I was sent here to arrest him and take him back to a court martial, but I am now convinced he was innocent—especially now—and the least I can do is to help his family."

"What the hell can you do? He's dead!" Dennis exclaimed.

"What I can do is this: I will arrange to have him flown back to the states for a proper military funeral. I will use my influence to have his case investigated and his name cleared. I'm sorry I was not able to prevent his death, but clearing his name will make a difference to his family and friends. I'm sure that Captain Ramsy will be freed in spite of what the Afghan officer said. He's well connected, and our embassy will most likely intercede on his behalf. When that happens I give you my word that I will make sure the captain is investigated and convicted of his crimes."

"May your captain die like a rat in the Kabul jail! He will not last too long there—some one person will see to that!" Shamsher declared, and spit onto the street.

"That would be a kind of justice I suppose, but believe me, it will not work out that way. If I don't get custody of him he will be sprung from that jail very quickly. Captain Ramsy has powerful connections in Kabul and plenty of money for baksheesh. If I don't get him back to the states for trial he may never pay for what he has done here today, or his atrocities in Viet Nam."

"Let's just calm down for a minute, Shamsher. We should think about this. What if he is right? What do you think, Conrad?" David interjected.

"I hate to say it, but he is probably right. As a high ranking officer that captain will have the embassy demanding his release, and General Daoud probably will not risk pissing off the Americans to keep him in prison for long. I know it's tough, but we can either trust this man, or run the risk that bastard Ramsy gets away with everything."

"What do we have besides your word on it?" David said, turning to Paul.

"For one thing, I have already arranged to have Reshtina and Dennis on the next available flight out of Kabul, and I have secured a visa for Reshtina. Those documents are at my hotel room, and you are welcome to have them as proof of my sincere intentions. I'm also willing to put my suspicions about Captain Ramsy into writing if that is what it takes to gain your trust here. Regardless, we don't have a lot of time, and unless you have a better idea, I need to get custody of Ramsy, before he is set free and spirited out of the country."

CHAPTER 26

General Daoud

I feel the happiest when I can light my American cigarette with Soviet matches.
—President Sartor Mohammed Daoud, July 30, 1973

After a short wait in the anteroom Paul was ushered into the large ornate office, so recently occupied by King Zahir, General Daoud's uncle and brother-in-law, but now the prerogative of the general. Sartor Mohammed Daoud Khan looked up from the immense desk and rose to offer his hand to Paul. The general was an impressive looking though slight man in his early sixties, bald and clean-shaven, with heavy dark eyebrows and a raptor nose. He was dressed in a well tailored suit and silk tie.

"I am sorry to keep you waiting for so long," he greeted Paul in French, though the wait had been no more than ten minutes at most.

In the waiting room Paul Sherman had been informed that Daoud, though multilingual, having been educated in France, preferred that language to all others. Paul, for his part, spoke the language reasonably well, though not as fluently as Daoud.

"You must understand it is a hectic time for me," the new ruler of Afghanistan continued with a smile, spreading his hands to indicate the disarray of the desk, which was cluttered with file folders and loose paper.

"Thank you so much for taking the time to see me, especially with such short notice," Paul responded deferentially.

"It is, I am afraid, a delicate matter—a most unfortunate thing. You see of course, in my situation I cannot afford to begin by offending your government either through action or inaction on my part. Would you care for a cigarette?" he asked, offering Paul a pack of Gitanes.

"Thank you, but I do not smoke," Paul replied.

"A bad habit indeed, but perhaps not the worst a man can have. What did your great writer Mr. Twain say? One should have a few bad habits in order to have something to give up if necessary, for otherwise one should simply become ill and die—but the man with a few bad habits can give up something and perhaps recover! You see, I am a great admirer of your frontier writers, Mr. Sherman. Ah—a noble name! Are you some relation to the great general of America's war to free the slaves?"

"Not that I am aware of. It is a common enough surname in America," Paul replied.

"I wonder how your wise namesake would have handled this situation? You see, I have looked into this matter personally. I have a communication from your officials informing me a Mr. Peccanter was wanted for various serious crimes against your government. Yet this same Mr. Peccanter, whom I gratefully thanked afterwards, was wounded in helping my soldiers overcome King Zahir's guards, and now has apparently been murdered by your American Navy captain, whom we now have under guard. To the people—the supporters of the revolution—your Mr. Peccanter is a hero, even a martyr! Yet I have been assured by these same communications that your country will be most displeased if anything were to happen to your Captain Ramsy, apparently the same man who has killed the unfortunate Mr. Peccanter. Is my information on this matter accurate in your estimation, Mr. Sherman?"

"You are correct, and I believe I understand your predicament, general," Paul replied.

"Perhaps you do after all, for my contacts tell me you have some experience in these sensitive matters of state, and that you have some authority to speak for your government here. I have also been informed you were in Afghanistan to find and arrest Mr. Peccanter. Is this also true?"

"It is. But I would be less than honest with you, general, if I did not tell you I have some doubts about Mr. Peccanter's guilt."

"But I understand this Captain Ramsy is in fact a friend of yours," the general said, gazing intently at Paul.

Paul wondered who the new ruler's informant was. He could not think of anyone at the embassy who would have revealed such information. He surmised Daoud himself or one of his advisors must have spoken to Cecil. The general certainly had done his homework.

"You are indeed very well informed, Mr. President."

"Yes, a most awkward and difficult matter—not an easy case at all," the general continued.

He rotated in the heavy wooden office chair away from Paul, and gazed for a moment out the window, as if trying to draw inspiration from the bright sun's illumination of the courtyard, before turning back to face Paul again.

"It seems to me significant that today is my birthday. I am now sixty-four years old. Too young perhaps to have the wisdom of an old man, for I might have continued to enjoy the comforts and pleasures of life in Europe, and stayed away from this troublesome land. Perhaps you know my father was assassinated many years ago by political enemies. I am still young enough to feel the need to accomplish one more thing in life, and to take joy in life's pleasures, but I am not unaware of the risks. I had hoped to spend part of this day celebrating the beginning of a new era for our country as well as my birth date, but I see I cannot escape for even an hour the demands and worries of my new office."

He inhaled deeply from his cigarette and exhaled again with a sigh of resignation before continuing.

"Perhaps our security is not so very good as yet," he continued, looking deliberately at the American agent and arching his distinctive eyebrows.

"We may not have sufficient police or the means to closely guard a man of the captain's resourcefulness and determination. It might be best if he could be escorted out of Afghanistan in a timely manner. The airport is not yet open to commercial flights, but the main roads have been secured and are safe for travel. We can arrange it so the captain is transferred to your responsibility without interference later tonight. We cannot guarantee his safety or protect him from the wrath of my soldiers should he be recognized in the days ahead. The sooner he is in the custody of yourself or other American authorities, the better, of course. Do we understand one another?" the general said, stubbing out his cigarette and rising to signal the interview had ended.

"Congratulations on your birthday, general, and may you have many more. You can count on me to handle this quietly and quickly, as you advise. I appreciate your candor and sensitivity. I believe you are the new leader Afghanistan has been hoping for," Paul replied, standing up quickly to take the ruler's proffered handshake.

Although he by habit spoke with formality and tact from long experience of dealing with government officials, Paul found himself actually believing his own words. His first impression of General Daoud was of an intelligent, urbane, and politically astute individual—

personable and even charismatic. Just as importantly, he appeared to have a sense of humor, which seemed to Paul to be an important signifier of an adaptable and adroit politician.

"Let us hope you are right. My assistant will arrange for the captain's transfer to your custody. Good luck to you Mr. Sherman," the general said in parting.

To Paul general Daoud seemed to be an improvement over the previous ruler, King Zahir, who it was well known had no real interest in the country, except as a convenient source of income. Of course Paul was aware from his intelligence sources that this latest leader had a love of extravagant parties, a fondness for young women, and a habit of nepotism when it came to allocating high or well-paying offices. But then he was no different in those respects than many, perhaps the majority of powerful men Paul had dealt with. As to hubris, he also seemed no worse than most in his position, and perhaps a certain amount of hauteur might be necessary in a country long inured to the rule of royalty. Daoud, he knew, was a first cousin of the king he had deposed, and married to that former ruler's sister. He was also a member of the powerful Durrani clan, which had ruled Afghanistan for over two hundred years.

A uniformed man entered the office, ushering Paul back into the waiting room.

CHAPTER 27

Another Taxi Ride

Paul had been instructed by General Daoud's representative to pick Captain Cecil Ramsy up at the prison at two AM. Flying was out of the question, as the general had pointed out. Since the coup all Ariana Airline's flights had been cancelled, and no one seemed to know when the airport would once again be open for commercial flights. Regardless, a daytime flight would have been too risky, for there was the danger that Captain Ramsy might be recognized at the airport. So, as Daoud's advisor had recommended, Paul had arranged for an early morning taxi ride through the Khyber Pass and into Pakistan. Once there, they could catch a flight back to the states from Peshawar.

At the exterior prison gate he was met by a military officer, apparently of high rank, and an interpreter. After the briefest of greetings and an identification check he was led to the same cellblock where Brian Peccanter had earlier been held. Coincidentally, Cecil now occupied the very same cell that had been Brian's only a few score hours earlier.

"Jesus, it's about time you got here!" Cecil exclaimed when he saw the men.

"I got here as quickly as I could, Cecil. It is too dangerous to have you out in the daylight," Paul answered.

His friend looked terrible—bruised, scratched, disheveled, and dissipated. It had been way too many hours since his last drink.

The gaoler unlocked the cell. Cecil Ramsy exited, turning and spitting into the cell as he left.

"Really Cecil, is that necessary," Paul said.

"Damn right. Fuck these towel-heads! I haven't even had a meal since I got here. The fuckers tried to feed me dog food or worse! I can't eat that crap. I had to piss in a bucket, for Christ's sake!"

"Just can the bullshit until we are out of here, if you want to survive this, Cecil. You are not in the best of positions. You have no status or authority in this country, and if it were not for our connections at the embassy and the new ruler's wish to get off to a good start with us, you'd be a maggot buffet by now. As things stand, I only just managed to get the authorities here to look the other way for a few hours—hopefully time enough for us to make it to the Pakistan border."

The taxi they took had been rented at an exorbitant rate. Local drivers seldom went far from Kabul, rarely at night, especially now with the added uncertainty of the coup. The Khyber Pass was a long drive, steep in places, with a reputation for being hard on vehicles—especially brakes. Only by offering the equivalent of better than three months worth of normal fares had Paul been able to negotiate a cab to the border.

"Well, the sooner we're over the border the better. I can't wait to see the last of this country," Cecil said as the cab headed out of Kabul.

The moon shed its weak cold silver light on the empty streets and dark buildings as they left the city, and made their way to the Kabul-Jalalabad highway.

"So far so good, but we can expect to hit a couple of check-points on the way. Things will take a while to settle down I'm sure. There could even still be pockets of resistance to General Daoud and his new regime," Paul remarked.

They drove on for some time in silence through the outskirts of Kabul. Their driver was competent, and the taxi, a newer model Toyota, was in better shape than most Paul had experienced here.

"Well, when we do get to Peshawar we will have to part ways. I need to get on back to my ship. I've been away too long as it is, and now that things are settled I should get back to my duties," Cecil remarked.

They had progressed to the very outermost fringes of the city, where the farmland began.

"What? Cecil, you of course know you are technically under arrest! You will be going when and where I take you. What the hell do you think—you can just shoot a man in the street and then go on about your business as if nothing has happened?"

"I hoped you might see it differently, Paul. I did what I did for the good of our country, and I thought you might understand that what happened was all for the best. The court-martial would have sentenced him to death or life in prison anyway. We go back a long way, Paul. I don't suppose I can persuade you to see it my way—for old times sake if nothing else?"

Paul got a glimpse of Cecil's face as they passed under an isolated street light at a desolate intersection. His expression was grim, and there were beads of perspiration on his face, though the temperature in the back seat of the taxi was cool.

"Come on Cecil, you know I can't just let you walk away from this thing. You will have to hope the courts agree with you when we get back state-side. There is no point in bringing our friendship into this. I can't condone your actions, and I'm not even sure if I believe your story about the late Mr. Peccanter's supposed crimes. I heard an entirely different story from him, and if what he said is true, you should be the one behind bars."

"If that's really what you think, then I guess this is the end of our friendship. It's too bad—I thought that after all these years and all I've done for you, you might have given me a little more benefit of the doubt, and perhaps given my word more credibility than some fucking stranger you had only known for what—a few hours? I killed a traitor and a deserter, and also saved the taxpayers the expense of a trial! An officer has the right and duty to make life and death decisions in time of war!"

"I wish it was that simple Cecil, but this is not the battlefield, and you have no authority or special status here. You ruined any remaining credibility you had when you murdered Peccanter. I'm afraid the courts will have to decide your fate."

"In that case I'm going to ask you to tell the driver to stop this car. I'll have to go on from here without you."

Cecil produced a short-barreled pistol—the same weapon Paul had discovered earlier in his friend's luggage, the revolver he had killed Peccanter with— and aimed it at Paul's chest.

"Don't try anything Paul. We may no longer be friends, but I would hate to have to shoot you, but I will if I have to. Tell the driver to stop the car. I'm sorry, but you'll have to walk back or find another ride to your hotel."

Paul silently cursed himself for not searching Cecil in his haste to get away from the prison and Kabul before daylight.

Cecil must have somehow bribed one of the guards to get his weapon back—or had General Daoud or someone in his administration double crossed him?

Paul thought quickly before speaking to the driver in Farsi, a language he spoke with reasonable facility and which Cecil understood not at all.

"The man is pointing a gun at me. He will kill us both if you do not do exactly as I say. Slow down now and pull over to the side of the road. When I start to open my door you must accelerate very quickly. Do you understand?"

"I will do as you say. May Allah protect us!"

"What the hell did you say to him?" Cecil asked suspiciously as the car slowed to a stop.

"I told him to stop the car—I have to take a piss —which is in fact true," Paul replied.

The taxi pulled over on the narrow shoulder and slowed to a stop.

"Okay now—out of the car—no funny business! I'm sorry it had to end this way Paul—I really am."

As Paul pulled the handle and opened the door Cecil cocked the pistol. At that instant, as Paul had directed him to, the driver revved the engine and popped the clutch. The gun discharged, but Cecil was thrown back by the acceleration of the taxi. He shot wide and high. Paul barely felt the bullet as it grazed his neck and smashed through the car roof. They struggled together briefly and the gun went off again. Paul watched as Cecil convulsed briefly from the effects of the .38 caliber slug, which had passed through his right eye and exited through the top of his head. Blood and brain matter dripped from the ceiling of the taxi and back onto Cecil Ramsy's convulsing body. The quick-witted taxi driver, who had pulled off the road again as the two men struggled, watched in horror.

"There is no reason to continue on, but I of course will pay you the agreed fare," Paul told the driver when Cecil's death throes had ceased.

"We will have to take the body back to Kabul. Come now, there is not a moment to be lost. We must get there before it is light!" Paul insisted.

The pistol was now in Paul Sherman's hand, and the frightened driver was in no mood to argue. They were soon safe within the large gated compound of the home of Paul's most trusted Agency contact in Kabul; a man whom Paul, since his recent promotion now officially outranked, but who for the most part operated independently, and who had much more experience in Afghanistan and Central Asia than did Paul. Paul was not even sure who the man, known to him only as 'Bill Green' reported to in the Agency's byzantine chain of command.

Together they moved the begored body into a small tool shed. The taxi driver was sent away with a large wad of greenbacks and a warning to keep his mouth shut.

"My God Paul, this is a hell of a mess!" Mr. Green exclaimed.

They were both soaked with perspiration from the effort of moving Cecil's lifeless body, even though the sun had not yet risen above the mountains and the morning was still cool.

"Couldn't you have just taken him out somewhere in the desert and buried him, or let the vultures do their job? My instructions are to help you out in any way I can, but this—Jesus Christ! I hope you know what the hell you are doing!"

Mr. Green—over sixty, balding, out of shape and twenty pounds overweight—wiped his dripping face with the sleeve of his bathrobe, which he had hurriedly thrown on when the sound of the gate alarm had awakened him. One side of the blue terrycloth robe was now stained purple with the dead man's blood.

"Cecil was an old friend. I want him flown home to a proper funeral in the States. I want his family to think he died honorably in the service of his country. He has a wife and three children. Make up any story you have to. I know you have the authority and the connections. That's why I brought him here."

"Well, it seems you are the man in charge here now, though why anyone would want to be in command of such a fucked-up mess is beyond me. I can certainly get a sealed casket and some dry ice, and arrange to have him flown back as soon as the airport reopens. As for the rest—best just to say the cause of death is classified and in the line of duty. Maybe you can tell me the real story inside. I don't usually drink before noon, let alone before breakfast, but I'm going to make an exception this morning, and I would advise you to join me. Anyway you can't go out looking like that in public. You had better come in and clean up at the very least."

Agent Sherman followed Agent Green into the house. Paul became aware of a stinging sensation. He reached up to his neck where a scab was beginning to form over the place where the bullet had only just nicked him. A fraction of an inch over and he would have been breakfast for the vultures, and the late Cecil

Ramsy might have been safely away. He did not feel at all fortunate though, only a conflicting mixture of sorrow, regret, and relief; as though his old friend had finally died after a lengthy, debilitating, and incurable disease.

CHAPTER 28

The Zealot

Through the embassy Paul Sherman and Mr. Green did arrange refrigerated storage of both Brian and Cecil's corpses until they could be shipped home for burial. General Daoud's new administration had plenty of more pressing concerns to deal with, and was willing to ignore the fact that two murders had been committed on Afghan soil by foreigners, in exchange for a certain amount of intelligence on the PDPA, which Mr. Green, at Paul Sherman's urging, provided. They were easily persuaded that the deaths were matters of concern only to the United States government. Moreover, there were those in the Kabul police department who felt justice had been served in the case of the dead policeman by Brian Peccanter's death. The dead police officer's family were also satisfied with the morality of the eye for an eye retribution, but there were those in the military who would always remember the unlikely American hero of General Daoud's overnight coup.

The airport was scheduled to open again July 21. Paul had arranged for himself, Dennis, Reshtina, and the remains of the two men to be on the same flight. They would travel first to Istanbul, then to Rome, and finally to Frankfurt before changing planes and departing to London and Washington DC, where Paul would turn the bodies over to a naval officer.

Dennis and Reshtina's friends arranged another party—a combined bon voyage celebration for the couple and wake for Brian Peccanter—for the evening before their flight. Paul had also been invited to attend. He had been especially moved by the invitation. He suspected Conrad had made the suggestion, but he knew the group could have excluded him and had not, and that is what mattered.

The USAID bar was the logical choice. The bar was busy. A local rock band, "The Lumberjacks," made up of a group of expatriate Americans, was slated to play. There was an air of celebration now that it was clear things were getting back to normal in the city.

It was a bittersweet gathering—the last night that the group of friends who had experienced so much in the past few weeks would be all together in Kabul. Conrad thought it just as well that the music and crowd were so loud it was not possible to have a real conversation. He feared any talk would run the risk of becoming melancholy and maudlin. The women—Karen, Aletheia, Reshtina, Cindi, and several more he did not know, all danced with each other song after song, and periodically one or another of the men would join them in a drunken dervish. Even Paul, not a fan of rock and roll or the new style of free-form tribal dancing, joined good-naturedly in the fun for several songs. The band blasted through exuberant renditions of the Rolling Stones, Beatles, Chuck Berry, and The Animals, for their ecstatic and uncritical audience.

David, Dennis, and Tony quickly became drunk, but Paul, Shamsher, and Conrad were more circumspect. Conrad was especially reticent, only nursing a couple of drinks. He was worried about Reshtina and felt he had to remain on his guard. Two nights earlier his lover, Ameena, had reported that she thought she was being followed as she made her way to his apartment. She had seen the same man, in traditional Afghan dress but wearing dark glasses and tennis shoes, three different times on her way there. Of course she could be mistaken, or it could have been one of the hordes of spies that infested the city out on an entirely different errand, but Conrad's intuition was that it probably did have something to do with Sartor, Reshtina's would-be fiancé.

It was past one in the morning when their group finally left the bar. Karen and Cindi, arm and arm, led the way singing "Day Dream Believer" by The Monkees at the top of their lungs. Dennis and Reshtina lagged behind the rest, talking of the arrangements for their flight out, now only hours away. As they exited the compound Conrad saw a quick movement behind a nearby tree. Suddenly a man, face masked by a scarf, came running at them. Shouting curses in Pashtu he threw liquid from a plastic container at Reshtina. She cried out as the acid burned through her clothing, but fortunately she had turned slightly at hearing the stranger's shouted insults and the fluid, instead of hitting her face as he intended, splashed on her shoulder and back. The man dropped the container and sprinted off down the dimly lit street.

"Get her back into the building—get her coat off and call the doctor!" Paul instructed the group as he herded them back to the bar.

Paul had drawn his Beretta. Once the others were inside he enlisted the aid of the lone night watchmen, and began to methodically search the compound grounds.

Conrad immediately raced after the assailant. The man, whoever he was, ran well. He was young and fit, and for a time Conrad thought he might get away, but after his rapid initial sprint the attacker's pace gradually slowed, and Conrad began to gain. They ran several blocks into a darker and older neighborhood, with no streetlights, and only the occasional porch or gate light illuminated intermittently small segments of the streets. The neighborhood was quiet and deserted at this hour. The only sound was the rapid slapping of their shoes on the pavement. The man obviously hoped to lose Conrad in this labyrinth quarter of the city, but Conrad paced him tenaciously.

After several minutes both men were nearly out of breath and tiring, however Conrad had closed to within a few yards of Reshtina's assailant. Mustering the last of his strength, the man cut though a small park, made a desperate leap to clear a low hedge and missed his footing, falling hard onto the pavement beyond.

Conrad was on top of him instantly, pinning him down, with his knife pressed against the man's neck.

"Did Sartor send you! Speak now or I will slice open your jugular this instant!" Conrad panted in Pashtu.

He was nearly overcome with a fierce upwelling of rage which rose up suddenly and seemed to take brief possession of him, along with a compelling urge to plunge the knife into the youth's exposed neck, but the sensation passed quickly, and Conrad regained his composure. He needed to find out if, as he suspected, Sartor was really behind the attack, or if the attacker was motivated only by his fanatical beliefs.

"No one sent me. It is the will of Allah! She goes in public without covering her face—in the company of infidels!"

The voice sounded familiar. Conrad ripped the scarf from the man's face. It was one of the young fanatics of the Muslim Youth Organization. He did not know the man personally, but had seen and heard him speak on the campus of the Kabul University more than once. He was one of a group of radicals who regularly held forth on the necessity of returning to a severe and puritanical version of Islam.

"I ask you again, why this particular woman when so many in Kabul go without the Burqa. Did Sartor send you?"

This time Conrad emphasized his question by lightly slicing open the man's cheek. The man opened his mouth to scream, but Conrad pushed the knife into his throat until the blood oozed again.

"If you scream you are dead. For the last time answer my question!"

"It is as you say. Sartor did send me, but she deserves her fate—they all do, and worse! As Allah commands, I obey!"

"And just where is Sartor tonight?" Conrad continued, putting slightly more pressure on the knife.

"He has gone to the woman's apartment to await my arrival. That woman was promised to him, but she has whored herself to an infidel. Sartor knows that she deserves death, but he will be satisfied with her disfigurement, as a warning to all Afghan women who ignore the Koran and the true words of the prophet!"

"How much money did he promise you?"

"I would not do such a thing for money—my reward shall be in heaven!"

"Then you should not object to collecting your reward today!" Conrad replied.

He pushed the knife all the way through the man's neck and out the other side, cutting through the arteries, windpipe, and bone with the sharp blade. The dying man gurgled and coughed blood. The warm liquid spouted from his neck and ran onto the pavement and into the shallow drainage ditch. Some spilled on Conrad's shirt and pants. The man shuddered a last time and was still.

Several times in his past Conrad had been involved in violent altercations, and on at least two of those occasions his attackers had landed in hospital emergency rooms, but he had never killed before, and he was surprised how little emotion he experienced at the act. He knew only that if he had let the man live more women and girls—who knew how many more—would be disfigured for life by this madman.

Conrad felt he had been an agent of justice and the fates, and that somehow he had been in the right place at the right time—both to exact this vengeance for Reshtina (for he had given chase without knowing that her attacker had not succeeded in getting any of the fluid on her face), and to prevent the young zealot from disfiguring yet more women. Either reason by itself would have been enough motivation for him to kill the maniac; together they were absolutely compelling. Conrad rolled the body under the thick hedge that had tripped up the fanatic, looked carefully around to be sure he had not been observed, and left the scene by another route. He wanted to get to Sartor before the man got wind of his villainous emissary's fate.

While Conrad was occupied with his lethal errand, the women hurried Reshtina into the bathroom. On the way inside they removed her jacket, as Paul had insisted. They helped her with her light sweater and blouse. Fortunately very little of the acid had penetrated the layers of her clothing, and she had escaped with only some minor burns to her shoulder and arm. The women rinsed her thoroughly, and decided there was no need to call the doctor. The bartender, though he had already locked up, had let them back in immediately after Paul placed an impressive looking badge against the door window. He had provided an emergency first aid kit from behind the counter, which they used to treat and bandage Reshtina's scattering of small blisters.

The band members were still packing up their gear and finishing their final drinks. One of the men came up to the group. Joe Tipoplo, the drummer, and David were casually acquainted. They knew each other mostly from previous encounters at the bar, and parties at the homes of other expats.

"Hey what's going on—what happened to her?" he asked nodding towards Reshtina, who was now sitting at one of the tables quietly sobbing, while the women and Dennis did their best to comfort her.

"Someone threw acid on her," David answered.

"Is she okay?"

"Luckily he missed her face—just superficial burns, but of course she's really shaken and upset."

"Shit—that just happened last week to my housekeeper's daughter! She was coming back from Salim's. She lost an eye and her face is destroyed. What a fucking tragedy! She was a beauty—only eighteen and a student at Kabul University. I've heard it is the Islamists. They say it is just a few young fanatics doing it, but the leaders don't discourage it—the bastards!"

"I've heard the same. I hope their movement doesn't take hold. It would be a big step backwards for Afghanistan," David replied.

"I'm glad she was not badly hurt. I hope this new president, Daoud can get those people under control before they do any more damage. Kabul used to be pretty nice in its own way, but I'm not so sure anymore. I'm starting to think it might be time to move on. Great thing about playing in this part of the world is that there are so few rock bands, you can always find a paying gig at places like this. The rich folks hire too, because they want all their friends to see how hip they are to modern music and styles. Shit, we make five times the money here we ever could back home, and it's a lot cheaper to live besides."

"Well, for what it's worth, you guys sounded great tonight," David offered.

"Thanks, but if so, it wasn't because we or the crowd stayed sober—but I'm glad you enjoyed the music. The guys are waiting for me. I'll see you around David. I'm really glad your friend is okay."

The band members left carrying guitar cases and miscellaneous musical gear. David joined the rest of his friends, who had gathered together around the same table.

"We are trying to figure out if Conrad will come back here or go on home," Tony said, as David approached.

"It seems like he's been gone quite a while. I wonder if he caught that man?" David answered.

"Man—that was no man! Only a chicken-shit mother-fucker attacks women! He's no man at all—just a rabid cur that should be put out of his misery for everyone's sake! I hope Conrad catches him and sticks his Koran up his ass!" Dennis exclaimed.

"Allah willing," Tony quipped caustically.

"I do not believe he acted alone or strictly because of his fanatical views," Reshtina said. She had recovered her composure for the most part and ceased her sobbing.

"What do you mean?" Paul asked.

"I'm sure Sartor is behind this. It could have only been him who gave that man directions to find me tonight!"

"If that is true you may not be out of danger yet. We can only hope that crazy bastard thinks he was successful in his cowardly errand tonight. Even so, you should not be left alone until the plane leaves tomorrow," Tony offered, and the others agreed vociferously.

The friends decided, after a last round of drinks to calm their nerves, that it was time to go. The relieved and well-tipped barkeep was happy to usher the group out into the night a second time. Conrad would show up when and where he wanted, they all concurred. Although Reshtina had a key to Conrad's apartment it was decided she should spend the night at Cindi's home. Since the attacker had obviously known Reshtina was at the USAID complex, and they had no idea if or how Conrad had dealt with him, they reasoned the thug could still be at large, and might also know the location of Conrad's flat.

Although Paul too was disturbed by the turn of events, he was even more concerned with Conrad's activities and whereabouts. He was not sure what to expect from his new recruit. He was well aware that the young agent was capable of violence. Paul fretted that Conrad might compromise his usefulness for the Agency here if the Muslim Youth learned his identity. Paul was not much concerned with what Conrad did to the attacker, as long as he did not jeopardize his role as an informant and intelligence agent. He figured the acid tossing radical deserved whatever happened to him if Conrad caught up with him. On the other hand, Paul mused, the Communists and Islamists were mutually distrustful and more and more at odds, and Conrad might still be useful for gathering information with one group even if he fell out of favor with the other.

Before catching a taxi outside of the USAID compound Paul got directions from Reshtina to her apartment, where she believed the corpulent culprit, Sartor, must be waiting for her to return for the rest of her possessions. Paul's hunch was that Conrad would go after Sartor after he had dealt with the acid tosser, and he hoped he might be able to intercept him, and talk him out of any imprudent action he might be contemplating.

Paul's dossier on Conrad Slocum had detailed several incidents during Conrad's school years which had resulted in problems with authorities, although Conrad had never been charged with any crime, and had somehow managed to avoid any serious legal problems. Paul had no doubt that his new protege would not hesitate to take violent action if he thought it necessary or justified, and this was definitely such a time.

Paul's timing was perfect. Only a few blocks from Reshtina's apartment he saw the dark form of a man walking, obviously avoiding the light as much as possible, yet proceeding at a normal pace in order not to draw undue attention to himself. Paul ordered the driver to stop and stepped quickly out of the taxi.

"Slocum—stop!" he hissed. "Think about it! You will have another better opportunity!"

"Stop what?" Conrad replied nonchalantly.

"You know what I am talking about. I'm pretty sure I have some idea of what you intend, but why not wait for a more opportune time. Reshtina is safe and uninjured. She will be on that plane and out of Kabul tomorrow—entirely out of Sartor's reach."

"Safe?" Conrad hesitated.

"The acid missed her face. She's fine, and staying at the Webster house tonight. Why not call it a night? It's late."

"Or early, depending on your point of view I suppose," Conrad replied. "But you are correct about one thing. My rendezvous with fatso can wait a little while longer."

He joined Paul in the taxi. Now that he knew Reshtina had not been badly hurt, it seemed to Conrad that Paul made a valid point. There would ultimately be a better place and time to deal with the savage Sartor.

"I suggest we head up to my hotel room. Reshtina reports that Sartor might know your address, and he could decide to pay you a visit when he does not hear back from his nasty emissary."

"Let him come. He might find me slightly more difficult to deal with than Reshtina or her brother. But what the hell, let's go to your place if you want. My late house guests have drunk up most of my booze, and I could use a nightcap."

"I'm assuming you took care of the, ...um, immediate situation," Paul said, eyeing the dark stains on Conrad's clothing, after they had arrived at Paul's room back at the hotel.

"You are correct. One down. One to go."

"It does not pay to make enemies unnecessarily—especially in our line of work."

"I don't agree with that. I happen to think a life without enemies is no life at all. How the hell can anyone with even a mote of character get through life without making some enemies? Besides, this is a personal matter for me. It has nothing to do with politics, or your idiotic cold war games."

"Unofficially at least the Muslim Youth and their supporters are our allies against the communists here. They certainly cannot be regarded as enemies. Or were you referring only to certain individuals? I realize they are not the most savory of bedfellows, but I should not have to remind you that sometimes such alliances are necessary, if only temporarily."

"You don't have to lecture me about realpolitik, and I've read Machiavelli. Although we barely know each other, we've discussed this before, and you know I don't accept your rationale, which in any case I believe is more the Agency's line than your own. It is, as I said before, a Faustian bargain, and nothing is to be gained by courting the reactionary factions here, only more misery for the Afghan people, and failure worse than even Viet Nam for our country if we continue with this stupid strategy. I don't see any of the communists throwing acid at women, or stoning them for attempting to leave abusive husbands, or any number of such behaviors which are the norm among our supposed allies here. You can bet that as soon as they get enough weapons from us to run the communists out, they will turn those same weapons on us or any other force that dares to challenge their archaic ideas of social order."

Paul did not respond. There was no point in further discussion. In any case Paul did not completely disagree with Conrad. He too had reservations about the Islamists, though his distaste for the communists was even more pronounced. For the time being at least the young agent was a valuable asset, but Paul wondered how much longer he would remain so if he continued to take the side of the socialists and communists against the resurgent forces of conservative Islam, which were on the rise in Afghanistan as elsewhere in the region. He hoped Conrad would at least continue to provide intelligence for the next few months, while the new regime of General Daoud was consolidating its power.

Paul sighed inwardly. Some things were out of his control. Regardless of how his new protege performed in the future, and after all that had occurred during his short stay in Kabul, Paul was grateful he would be on a jet out of the city in the morning.

"What's going to happen to Captain Ramsy?" Conrad asked later, as they sipped their second round of drinks.

Paul considered the question. His emotions were still raw from the loss of his friend, and he felt no compunction to answer truthfully. He stifled an urge to snap back, but it occurred to him that Conrad was making a genuine effort to be friendly, perhaps regretting his sharp comments earlier. No matter how hard it was to talk about the death of the Cecil, Paul saw an opportunity to improve their relationship. In any case, he rationalized, Conrad would find out the details soon enough from Agent Green or one of his other contacts.

"Cecil Ramsy is dead. I had a chance to get him safely out of the country, but he didn't like the idea of going on trial back in the states for killing Peccanter. He tried to escape. I had no choice. It was him or me."

"Jesus—we've left a bloody trail between us these last few days."

"It gets worse. I'll level with you. The captain, Cecil Ramsy, was my closest friend. I owe my career to him and his influence. We had known each other since our school days."

Conrad downed the rest of his drink in a single gulp.

"Man, that is harsh. I don't know what to say. It's a fucked-up world. I can't even imagine being in your shoes. I suppose you will have to report on all this back in Washington, right?"

Conrad held his empty glass and studied the other agent's face closely. Perhaps Paul blinked at a slightly faster rate, but otherwise his expression did not change.

"Of course. I'm not looking forward to it, obviously. Cecil has a family back home too. Family that I am as close to as my own."

Paul finished his own drink, stood quickly, and sat the glass deliberately down on the end table.

"Well, I'll have the whole flight home tomorrow to think about that report. I'm going to bed now. I've had enough for one day. I can call room service if you'd like another drink."

A glimmer of an idea had occurred to Paul. A way he could restore the reputation of seaman Peccanter, while still protecting Cecil Ramsy's family, and he wanted to contemplate it in solitude.

"No more drinks for me. I'm ready to crash. It has been an eventful day, to say the least."

"Then I'll see you in the morning, Conrad. I've got a wake-up call scheduled at seven. I can tell you from experience that the couch is pretty comfortable, and there are extra blankets and pillows in the closet. We'll have time for quick breakfast before we head out to the airport. I imagine you'll want to see your friends off."

Neither man fell to sleep immediately. The couch was comfortable, but uncharacteristically Conrad could not calm his thoughts, and he found himself worrying about his mistress, Ameena. He would have to tell her to stay away from his apartment until Sartor could be dealt with.

Paul's mind was occupied with memories of his late friend. Cecil Ramsy had been his brother in spirit if not blood, and Cecil's wife and children were also family. His only confidant was dead. Paul had always been a very private man, had never married or had a long lasting relationship with any of his many dates or girlfriends. He traveled constantly, and his line of work did not encourage close relationships, so his bond with Cecil had assumed a special significance. He felt utterly alone.

Ironically, the newly recruited young agent in the adjacent room, difficult and abrasive as he was, seemed to be the only person in the world Paul could confide in—the only person who could be trusted to any degree.

But perhaps I'm just getting old and sentimental, Paul corrected himself as he finally drifted off. *In the end no one can be fully relied on, nor can another's motivations ever be fully understood. We sail alone over a dark sea, with rocks and reefs close at hand.*

CHAPTER 29

Epilog: Washington

Agent Paul Sherman sat quietly watching the man from the other side of the massive old mahogany desk while his boss finished reading his report. His superior's expression changed little while he read, but Paul had worked under him long enough to notice the tightening of his grip on the pen and the subtle shifting of posture—signs of great uneasiness in this normally self-contained man. At last he let the papers fall to the desk. He shook his large bald head and swore softly under his breath.

"Of course you realize none of this can come out," he said at last. "My God, between Watergate and our continuing problems in Southeast Asia we can't afford a scandal like this. The last thing we need is another My Lai type affair. Goddamn—what a can of worms you've opened, Paul!"

The man paused for a few seconds as a new thought occurred to him.

"Besides his girlfriend how many people do you suppose know the full story?"

"I would say no more than a handful of people—a few friends he made in Kabul, but he wasn't there long. Why do you ask?" Paul replied, suspecting he knew the answer but curious to see if he was correct.

"I suppose they could be persuaded to keep their knowledge to themselves, for the present at least?"

"If you mean money or threats, or even appeals to their patriotism, I don't think so, but they have no reason to talk if certain conditions are met," Paul replied. His heart beat faster. Everything depended now on how the next few minutes went.

"Conditions? In my experience the Agency makes decisions and sets conditions, not outsiders," he replied, observing Paul closely.

"As you said, these are extraordinary times. Perhaps extraordinary measures are called for," Paul parried.

"Just for the sake of discussion, what might these 'conditions' be?"

"Death in the line of duty for Brian Peccanter, and all the usual benefits to his wife and child, including a military funeral. I don't think his friends would insist on a decoration, although he was wounded fighting for General Daoud's forces."

Paul's face was immobile, but he could not control his heart beat or the perspiration on his palms.

His boss swore again.

"Jesus Christ—you've got balls Paul! I've got to give you that. What makes you think the Agency can get the Navy to agree to those terms? Hell, what makes you think we can even present those terms?"

Paul was encouraged by the supervisor's use of 'we' in his response.

"I don't really see that we have a choice. We can't silence all the people who know the story, and Karen's parents are well connected here in Washington. If she decides to talk to the press, you can bet the story will be front page news," Paul replied with more confidence than he actually felt.

"I suppose the admiral might be persuaded to our point of view, if he could be absolutely assured there would be no leakage of the actual circumstances of their deaths, but there is the matter of Peccanter's court martial to deal with. Even the admiral might have his hands full there."

"I've given that some thought also," Paul said. "What if the Agency could convince the concerned parties that Peccanter was a secret agent even nominally under our employment?"

Paul could relax a little now that his superior seemed to agree that the best interests of all might possibly be reconcilable.

"I see the beauty of it," he said, thoughtfully. "I am beginning to understand why you were promoted, Paul. Your idea would also explain the secret codes in Peccanter's possession, and the Agency could tell the Navy as little as they want, merely replying that the information is classified. The Navy has a vested interest in keeping things as quiet as possible, in any case. You realize of course, this is going to have to come down from a lot higher up, but I believe we can make the necessary people see things our way."

This was not exactly true. Paul was aware that his supervisor, being a personal friend and trusted confidant of a certain member of the president's cabinet, had nearly carte blanche in most Agency matters.

The supervisor stood up, having made his decision.

"You did the best you could under the circumstances, Paul. I understand that Captain Ramsy was a close friend. I am truly sorry that you had to be involved with this affair, but perhaps after all there was no painless solution possible. Take a couple weeks off. Get some rest. Get the hell out of this damned town and go lay on a beach somewhere. I may need your help on a particular matter in a few weeks, but for now you've earned some R & R. Just make sure I can get a hold of you if I need to."

He shook Paul's hand and ushered him out of the office.

Paul stepped out into the August heat and humidity. *That went about as well as I could have hoped,* he thought, hesitating on the landing of the federal office building.

Around him spread the city that had been at the epicenter of so many changes that year. In March the last US ground troops had left Viet Nam. Congress had finally voted on July 31 to stop all the bombing, and to ban future military moves in Indochina without their approval. It was obvious Lieutenant Calley's conviction of two years earlier would be considered again in a military court of appeals. A month earlier Nixon had refused to turn over White House tapes to the special prosecutor, and it was beginning to look like the Watergate hearings might signal the end of the president's grotesque and fantastic political career.

Seaman Brian Peccanter's wife and parents would get the news of his death delivered formally and in person by the Navy. His death was tragic, but he would be officially memorialized as a patriot who died in the line of duty. The real circumstances of his death would remain classified. Paul himself would have to console Captain Cecil Ramsy's family. They would never know the depths of his depravity. That too would be classified.

Thinking ahead to the two funerals he would soon be attending, Paul was not sure which he dreaded more. He squared his shoulders and set off, dismissing those gloomy concerns from his mind, focusing instead on the far more pleasant prospects of the holiday he had coming, once he had discharged his sad and onerous responsibilities.